STEALING
LIFE

An Abaddon Books™ Publication
www.abaddonbooks.com
abaddon@rebellion.co.uk

First published in 2007 by
Abaddon Books,
Rebellion Publishing Ltd,
Riverside House, Osney Mead,
Oxford, OX2 0ES, UK.

Revised edition published in 2018
by Abaddon Books.

10 9 8 7 6 5 4 3 2 1

Creative Director and CEO: Jason Kingsley
Chief Technical Officer: Chris Kingsley
Head of Books and Comics Publishing: Ben Smith
Editors: David Thomas Moore,
Michael Rowley and Kate Coe
Marketing and PR: Remy Njambi
Design: Sam Gretton, Oz Osborne and Maz Smith
Cover Art: Sam Gretton

ISBN: 978-1-78108-520-2

Printed in Denmark by Nørhaven

STEALING LIFE

ANTONY JOHNSTON

ABADDON
BOOKS

WWW.ABADDONBOOKS.COM

CHAPTER ONE

HE'D BEEN TOLD the apartment would be empty while he robbed it.

In fact, it was the young woman sitting on the edge of the bed who'd said it. She was pretty, with long, dark hair, a slim boyish figure, dark brown eyes and pale skin. Her figure was a little too straight, perhaps—her mouth a little too large—but it suited her.

"Hello, Nicco. Right on time."

But Nicco wasn't looking at her. He was looking at the fat man sleeping next to her.

Nicco reached through the hole he'd made in the glass and opened the window, then swung his legs over the windowsill and tip-toed toward the woman across a deep pile carpet. "Keep your voice down," he whispered. "What in the fifty-nine hells are you doing here? What's *he* doing here?"

"Relax, lover." She wore a silk slip that barely covered her, and as she spoke she crossed her legs and looked up at Nicco. "I drugged him. He'll be out for about four hours. I wanted to see you. I never see you at work."

Her name was Tabathianna, but everyone called her 'Tabby.' She and Nicco were what he called 'part-time' lovers, which meant they slept together occasionally, but he didn't return her calls. And she was also a hooker.

"I could have just walked through the front door if I'd known," said Nicco. "You were supposed to take him out! What if he wakes up?"

Tabby gripped Nicco's collar, pulled him down and kissed him. "I told you, he's drugged. I put enough dope in his beer to keep him out for hours. He just didn't want to go out. Not even for a romantic walk on the harbour."

Nicco looked at the sleeping man and thought of Azbatha's northern harbour front, a ghost town of empty warehouses and docking platforms punctuated by rusting cranes and shipping cartons. The only major business still operating there was an old shipbuilding firm that had diversified into airships just a couple of months before the bottom fell out of the surface cargo industry. All the other shipbuilders had gone under, and with no ships there was no cargo, and no work for the docks. The city council was desperately trying to reinvigorate the area with 'business incentives' and backhanders, hoping that surface trade would pick back up in these unfamiliar times of peace. But the smart money had already moved to airships. Azbatha International, the city's central airship station, saw hundreds of vessels packed with cargo come and go every day.

By this time of night the harbour's regular inhabitants would rob a man like Tabby's client blind, deaf and dead. Nicco wondered about her idea of romance, and figured the man had gotten off lightly.

Nicco gently removed Tabby's hands from his collar, stood up and looked around the apartment. He was here now, so he may as well steal whatever he could. He certainly needed the money, and the whole thing would be a waste of time if he left empty-handed. Besides, it would upset Tabby, and he didn't want that.

Whatever the state of their relationship, Nicco had known her since they were both children.

He opened the bedroom door and walked into the lounge. Tabby followed him, pulling the door closed again behind her, and together they looked around at the sumptuous decor.

"Was I right?" asked Tabby. "It's all worth something, isn't it?"

She was right. Nicco could see the man had spent a lot of money to make this place look legitimate. But for a thief, everything had a catch. Two original paintings by the famed Varnian painter Arno Ven Ladall hung on the walls, one above the fireplace and one adjacent to the window. They were worth thousands... but would be hard to fence. Nicco was no expert, but the design on the hearthrug looked like a hand-woven depiction of the Three Praali Mountain Kings myth, worth almost as much as one of the paintings... but Praali rugs were thick and heavy. Nicco had brought a backpack, not a truck. Next to the holovid unit was an art deco statuette in the central Varnian style, a high-foreheaded caricature carved from the region's famous white, heavy stone... but the stone was just as famous for its brittleness. It would take at least two men to remove it safely, and there was only one of Nicco.

His mind turned to smaller things, looking for jewellery, valuable books, cash. But if there was anything like that in the apartment, it wasn't in this room. He glanced in the kitchen, but as he'd suspected, there was as much chance of this man lighting an oven as Nicco marrying a cop.

"It's not looking good," he said. "It's all worth a lot, but I can't take any of it. This isn't a home for him, it's a place he visits. It's got about as much soul as my mother's corpse."

Tabby tutted. "You shouldn't say things like that. It's bad luck to speak ill of the dead."

Nicco ignored the admonition. He'd spoken ill of his mother often enough when she was alive; he didn't see what difference it would make now that she rested at the bottom of the Nissal Straits.

He moved through to the bathroom. The bath had gold taps, which could fetch a tidy sum, but with the man still inside the apartment Nicco wasn't about to wrench them off and flood the place. Drugged or not, some things just made too much noise for a thief's comfort. He settled for the bath plug and soap dishes, also made of gold.

He heard Tabby calling in from the lounge. "What about this?"

Nicco walked back to see her pointing at an enchanted orb, floating three feet above the coffee table. It was a couple of inches in diameter and pulsed with a soft, blue-green iridescent light. The enchantment was beautiful, subtle. Probably not from Turith itself. Varn, perhaps? Or Praal, like the rug? One of those weird places where everyone used magic, no doubt.

"This must be worth something," said Tabby, "and you can easily carry it out. You could probably fit it in your pocket."

Nicco hesitated. "I'm not sure... I only know one wizard who's a fence, and frankly I don't trust him that much."

Tabby frowned. "It could be worth a fortune!"

"Magic just gives me the creeps. You can't touch it and half the time you can't see it. How can you trust something like that?"

Tabby giggled. "Big Nicco Salarum, frightened by a little magic. Come on, it's not going to bite you, is it? It's just a bit of glass."

Nicco supposed she was right. He sighed and reached for the orb.

It shrieked.

Nicco let go, but the loud, high-pitched whine didn't stop. Some kind of alarm.

It was the final straw for Nicco. With a silent vow never to take job suggestions from Tabby ever again, he headed back to the bedroom door. Then he realised it was slowly opening.

Naked as the day he was born, Tabby's client opened the door and blinked at Nicco.

It had been Tabby's idea. She'd been with the mark before, a wealthy industrialist from Jalakum, in the centre of the Turithian archipelago. A wealthy *married* industrialist, more to the point, and so he came to Azbatha—famed city of vice, the 'Pit-on-Stilts,' the most dangerous and overcrowded city in Turith—to satisfy his lust. Which was often enough that he'd bought an apartment in Riverside, Azbatha's wealthiest neighbourhood, to use while he and his libido were in town. He'd bought the apartment under the guise of needing a place to stay while doing business in Northern Turith, and certainly no-one would argue that in Azbatha, an apartment was probably more secure than a hotel. In fact, he really did use it for legitimate business sometimes, so the apartment was filled with expensive goods. From the art hanging on the walls to the gold bath taps, from the Praali hearthrug to the enchanted floating orb in the lounge, when Tabby had seen the apartment she figured a good thief could turn its contents into a tidy sum of money.

And Nicco Salarum, as Tabby well knew, was a very good thief.

She'd told Nicco about the businessman's apartment four months ago. He'd come to town and called on Madame Zentra, asking for a young woman with dark hair. Madame had sent Tabby, one of the brothel's more experienced girls. The john had picked her up on a crowded street corner in a hired groundcar and taken her back to his apartment. It was forty-five stories up, but when Nicco went to case it, he figured the building was eminently scalable with monofilament wire and omnimag grips.

(Nicco knew some burglars who used enchanted tools to get them up Azbatha's ubiquitous skyscrapers—floating boots, sticky gloves, even light-bending cloaks that rendered the wearer invisible—but he was a traditionalist at heart. He preferred technology to magic. Even in Azbatha, the paths of thieves and wizards crossed often enough for Nicco to know he wouldn't trust any of them as far as he could kick them. What happened when your floating boots suddenly stopped working at the fourteenth floor? Even assuming you survived, wizards didn't exactly hand out receipts.)

That evening, Nicco also saw what Tabby *hadn't* told him... That it really was about the most expensive place you could find in Azbatha, complete with high-tech security and a permanent guard patrol. Getting in via an apartment window would be easy, but doing so without tripping an alarm was an altogether different challenge. Social engineering to disable alarms, like the old 'unexpected electrician call-out' ruse, worked well enough... on the lazy, the gullible and the downright stupid. But no Azbathan security firm got very far hiring stupid people.

So Nicco decided to pass. Good thief or not, he didn't think the profit margin was high enough to risk being target practice for a bunch of bored, trigger-happy ex-cons playing at guards.

But the reason Tabby hadn't told him about the security was because she hadn't seen it. It transpired that the businessman had an arrangement, no doubt an expensive one, with the in-house security firm to preserve his dignity and minimise the risk of wagging tongues. When he was in town and 'entertaining,' the security patrols ignored him and anything going on in his apartment. Cameras were switched off, patrols innocently missed out his corridor, and guards made themselves scarce when they saw him walking up the steps to the lobby. The apartment was extremely secure—but only when it was vacant.

Nicco found all this out the next time the businessman visited Azbatha, six weeks later. Six weeks was a long time in crime, and Nicco had all but forgotten about the man by then. But that night he was casing a warehouse on the other side of town, clambering around in the eaves doing his due diligence, when a dark blue groundcar pulled up at the roadside and waited. Nicco froze. It wasn't a part of town known for streetwalkers or kerb crawlers, and for a moment he thought perhaps he'd missed a security camera, that he was about to be chased down by an over-eager guard.

Then Nicco heard the clatter of high heels. He craned his neck out and saw a tall, dark-haired woman in a long coat and evening dress walk toward the car. Nicco didn't recognise the woman—some high-class escort from the other side of town, by the look of her—but he did recognise the businessman's face as he opened his car door and invited her in. Nicco wasn't an overly spiritual man, but he could take a hint from the cosmos. He followed them, this time focusing on any changes in the security pattern when the man was at home. That night, he observed all the deliberate lapses. But he still wanted more certainty of the arrangements before he'd consider the job a good one, so he shrugged it off and moved on.

The next time he came to Azbatha, the businessman called Madame Zentra's again. Tabby, by now convinced he was an easy mark for someone like Nicco, was ready to connive her way into the job if she'd had to; but it hadn't been necessary. The man had asked for her by name. Apparently, the high-class escort had been a little *too* high-class for his particular peccadilloes.

A plan was hatched. The john always paid for a full night, so Tabby would get the sex over with, then insist he took her out on the town. A holokino show, a quick drink, a walk along the sea front perhaps; she'd come up with something. And as she explained her foolproof idea to Nicco over several jars of beer in the bar next to Madame Zentra's, tossing back her hair and giggling about how much money he could fence it all for, Nicco had decided that, by the watery saints, she really *would* think of something and it really *was* a foolproof idea.

When he woke the next afternoon, it was with a clearer and

more sober view of Tabby's plan. But he also knew she was trying to help his current, somewhat dire situation. Nicco was in a sizeable debt to Wallus Bazhanka, the famed mob boss of Azbatha, after losing a trailer full of high-performance skycars. The loss was unavoidable—the only alternative that didn't involve being arrested was to silence the guard who saw him, a guard who shouldn't have been on duty in any case. But Nicco had never even seriously injured anyone in the course of his work, much less killed someone. It was a badge he wore with pride, and he wasn't about to start now.

So Nicco dumped the trailer in the ocean and made a getaway. To him it was the only viable option, but Bazhanka didn't see it that way. To Bazhanka it was the careless and unnecessary loss of one hundred and fifty thousand lire; and he expected Nicco to compensate him. Nicco gave Bazhanka sixty thousand straight away, almost everything he had saved. But it wasn't enough to get the mob boss off his back. Now he wanted the balance, ninety thousand lire, and the deadline was running out.

Bazhanka offered Nicco the chance to pay it off in kind by working for him, but Nicco refused. Owing Bazhanka was bad enough, but the thought of being on his payroll made Nicco sick. He'd find the money some other way. Nicco had already amassed fifteen thousand in loot, all of it fenced and converted into money as quickly as possible, but if he was going to meet the deadline he couldn't afford to turn anything down.

So he decided to go ahead and rob the businessman. Maybe Tabby's plan would work after all.

NICCO WOULD NEVER know. Because here he was, having climbed forty-five stories in the sub-zero temperatures of a Turithian winter to get through the poxy window, and not only had Tabby not taken the man out, but he'd already recovered from whatever she'd slipped him.

Nicco weighed his options. He could clobber the man and make a hasty exit, but that would leave Tabby in potential danger. Nicco couldn't abandon her, not if the john worked out the scam. He hesitated.

Too late. Nicco had given him enough time to work out what a black-clad man with a backpack was doing in his apartment. He punched Nicco in the guts.

Nicco lost his breath in a single gust, and his knees buckled. The bodyweight that had shaken off Tabby's dope so quickly also gave the businessman's blow a hefty power.

Tabby's voice rose a couple of octaves as she shouted, "Hit him! Hit him!"

Nicco could barely hear her over the shrieking orb. Was she talking to him? The man loomed over him, and Tabby was still screaming. "I got up for a drink of water and I found him in here. He was trying to rob you and he had a gun and I couldn't scream or he'd kill me!" She backed into a corner as she screamed, circling round toward the holovid box.

Nicco scrambled backward on his hands and heels as the man advanced on him. Clever girl, he thought. Obvious, but plausible. He only hoped the man would overlook the complete absence of a gun in Nicco's hands.

Now that Tabby was above suspicion, he turned to the situation at hand. He kicked upward, driving his foot into the businessman's groin with enough force to turn the man a darker shade of pink. He also made an 'O' shape with his mouth, but no sound came out. Or perhaps Nicco just couldn't hear him over the screeching from the enchanted orb. He could hear Tabby though—the girl could scream—and suddenly, she stopped.

Then he saw her calmly walk up behind the john and smack him over the head with the Varnian statuette.

It smashed into a hundred pieces, covering the floor with fine white powder. The businessman stood stunned and motionless for a moment, then collapsed on top of Nicco, knocking the wind out of him again.

Tabby helped Nicco out from under the man's unconscious body, then ran into the bedroom. Nicco paused a moment to grab the orb and throw it down on the floor. Like the statuette, it smashed, and the piercing alarm finally stopped. Nicco sighed, caught his breath and followed Tabby into the bedroom. He expected her to be dressing, ready to make a quick getaway. Which she was, but not in the manner Nicco expected. Tabby stood by the window, still in her slip, ready to climb out.

"What in the fifty-nine hells are you doing?" Nicco said.

"Well, we'd better escape, hadn't we?"

"We're forty-five stories up and it's minus eight out there! No, get some clothes on and leave through the front door. The guards will just think he's finished with you." Tabby paused, considering his suggestion, so Nicco pulled her towards him and kissed her. "Trust me."

That did the trick. As Nicco moved to the window, Tabby pulled her clothes out from an untidy pile on the floor, starting with a sequined top. "All right," she said, "but what about you? You could come with me."

Nicco shook his head. "Too suspicious. And there's no way I could pass for your pimp in this get-up." He stepped onto the windowsill. "I'll see you soon, all right? Just get out of here and back to Zentra's as quickly as you can." Then he leapt out of the window.

Nicco was confident Tabby would be all right. Even if the businessman did suspect her, he was hardly likely to call the police. Besides, half of the Azbathan force was on Madame Zentra's client list.

Nicco caught the monofilament he'd left hanging from the window frame and slid down it at full speed. Sparks flew from his steel-palmed gloves. As he passed the twelfth floor he hit the switch on his semigrav belt to slow his descent, then hitched his belt clip to the wire and casually rappelled his way toward the ground. At the sixth floor he stopped completely, hidden from view behind one of the city's ubiquitous gaudy holo-billboards. Those billboards pumped out enough light to fill a stadium, keeping Nicco safe from the prying eyes of police skycars.

He pulled the omnimag grips from his belt and hit the seals. There was a low hum, then a soft liquid sound, and a soft green light signalled the grips were in place and bonded to the building's cladding. Hanging by one arm, he cut the monofilament—let it hang there, it couldn't be traced back to him anyhow—then used the grips to move across the wall, ignoring the crowded street below.

With four million people crammed into a hundred square miles and nowhere to build but up, the streets of Azbatha were always crowded whatever the time of day or night. No floating housing projects or thought-form supported malls here. Azbathans were nothing if not arcanophobes, and with the serious business of rebuilding society in a time of peace foremost on the agenda, any city councillor stupid enough to suggest paying wizards to maintain flying cities would be lynched before he got the words out. Luckily for Nicco, and the city's myriad other thieves, this peculiar brand of pragmatism meant Azbathan architecture was born more of necessity than aesthetics. It did nothing to invite admiration, and the added dangers of pickpockets, muggers and beggars kept the collective Azbathan gaze aimed firmly at street level. The surest way to tell a tourist wasn't by their clothing or accent, but by the angle of their neck.

Nicco moved round to the rear of the apartment building, away from the bright lights, and dropped to the ground behind a refuse canister just to be safe. He replaced the omnimag grips on his belt and put the belt in his backpack, then opened his jacket, reached inside and squeezed a small, fabric-covered nodule attached to the lining. Colour spilled across the coat from the collar downwards, turning black to red. A few seconds later, the jacket was bright crimson.

It wasn't exactly a disguise, but Nicco's tanned skin already marked him out in most cops' eyes as trouble waiting for the right moment. Anything he could do to break up his all-black ensemble and make himself look less a potential criminal would make his journey easier.

And it was only a short journey. Eight blocks east, catch a sky whale ferry across the Nissal River, then ten blocks south to his equipment lock-up. Normally he might have taken a more circuitous route to avoid being seen or followed, but it was very unlikely that the businessman would even raise the alarm, much less involve the police. Nicco relaxed, hauled his backpack onto one shoulder, shoved his hands in his pockets and stepped out to join the heaving foot traffic on the main street.

He was so relaxed that he didn't notice the large groundtruck start to follow him six blocks from the ferry port. He didn't even notice when the truck stopped and ejected four identically tall, thin, pale-skinned men two blocks later.

He noticed their footsteps when they ran up behind him, but by then it was too late.

CHAPTER TWO

WHEREVER NICCO WAS, he couldn't see or move his arms, and something solid was hammering repeatedly against his back. After a moment's disorientation, he realised he was lying on his back, bouncing around on a metal surface. He was tied up in the back of a groundtruck, driving at speed.

Someone was playing an anvil symphony in his head, foiling his efforts to listen to sounds from outside the groundtruck. He sniffed the air, hoping for a hint of sewage, the various tangs of industry, the sickly smell of stale alcohol, and tried to remember the directions his captors turned. Where was he being taken? Who in the fifty-nine hells would do this to him anyway? Nicco was a known thief throughout the Pit-on-Stilts, a young man with a knack for deft, subtle robbery... and for being careful. He didn't make enemies, he'd never ratted on a fellow thief and he'd only ever been arrested once—for a bank vault job six months ago. But the police couldn't make it stick, thanks to some fancy lawyers courtesy of Wallus Bazhanka, and Nicco walked. His rap sheet was still clean as a whistle, another badge

Nicco wore with pride. So who would snatch him in full view of a crowded street?

Bazhanka himself? Possibly—the mob boss was nothing if not mercurial—but the blindfold, the restraints and the distinct lack of meat-headed wise guys telling Nicco how much they were going to enjoy cutting on him just didn't seem Bazhanka's style.

The groundcar blundered to a halt. Nicco was thrown forward by the sudden stop and slammed into another metal surface. He tried to stand. Maybe they were going to leave him here for a while. Maybe they'd stopped for a bite to eat. If he could just get the blindfold off, he could probably undo whatever it was binding his wrists behind his back. But a clatter from behind him signalled the doors opening, and without a word two men grabbed Nicco by the arms and pulled him out.

He stumbled onto the street. A strong odour filled his nostrils and Nicco realised what had been bugging him during the ride. When he'd tried to smell the street, all he'd been able to identify was the waxy smell of paraffin. It confused him because one thing Azbatha definitely didn't have was any kind of candle-making district. But now the smell was even stronger, and the pieces of the puzzle slotted into place: the scent, the lack of conversation or threats, the awkward handling. Nicco had been snatched by thinmen.

Thinmen were short-lived magical golems, sometimes used as errand boys and disposable heavies. And like everything else magical, they creeped Nicco out.

The thinmen frogmarched him through a heavy metal door, which rang dully as it groaned shut behind them. After entering, they turned a couple of times, then Nicco almost fell as they walked down a flight of stone steps. All sound from outside was now completely blocked, and there hadn't been much to start with—which Nicco also found odd. Unless he'd been out for four or five hours, they had to still be in Azbatha, and any local street would be noisy and crammed.

So maybe I'm not in Azbatha.

It was possible, certainly. They could have taken a short hop sky whale ferry to a nearby island, or drugged him and thrown him on an airship to Rilok. Come to that, they could have knocked him out and taken him to the wastes of Hirvan. He could be anywhere. Worrying about it was pointless until he found out why he'd been kidnapped.

Nicco felt the clammy hands of a thinman on his face. The golem removed Nicco's blindfold and he blinked, expecting bright interrogation lights or a fist to the face. But neither came. Nicco was in a large, windowless chamber lit by flaming torches. The walls and floor were grey stone, lined with thick rugs, shelves and draped tables. Books, ornaments and curios covered every surface, flat or otherwise. Ceremonial robes hung from a stand set between two tables. A wooden cabinet displayed jewellery and crystals. Arcane symbols filled otherwise unused spaces on the walls. Nicco had no idea what any of them meant, but it was probably safe to assume they were magical. Half of the stuff on those tables was probably enchanted too. Nicco shivered, looking sidelong at the thinmen who had brought him here and still held his arms.

They were pallid and tall—like all such golems—but at least they had a face. Most of the thinmen Nicco had previously seen were Bazhanka's, and the mobster never bothered assigning features. Many people had thinmen created in their own image in order to identify them easily. Nicco had always assumed Bazhanka's golems were blank-faced for precisely the opposite reason—so they couldn't be traced back to him. But looking now at these emotionless quadruplets with their thick black hair, piercing blue eyes and neat black beards, Nicco also wondered if it wasn't just because Bazhanka was, to put it kindly, ugly as a squid. These thinmen looked better, and closer to human, than anything wearing Bazhanka's face ever would.

"Welcome, Nicco Salarum. My name is Xandus."

Nicco stood at one end of a long, crimson Praali rug, flanked on both sides by the thinmen. The rug led to a set of low stone steps. Atop those steps was a large, ornate chair that Nicco guessed was supposed to resemble a throne. Behind this was a large fireplace, stoked and roaring.

But it was the man who stood in front of the chair that Nicco focused on—the man who called himself Xandus.

He had thick black hair, piercing blue eyes and a neat black beard, framing a face almost as pale as those of his thinmen. Xandus wore a long silk cloak—deep red, to match the rug— and a black silk tunic cinched at the waist with a wide leather belt. His trousers were black leather, and heavy, thick-soled boots finished off his ensemble. It seemed an odd combination to Nicco, a mixture of hardy outdoor wear and indoor finery. Still, he didn't need any further explanation to know Xandus was a wizard; and if there was one thing you could rely on with wizards, it was their atrocious dress sense.

Xandus walked down the length of the rug, smiling. "You are recommended to me from... a friend. Of your high skills they speak, very good." His voice was a deep drawl, his syllables hard and deliberate.

Nicco struggled against the thinmen's grip. He didn't like where this was going one bit. He wrenched his left arm free, but one of the golems standing behind him reached out and grabbed the collar of his jacket. The thinman pulled Nicco backward and slammed a knee into his back. Nicco winced and dropped like a sack. Only the remaining thinman's grip stopped him head-butting the floor.

"Enough! Let him go," said Xandus to the thinman. The golem did as ordered, and Nicco dropped to the ground. He stared up at Xandus.

"I don't do... referrals," he said. His back ached from the thinman's blow. "Who was it?"

Xandus stood over him. "I am not at liberty to say. But I

am confident that my offer will agree with, once you have it heard." The wizard's accent and dialect were odd, out of place somehow. "Allow me." He offered Nicco a hand.

Nicco took it and stood. Xandus' hands were long, thin and exceptionally smooth, almost delicate. Struck by the thought, Nicco studied the wizard's face. Xandus was wearing a lot of make-up, it was true, but the beard was definitely real. The wizard was middle-aged, and Nicco could tell the make-up hid some of his lines. So perhaps he was just vain and affected. It wasn't as if wizards had ever done a day's honest work in their lives.

Not that Nicco had either, of course.

Xandus smiled as if sensing Nicco's curiosity. "I am first from the Shalith, young thief," he said. "To the eastern side of Turith, and came to Azbatha when I was grown already. Pardon if my words are strange."

Nicco nodded. It wasn't just the wizard's words that were weird, but now it made sense. The Turithian archipelago was wide, almost a thousand miles from west to east. Azbatha was a small island on the very tip of the north-west, and if Nicco remembered his geography correctly, Shalith was its counterpart in the south-east. Shalith was almost as close to the continent of Praal as it was to Azbatha, and Nicco had never met anyone from that side of the country before. Looking at Xandus, he guessed he hadn't missed much.

Nicco noticed the wizard staring at his chest. He looked down and saw his charm pendant hanging out over his shirt. It must have shaken loose when he was trying to escape the thinmen's grip.

Xandus gently lifted the charm. "What is this? Do you know what it is means?" The charm was engraved, an abstract interlocking pattern of thick lines braided around a golden teardrop-shaped pendant. Xandus looked at it, then back up at Nicco.

Nicco glared at him. "It was my father's. And it's just a pattern, it doesn't mean anything. Now, are you going to get on with this or what?"

Xandus smiled and let the pendant drop back to Nicco's chest. "Very well," he said, and walked back along the thick rug. "You know the Hurrunda? A city on the near coast of Varn?"

"I've heard of it. Used to be a big trading partner of ours before the wars."

"Yes! Yes, exactly, before the airships and guns. And now the wars are ended, and all is peace. Trading will soon start again. So a visitor comes to Azbatha, from Hurrunda. His name is Governor Werrdun."

"I'm a thief," said Nicco. "I steal things. I don't kidnap people."

The wizard shook his head and laughed. "No, no, no, no! Not kidnapping. Stealing, exactly. Werrdun wears like you a necklace, symbol of power for governor, but enchanted necklace is his. I am a collector, young thief. All wizards are collectors, you know?" Xandus swept his arms out, gesturing to his hoard of books, jewellery and magical miscellany. "And I want this necklace."

Nicco shook his head. Xandus' grammar worsened as he became excited, and Nicco had to concentrate to get the gist of his speech. He'd understood enough. "I don't even know who this guy is. I don't know who *you* are. Why should I?"

"Governor of Hurrunda, that is Werrdun's name. He comes to Azbatha for strengthening trade relations, as you say, now the wars ended. He is an old man, and with security always. But you are special to get past."

"Rubbish. You're a wizard, why can't you just magic it from his neck to your display case?"

"Not so simple. Magical is the necklace, and Werrdun is of Varn, land of magic. His security is much of magical, too. But you, you are not use magic at all. This I was told."

Nicco shrugged. "Never touch the stuff. So what?"

"So magical is useless. But a special man, with no magic, cannot be detected by him. You can be the man."

Typical. Even with all their power, wizards still needed men like Nicco to do their dirty work.

"I give you forty thousand lire," said Xandus. "Half now."

Nicco stared at the wizard. That was a lot of money. Added to the money Nicco had already built up through burglary, it would almost pay off his debt to Bazhanka. Hells, twenty grand in one hit might even be enough to persuade Bazhanka to forget the rest.

But not if Nicco got caught. And this job seemed very risky for a mere collection piece. An ambassador would have two levels of security, his own and an Azbathan detail. Not to mention that wherever he was staying in town would be secured to the hilt. Magic or no magic, it would be a difficult job. Even impossible.

But that wasn't the real problem. Given time, Nicco was confident he could find a way round the security, figure out a way to get the necklace. It was what he did. No, the real problem was working for a wizard, especially one whose grasp of West Turithian hung by an increasingly slim thread.

"No deal, Xandus. Find some other mug to play patsy for you."

"But you must! You must, you must! Very valuable to me, is necklace! And you are best thief in Azbatha, this I was told!"

"Sure, very flattering, thank you. The answer's still no, so if you can just get your thugs to show me out I'll be on my way. Don't worry, mum's the word. I won't tell a soul about your little scheme."

"Fifty thousand, I give!"

Nicco sighed. "No means no, Xandus. Money isn't going to change my mind." That wasn't entirely true—if Xandus had offered a million or so, Nicco could probably have overcome his principles—but it made the point sufficiently. The wizard fell quiet, looking crestfallen.

"You sadden me, Mister Salarum. But I am confident that your mind will change." Xandus settled himself into his ornate chair. "We will finish speaking now."

"Fine. Now, let me—"

Before he could finish, one of Xandus' thinman cracked Nicco over the back of the head. Not again, he thought as he dropped to the ground.

CHAPTER THREE

"HEY, THIS IS my spot! Get out!"

Nicco felt a hand pull him upright by the collar. Through bleary eyes, he stared into the heavily lined face of a tramp. The man's beard scratched at Nicco's cheeks and his breath stank of booze. "I've been sleeping here for fifteen years, you son of a squid!" shouted the tramp. "This is trespassing!"

Nicco blinked in the harsh sunlight. "All right granddad, no need to get personal. Anyway, it's broad daylight. Shouldn't you be out begging?"

The tramp threw Nicco to the ground. "I've got my pride, young 'un! Don't you give me no lip!"

Nicco's pack lay on the floor where he'd been dumped. He snatched it up and backed away. "Whatever. Keep your whiskers on."

Nicco rubbed his wrists and walked toward the main street. A cold breeze made him gasp and shiver, and shove his hands into his pockets. At least the thinmen had cut his arms loose, even if they hadn't been smart enough to drop him back where they'd picked him up. And they'd left his pack with him.

The pack! Nicco felt a stab of panic and dropped to a crouch, opening the backpack's top flap. The omnimag grips were still there... and beneath them, the gold soap dish and bath plug. He sighed with relief. They may not be worth fifty grand, or however much that crazy wizard had offered him, but they should fetch enough to keep Bazhanka off his back for a week or two.

Nicco dusted himself off, walked out onto the main street and quickly realised where he was. Right in central Azbatha, in the shopping district. A holo-billboard, mounted high on the side of a mall, told him it was midday. It also told him how the new Soarus Bullet skycar would bring him the respect of his peers, not to mention the adoration of several women in very tight clothes. But Nicco wasn't in the market. Not for the car, anyway.

He took a right and merged into the sea of shoppers drifting slowly down the street. His stomach growled, reminding him he hadn't eaten or drunk anything since before setting out for the businessman's apartment. He sidestepped his way through the crowd, weaving with a practised air toward the door of a small café. A hand-written sign declared the owner's politics: *NO WIZARDS, NO VARNIANS*. Nicco reckoned he could get away with it. He pushed open the door, ignored the owner's grunted greeting and entered, letting the door shut behind him. He found an empty booth in the back corner, as far away from the street as possible, and sank into the leather seats with a tired sigh. A holovid projector above the booth was running a news stream with the sound turned off.

For the first time since the previous night, he thought of Tabby. Had she made it out of the apartment okay? Was she safely back at Zentra's? He considered calling her, but then remembered he was still wearing the same clothes from the previous night, and never took his phone on a job. He wasn't stupid enough to leave the ringer on, but that wasn't the problem. Every cell phone broadcast its location, accurate to within a few feet, to the network. Even switching the phone off didn't help. The only way to stop it broadcasting your location was to remove the battery, rendering it useless. So you might as well just leave it at home.

But Nicco was pretty sure Tabby would be fine. Even if the john had recovered before she left, what could he have done? Any cops he called would be more interested in him than a working girl. Azbatha was a pit, sure, and the police often turned the other cheek; but that didn't mean they'd blatantly ignore a crime happening right under their noses.

Nicco decided to get the swag fenced first, but call in at Madame Zentra's before going back to his apartment. Tabby wouldn't mind that he probably stank like a tramp by now, especially if he showed up with pockets full of beer money.

"Sign says no Varnians."

Nicco looked up into the sour face of an old woman scowling down at him. She wore a faded pinafore, covered in twenty-year-old stains, and clutched a notepad to her bosom.

He was pretty sure it said *Café* above the door, not *Abattoir*, but she must be what passed for a waitress in this place. Nicco smiled up at her. "No, no, exactly! I am from the Shalith, you know. To the East of Turith."

The woman peered at Nicco, then sniffed in contempt. "All right," she said. "What do you want?"

He ordered a cup of coffee and a sandwich, and smiled to himself as the woman lumbered away to the counter. His impersonation of Xandus had been pretty poor, but there was as much chance of this woman having actually met someone from the other side of the country as Nicco himself—until last night, anyway. Added to his plain, rumpled wardrobe— Varnians were famous for their bright, garish costumes—it was enough to convince her.

Besides, he was only half Varnian.

Nicco leaned back to watch the holovid stream. Local news showed a few council members on the steps of City Hall. There was the mayor, smug as ever with his ex-model wife in her ridiculous hat, who happened to be half his age, on his arm. The usual rubbish, or so it seemed until a caption ran across the bottom of the stream. It read: *HISTORIC TRADE VISIT FROM HURRUNDAN GOVERNOR.*

The sour-faced waitress returned with his order. Nicco was ravenous, but kept his eyes on the silent news stream as he tucked into his lunch. Xandus wasn't kidding about Werrdun being old. The man's skin was paper-thin, tight across his bones and tendons. His skin had so many liver spots it would be easier to count the clear patches. Nevertheless he looked in comparatively good health, keeping good posture as his groundcar convoy rolled up to city hall, and when they showed him greeting the mayor he walked without sticks.

Not without bodyguards, though. Nicco counted at least ten burly, serious-looking men with suits as dark as their skin and one hand permanently stationed inside their jackets. Perhaps they were worried someone would try to steal Werrdun's magic necklace.

The necklace itself was a large, gold thing. It looked ceremonial, like it belonged on a tribal chieftain, and the news stream captioned it the *FAMOUS SYMBOL OF WERRDUN'S OFFICE.* It couldn't be too famous, at least around here; it had been so long since Turith had done any trade with Varn that he doubted anyone in Azbatha knew where Hurrunda even was, much less the gaudy necklace worn by its governor. Apart from Xandus, it seemed. Nicco wondered if the necklace really was magical. Even assuming it was, did Werrdun wear the real thing? Or was it just a paste and nickel copy, while the real necklace stayed firmly locked up in a secure Varnian vault?

Nicco finished his sandwich. It wasn't his job to worry

about it. Let some other mug take on the trigger-happy gorillas shadowing their governor; Nicco had stolen goods to fence. He slotted his card into the table's paypod, settled up and walked out. He didn't leave a tip.

NICCO HADN'T EVEN walked a hundred yards when he spotted two pale faces heading for him through the crowd. The mass of people parted as they advanced, backing away with startled expressions and low, uneasy whispers. "Thinmen," the whispers said. But these thinmen weren't Xandus'. Their faces were blank. Bazhanka's goons.

Nicco made a sharp turn, hoping to lose them in the crowd and make off down a side alley, but there were another two behind him approaching fast. He was cornered, and the rapidly-thinning crowd only made him more exposed.

"Salarum." The voice was a slightly deeper-pitched imitation of Bazhanka's own, the mob boss's one concession to vanity. "Mr Bazhanka is waiting for his payment."

Nicco was backed against a wall, with the thinmen crowding around him. The smell of wax hit his nostrils again. He felt sick. "I know, and I'm going to pay, I'm on my way to get some money now..."

"Mr Bazhanka has been very patient."

"I know. I appreciate that."

"But even a patient man has limits."

"I know. I'm going to pay. I just need to... dispose of some inventory."

The thinman cocked his head, considering this for a moment. Finally he said, "You have twenty-four hours. We will find you again. Do you understand?"

Nicco nodded, exhaling at last.

"Goodbye, Salarum."

Nicco watched them go, parting the street crowds like a royal procession and leaving gossiping afternoon shoppers in their wake. Those nearest Nicco looked at him with suspicion. No-one bothered to ask if he was all right.

THE EXTERIOR SIGN read *International House of Hair*. It was an upmarket unisex salon catering to the wives of rich men, the husbands of rich women and kids doing their best to make their parents less rich by the day. Nicco entered, ignoring the customers and approached the reception desk. A pale-skinned young woman with outrageously big hair—red as blood on snow—sat behind the desk. She wore a sharp suit and low-cut blouse underneath, and her name badge informed the world her name was *Shenney*. She gave Nicco a lopsided smile and raised an eyebrow at him.

"Good afternoon, Mr Salarum. How can I help you?"

Nicco rubbed a hand over his cropped dark hair and smiled. "Afternoon, Shenney. I'd like to make an appointment for follicle therapy treatment, please."

Shenney pressed a button on her desk phone. "One moment please, sir, while I check the diary." Nicco couldn't see it, but he knew that behind her was a monocell camera transmitting a stream through to the backroom. He exaggerated a smile for its benefit. "Mr Salarum wishes to make a therapy appointment," said Shenney towards her desk.

"*Eight o'clock tomorrow morning*," replied a tinny voice.

Shenney looked back up at Nicco. "Eight o'clock—"

"Actually, I was hoping you might have something this afternoon. Possibly even right away?" Nicco leant on the desk, emphasising the urgency.

Shenney pursed her lips. "As sir knows, we can only see clients according to the appointment calendar—hey!"

Nicco leant all the way over Shenney and hit the button himself. "Allad, you lazy son of a squid," he hissed into the microphone. "Let me in right now or I'll tell Shenney here where we really went for your last birthday."

Shenney looked at Nicco with surprise. "You told me it was a nightclub," she whispered. "Where did you take him?"

"*It was a bloody nightclub!*" said the tinny voice.

Shenney pouted. "A nightclub that just happened to be right above a brothel, I'll bet!"

"*Are you coming, or what?*" said the tinny voice. A door behind the desk buzzed, signalling the lock was deactivated.

Nicco strode through, winking back at Shenney.

Behind the door was a short corridor leading to store rooms and an office. A handsome man the same age as Nicco stepped out of the office and glared at him. "I should skin you alive, you sneaky son of a squid. What in the fifty-nine hells is so urgent?"

"I'm fine, thanks, Allad. It's great to see you too."

"Come on, into the back room." Allad led Nicco down the corridor to a heavy metal door with a keypad lock. He punched a code into the pad and the door swung open.

Nicco followed Allad into the windowless room. "You know," he said, "One of these days I'm going to come in here and actually ask for a haircut." The door swung shut behind them. The walls, floor and ceiling of the room were lined with the same metal as the door, and a metal table stood in the middle of the space. "What's wrong with a betting shop, anyway? Or a strip bar? I never understood the hairdresser thing."

Allad leaned on the table and sighed. "Your problem, Nicco, is that you're too old-fashioned. Card dens, gentleman's clubs, they're old hat. Too obvious. No-one suspects a hairdresser."

"Until they raid you for bad taste." Nicco hefted his pack onto the metal table. "Are we closed?"

"Hold on..." said Allad. He crossed to the back of the room and pressed a button set in the metal wall. A deep hum, barely above subsonic, vibrated through the floor. The button activated an omniscrambler loop embedded in all six sides of the room, surrounding it with charged black noise particles that shielded the space from recording and surveillance equipment. So long as the loop remained active, nobody could spy on them.

Allad returned to the table. "Done. So what have you got for me?"

Nicco opened his pack and took out the soap dish and bath plug. A scrap of paper tumbled out of the pack with them, and Allad picked it up from the table.

"Who's 'Xandus'?" he said.

"What? Give that here." Nicco took the note from Allad. In neat handwriting, it read:

Xandus
Phone: 207212-578707

Nicco felt violated. Being knocked unconscious and tied up was one thing, but the wizard must have rifled through his pack while he was out cold too. That was just rude. "It's nothing," Nicco said, shoving the paper into his pocket. "Just some crank I met."

"Cranks often give you their phone numbers, do they?"

"I can't help my raw sex appeal," Nicco said with a smirk. He held up the soap dish and bath plug. "Anyway, I got these from an apartment last night. I've got Bazhanka on my back, and I need to come up with some quick cash. What do you reckon?"

Allad picked the items up and turned them over, then shrugged and replaced them on the table. He walked to one of the metal walls and placed his hand on a barely-discernible plate in the surface; a green band of light moved down the plate, scanning Allad's hand, and a panel slid back to reveal several shelves full of goods: watches, holovid boxes, statuettes, paintings and more. All of it was stolen, some by Nicco himself. Allad bent to retrieve a gadget from the floor of the hidden cupboard and brought it back to the table, picked up the soap dish and held the gadget to it. It was small, black and smooth-cased, with only a tiny vidscreen to break up the polished contours.

Allad frowned at the vidscreen display. "Not solid, then."

Nicco cursed. "I thought they were. Still, even plated, that's a fair bit of gold. The wars may be over, but Varn hasn't exactly opened its mines to the public. There's enough there to melt down and sell..." Nicco trailed off. Allad was looking from the vidscreen readout to the soap dish and back again, his frown growing deeper. "What's up?"

Allad looked up at him in confusion. "Nicco, these aren't gold."

"You already said that. Come on, they're still worth a couple of grand. I just need—"

"No, no... It's not even gold plate. This is an alloy knock-off."

"What?" Nicco snatched the soap dish from Allad and stared at it. He rubbed it hard on the edge of the metal table. The 'gold' started to flake away. "But... but..."

"Sorry, Nicco, but these are useless to me. I'm not running a boot sale, here."

Nicco stared at the flaking alloy in disbelief. The cheap bastard! He thanked the watery saints he hadn't tried to lug the Praali rug out of there, or the Ven Ladall paintings. If even the soap dish was fake, chances were everything in that apartment was a cheap knock-off to impress girls and clients. Nicco cursed himself for not noticing. Tabby, the businessman, the screaming globe... He hadn't been thinking a hundred per cent. He should have aborted as soon as he saw Tabby in the bedroom, turned back and given it up as a bad job.

Except that he desperately needed to pay Bazhanka something, even just a few thousand, to keep those thinmen from breaking his legs. Nicco had no doubt they'd find him, if not at his apartment then at Zentra's, or in a club, or even on the street like they had earlier that day.

He cursed and took the scrap of paper from his pocket.

CHAPTER FOUR

"Salarum."

It was the same deep voice Nicco had heard the day before, but he couldn't tell if the thinman standing at the door of Wallus Bazhanka's club was the same one who had accosted him in the street. From what Nicco could remember, thinmen only lived three to four months before the charm ran out; for all he knew, the one who threatened him yesterday had crumbled to dust by now.

"I'm here to see—"

"Mr Bazhanka is expecting you." The golem opened the door to the club and stood back to let Nicco pass.

Nicco walked through the steel-backed door into a dark entrance corridor, past the cloakroom and through a pair of large glass doors into the main room. It was eleven-thirty in the morning, thirty minutes before Bazhanka's thinmen came looking for him and several hours before the club opened for business, but you could have been forgiven for thinking it was just a slow night. The lights were low, the music was playing and two dancers writhed and bumped up on the stage. But the only patron was a middle-aged man who sat in a dark corner far from the stage, with two heavies—real people, not thinmen—flanking him.

The man was grossly overweight and completely hairless. Even his heavy brow was bald, though it did little to improve the appearance of his small, heavily-lidded eyes—the left of which was lopsided, drooping down toward his cheek. The man's skin bore the washed-out pallor of a born-and-bred Azbathan: his thick pink lips and heavy jowls seemed almost to float on it as he devoured hishuge lunch. His lips smacked and sauce dripped down his chin, onto the napkin protecting his bulging suit.

Wallus Bazhanka.

Under normal circumstances, Nicco would never have taken the skycar heist job from Bazhanka. He was a lone operator, and he liked it that way. Also, the man just plain creeped him out. When Nicco was arrested for the bank job, Bazhanka sent his own lawyers to defend the young thief. He asked the mob boss why he'd helped him, but Bazhanka would only make some vague references to knowing Nicco's mother many years ago—which was odd, because his mother had only ever mentioned Bazhanka to Nicco once.

He was nine, and already a young thief, boosting holovids and fencing them for fifty lire apiece; and his mother had implored him not to join the mob, to never get in bed with the man who, even back then, already ruled Azbatha's underworld with a meaty fist. "A debt to Wallus Bazhanka will never be paid," she'd said. It was the first and last time she ever spoke his name, and one of the few pieces of advice from his mother that Nicco had listened to. And he'd never regretted it.

But when Bazhanka's lawyers had turned up at the city jail *pro bono*, what choice did he have? Nicco couldn't afford a decent lawyer himself, and the evidence included video footage that clearly showed him entering the basement of the building next to the bank carrying one tool bag, then leaving half an hour later with two.

Somehow, Bazhanka's men had cleared all that up. One of the holovid files went missing, and they argued the other one into a corner. Then they ran rings round the prosecution. Three days later Nicco was a free man—legally, at least. He knew he wouldn't be free of Bazhanka until that debt was paid.

And standing here now in the man's club, Nicco thought back to his mother's words. He'd tried to pay off the debt with the skycar theft, but it had only made things worse. Now he owed Bazhanka not just a favour, but ninety thousand lire.

He strolled across the floor of the club, one of Bazhanka's bodyguards watching him warily. When Nicco was ten feet away, the goon held up a beefy hand and motioned for Nicco to stop.

The mob boss replaced his cutlery and wiped sauce and crumbs from his mouth with the napkin. "Nicco," he said without looking up. "I am so happy to see you. So very happy. Always the eleventh hour with you freelancers, isn't it? Always just the right side of late. And you could have been so very, very late."

Nicco ignored the implied threat and held up a plain black briefcase. It contained twenty-five thousand lire in cash.

"*Cash?*" Bazhanka's eyes nearly popped out of their sockets. "You bring me cash, here? You are insane, dear boy, so very insane!"

Nicco let the briefcase drop back to his side. "You want the money or not?"

It had been raining when Nicco left Allad's place, a cold, sleety downpour that only blackened his mood. He threw the fake gold soap dish and bath plug in a recycling can and walked a block down to the nearest street phone. Xandus' number stared at him from the scrap of paper. Nicco stared back.

He picked up the headset, slotted his card in the paypod and thumbed the number into the keypad.

"*Mister Salarum,*" said a voice at the other end of the line. "*I know your mind would change.*"

"Hello, Xandus," Nicco said.

Silence filled the line.

"*You are still here, Mister Salarum?*"

Yeah. I'm still here. The words caught in his throat. "I'll do it. Meet me tonight."

"*I will arrange for you to pick up and come to me.*"

"No." Nicco knew what he was about to do was a gamble. Xandus could withdraw the offer, or send his thinmen over anyway, or just drop a rain of frogs on Nicco's head until he agreed to be blindfolded, tied up and probably knocked out again just to satisfy the wizard's paranoia. "You meet me tonight at eight, in the Silver Sky Whale on the corner of 84th and Kanan. You pay me there. If I so much as smell your thinmen, it's all off. Am I clear?"

Xandus paused. Then he said, "*Very well, exactly.*"

Nicco hung up.

He dropped his pack and equipment off at his lockup across the river, then staggered home for a jet shower. He couldn't strictly claim he hadn't slept at all in the last twenty-four hours, but neither of his 'naps' had exactly been restful. His clothes reeked of stale sweat, his head still ached and his mouth felt like the underside of a Praali rug. He reached his building, took the service elevator to the top floor and fell into his apartment.

Nicco's place couldn't have been less like the businessman's. The realtor Nicco bought it from had called it a 'bargain penthouse suite.' Yes, it was true the apartment was at the top of the building, with only the roof above. And, yes, it was cheap. What you wouldn't find in any brochure, though, was *why* it was such a bargain. The building was a converted aquatic slaughterhouse from Azbatha's golden period of trade and commerce—all cold steel and bare, damp stone, where millions of fish and sea cattle had breathed their last. It was also located right in the heart of the red-light district. Nicco's apartment was reached through a steel-grilled utility elevator from the ground floor. The steel roof sneered at fancy modern concepts like 'insulation' or 'water resistance,' because why on earth would a dead fish care if a little water found its way in? Or that Turith's extreme weather patterns baked the whole place like a cake in the summer, then froze it like a popsicle in the winter?

It was a sucker bargain. Even in the seller's market of Azbathan real estate, better apartments could be had for the same price. The list of people who might actually be willing to make a home out of this apartment held just one name: Nicco Salarum.

He liked the location. Some of his best friends—in fact, all of his best friends—were working girls.

He liked the exclusive entry and exit access as there was no need to fob off nosy neighbours with stories of working strange hours in the city (haha, yes, he supposed he did look like a burglar in this all black get-up—how funny, must dash, bye-bye).

And best of all, it was big. By the watery saints, was it big.

Nicco had left the apartment open-plan, with only a small area in one corner divided off for the bathroom. But somehow he still managed to make it feel cluttered. Shelves lined the walls of half the room, bursting with books, holovids and even old flatvids that he just couldn't bear to throw out. Occasional tables were piled high with printzines, reference books and more holovids. He had enough cutlery, crockery and cookware to feed a dozen people, even though Nicco only cooked once or twice a week, and only ever for himself. A holovid box and its audio system took up one side of the space, surrounded by more books and holovids. He didn't have a system to play his old flatvids; he kept promising himself that one day he'd buy one and convert them all to holovids, but 'one day' never came.

The far corner of the apartment was filled by what he jokingly called a shrine to his mother—a pile of boxes and bags filled with clothes, jewellery, newspapers, ancient audio discs. Antiques and memories. Nicco swore he'd sort through it all some day, to see if there was anything even remotely useful in there. But 'some day' seemed as elusive as 'one day.'

He showered, ate a vacpac meal from the fridge and left. No time to rest as such, but he was refreshed and alert again and the evening's cold rain kept him that way. He took a groundcab downtown, got out at 82nd and Kanan and walked the last two blocks. This section of Kanan Avenue was one of the few places in Azbatha where a man could walk without being in constant bodily contact with random strangers, or watching for muggers. It was clean, well-lit and respectable, because it belonged to Madame Zentra. And the Madame liked a clean establishment.

Nicco waved quick hellos to a few people as he walked, girls and marks from Zentra's place that he knew by sight—until he reached the establishment next door to the brothel. This was the Madame's other, more legitimate, business interest: the Silver Sky Whale Bar, affectionately known as the 'White Fatty' by locals. Nicco pushed the door open and stepped through. Blasts of warm air hit him from both sides, and in a few seconds he was at room temperature.

A pretty young blonde girl stepped up and greeted him by name. Gurinama worked next door four nights a week; all the girls did, moving back and forth between establishments from night to night. It made accusations of solicitation very hard to prove, and helped the girls find new clients. The only downside was the occasional furious spouse who spotted their partner in the bar and assumed they were also using the brothel. Which was true most of the time, but Zentra still ejected the offending parties on principle.

Nicco ordered a drink and made his way through to the booths.

It was a quarter to eight—Nicco always preferred arriving too early over too late, and in Azbatha you were always one or the other. He immediately headed for a table in the corner, with his back to the wall and a good view of the entrance. It was a regular booth for him, ideal for discretion.

But as he passed the other tables, a soft voice said, "Mister Salarum. Please, sit you down."

Xandus sat in an empty window booth overlooking the street. He gestured for Nicco to join him. It wasn't the booth Nicco would have picked, but then Xandus didn't look how he expected either. The wizard's clothes were discreet, dull and common, in stark contrast to the silken finery he'd worn the night they first met. Nicco noticed he was still wearing the make-up, though. Some things a wizard just couldn't do without.

"You understand what must you do? Time is small."

Nicco nodded. "How long's he in Azbatha for?"

"Not long, exactly. Four days more here, then he returns back to the Hurrunda."

It really wasn't much time. A job like this should be planned for months, not thrown together overnight. But it was this or a year in traction.

"Give me the advance." Nicco reached for his paypod, but to his surprise Xandus reached under the table and pulled out a briefcase. Nicco stared at it. "You've got to be joking. Cash?"

Xandus looked confused. "Is easier than your pods, exactly. Then no-one knows. This is how you are paid."

Nicco wondered at that. In the centre of the Turith archipelago squatted a barren, ugly little island called Shalumar. It had no great cities, no wide open shipping bays, no nearby reefs or feeding grounds. But Shalumar did have one big geographical advantage. Before airships, it had been on the route of every merchant boat sailing through Turith. It didn't take long for some bright spark to set up a permanent station, servicing the ships that passed through. And another, and another, until the immigrant population of Shalumar was a very wealthy population indeed.

And like many very wealthy people with nothing better to do, they decided to go into banking.

For six hundred years, since the miniature state declared sovereignty, Shalumari banks had been the biggest financial institution in Turith. Through merchant ships to airships, from coins to notes to cards and smartphones, the Shalumari banks adapted and survived. They were discreet, stable and utterly confidential. And far too many Turithian politicians had their own war chest stashed away in a Shalumari account to even think of passing legislation that would force them to open up.

Everyone with more than three lire to rub together had a Shalumari account. Tracking Shalumari-held funds was impossible. So why didn't Xandus have one? Wasn't it *magic* enough for him? Where did wizards bank, anyway—the Base Metals & Alchemical Trust?

Whatever. Nicco didn't have the time to wait for Xandus to fly to Shalumari and open an account, and he couldn't risk the wizard refusing to pay if Nicco didn't accept cash.

He waved Xandus away. "Leave it under the table. Goodnight, Xandus."

He watched the wizard slope out of the bar, looking nervous as all fifty-nine hells, then sighed. Bazhanka wasn't going to like this.

WALLUS BAZHANKA DIDN'T like it.

The mobster leaned back in his chair and folded ten fat fingers over his belly, staring balefully at Nicco. "Clarrum, please accept Mr Salarum's donation."

The bodyguard who had stopped Nicco's approach stepped out from behind Bazhanka and walked to Nicco, holding out his hand for the briefcase. Nicco gave it to him, and Clarrum turned, walked back to Bazhanka's table and put the briefcase down on it. But as he bent to open it, Bazhanka rapped the back of Clarrum's knuckles with a fork.

"Not right next to me, you idiot!" Bazhanka gestured at a side table, closer to Nicco than himself. "Go over there and open it."

Nicco tutted. "And I thought we were starting to bond. You don't even trust me to hand money over?"

Bazhanka stabbed his fork into a hunk of meat and stuffed it in his mouth. "Cash!" He snorted. "I'd have Clarrum whip you for impudence if I didn't think you'd enjoy it." He swallowed the mouthful with a loud gulp and looked up at the bodyguard. "Well?"

Clarrum opened the briefcase wide and held it up to show Bazhanka the contents. Twenty-five thousand lire in crisp notes.

"My, my. We *have* been a busy boy. Such a very busy boy. This money isn't dirty, is it, Nicco? You wouldn't just rip off a security skycar to pay your way?"

"No," said Nicco, cursing himself in silence for not thinking of that. He could have avoided working for Xandus at all. But it was too late now. "Money for a big commission," he said. "That's all."

"It's an awful lot of cash to be lying around in the open. Why haven't I heard about it?"

"Search me. Maybe you should keep your ear closer to the ground. Of course, that would require a waist that can bend in the middle." Nicco regretted the jibe even as the words left his lips, but he hadn't been able to resist.

Clarrum took a step toward him with a murderous glint in his eyes, but Bazhanka raised a hand to stop him. "No, Clarrum. Not in the club." He turned to Nicco, his sunken eyes burning with contempt. "You should remember where you are and why you're here. As you said yourself, this is only a fraction of the... donation you've pledged to my business."

"Oh, come on," said Nicco. "There's twenty-five grand in there! In one hit! You don't need the rest. Let's call it quits."

Bazhanka chuckled, a wet sound from the back of his throat. "So very funny... I was considering it, you see. I truly was, for my favourite young burglar. But not now, Nicco. No, not now.

"You have one week to present me with the balance. If you do not, you shall soon find your own waist remarkably flexible. Along with your spine. Get out!"

CHAPTER FIVE

GOVERNOR JARRAND L. Werrdun walked onto the stage next to City Hall and stood behind a lectern. The mayor, his wife resplendent in a silly hat, the head of the Trade Council, Werrdun's personal assistant and the assembled minor dignitaries all applauded him.

None of them had any idea they were standing on a bomb.

From behind a window on the 48th floor of a building overlooking the plaza, Nicco watched the ceremony through binoculars. The 48th floor was empty, awaiting refurbishment before yet another bunch of grey civil servants could move in and shuffle paper around, and Nicco sat on the floor next to a small transceiver, tuned to the PA down in the plaza, where Werrdun now stood facing a couple of thousand freezing cold well-wishers. Nicco wondered how many of them were employees of companies that stood to profit from this new trade agreement, 'incentivised' to attend by their bosses.

Nicco heard the applause through the transceiver and wondered if it was just the usual polite applause for a public speaker, or if they were as amazed as Nicco that the ancient Hurrundan governor could move under his own power. As he strode to the podium with an easy elegance, Nicco was reminded of the elderly Praali Archmage, Kathel, whom he'd seen during the Year Zero peace treaty broadcast. Perhaps Werddun was a wizard of some kind, too.

Thinking back to how the Year Zero fiasco had turned out, he hoped not.

Nicco had been unable to find Werrdun's exact age. In fact, two days of solid research had turned up very little about the governor's personal history at all, although it did unearth a wealth of information about the man's political life and Hurrunda's fortunes under his rule.

"*Mister Mayor... your good lady wife... Councillor.*" Werrdun acknowledged his hosts in perfect Turithian with a rich, sonorous voice, something else that had surprised Nicco when he first heard it. "*On behalf of the people and tradesmen of Hurrunda, I thank you for the hospitality shown to us by yourselves and the people of Azbatha. Though an ocean separates us, our cities are closer in character than we might think, and strengthening our relationship can only make us both stronger and more prosperous.*

"*Like you, we in Hurrunda labour under a mountain of bad press. Like the straits that separate you from the rest of Turith, the mountains that keep us apart us from our country are easily crossed in these times of magic and technology. But traditions live on, long after technology renders them obsolete, and so our cities share a tradition of isolationism. The Varnian people look on my city and they see a parochial place, with strange customs and an old man in charge. I know it's the same for you, here in Azbatha.*" Werrdun looked across at the mayor and smiled. The crowd picked up on his jibe and laughed along as the mayor's cheeks reddened. "*I believe we can use this common ground as a base, to grow our relationship and our commerce. Years of suspicion and fear have turned our great cities into strangers, and that saddens me—both as a governor and as an old man with distant family of my own right here in Azbatha. It feels good to be able to walk in their city at last..."*

Nicco had stopped listening. He was watching the security detail. Six of Werrdun's own bodyguards were on the stage, and Nicco guessed there were another half-dozen out in the crowd, watching for assassins and other shifty characters. There were also four Azbathan cops, a detachment sent to work alongside Werrdun's men, but Nicco wasn't worried about them. Azbathan police were lazy and corrupt; the governor's bodyguards would be better advised to keep an eye on them than the crowd.

Still watching through the binoculars, Nicco felt for the transceiver with his right hand and found the button that would detonate the bomb.

He pressed it.

NICCO'S RESEARCH HAD told him to expect Werrdun's guards to be top-notch. Serious professionals, not to be messed with. These men were used to dealing with threats.

Not that Hurrunda was some kind of battleground. By all accounts it was a wealthy city, with a good social improvement program and a leader who not only exercised some actual power, but whom most of the population genuinely liked. It was a far cry from Azbatha, where the mayor was a puppet for the city's largest crime and business interests, elected on the basis of being marginally less offensive than the other candidates.

Werrdun had served as governor of Hurrunda for sixty years, and in that time had turned the city around. Before he came to power, Hurrunda had been a wreck, a tiny sovereign state floundering on the vast shores of Varn, cut off from its own continent by the Hurrun Peaks—a wide swathe of hills and mountains that kept the city in isolation until magic and technology had made crossing the range safe and quick. Safe, because the mountains were thick with jungle, and the top indigenous predator was the groak—a lumbering carnivorous beast that happily ate anything in its path, be it human, animal or another groak. Quick, because the trails through the range were up to two hundred miles long, encircling Hurrunda in a fifty-mile diameter horseshoe of rainforest from coast to inland and back again.

Naturally for a population living in that kind of situation, the Hurrundans were very religious. So religious, in fact, that the priesthood ran the city as a theocratic dictatorship for over a thousand years. They followed the sacred Law of Kurreth, their strict—and, it seemed to Nicco as he read further, overly harsh—god. But the Kurrethi's grip on the city had slipped as access to the outside world became easier. Their attitudes to technology were backward, to say the least, and trade—even with relatively near cities like Azbatha—was a disaster. The Hurrundans were hungry, overworked, overtaxed and damn well sick of it all. A secular revolution was inevitable, and it finally came sixty years ago. Jarrand Werrdun didn't lead it, but he took part and was voted in as interim governor by a committee of the revolutionaries soon afterward, deemed a suitable, strong leader for Hurrunda's new age. Soon 'interim governor' turned into 'permanent governor,' and 'permanent governor' turned into 'governor for life.' Before they knew it the Hurrundans had replaced one dictatorship with another. Except they seemed perfectly happy with this one.

The difference, from what Nicco could find out, was in how Werrdun ran things. He directed the city well—well enough that Nicco, researching all of this on a library terminal in downtown Azbatha two days ago, couldn't find a single criticism of his rule from anyone who lived there. Not one. And the Turithian press, which barely acknowledged Varn's existence at the best of times, didn't seem to even know Hurrunda existed until last month when Werrdun's visit was first proposed.

Praise, by contrast, was plentiful. The Hurrundan media treated Werrdun like a benevolent god, publishing regular puff pieces that bordered on hagiography. The governor, Nicco read, had turned his back on superstition and invested in technology. Despite the war, he'd imported know-how and materials from Turith, Praal, Varn, everywhere. He'd encouraged business and science education, and done away with compulsory religious schooling. Three of the city's colleges were named after him. He'd encouraged free access, free trade and free expression. Over the last sixty years, Jarrand L. Werrdun had led Hurrunda to a golden age of wealth and quality of life, and everyone loved him for it.

Everyone except the Kurrethi, of course.

Fearing purges, the sect had gone underground. For the last sixty years they'd been a constant thorn in Werrdun's side, claiming oppression and resorting to violent protest. They bombed bars and shot at public officials, they reacted to secular policies with vague threats of retaliation in this life and the next. They released statements that accused Werrdun of making a pact with Ekklorn—the religion's adversary figure, an evil deity who was at constant war with Kurreth for the souls of humankind. They had quite literally demonised the governor.

Werrdun, his security and his citizens had all grown accustomed to these cranks. Life apparently went on as normal. The odd thing, to Nicco's eyes, was that Werrdun refused to actually outlaw Kurrethism. His police arrested plenty of the religion's soldiers, and funding them was illegal—though finding sympathetic donors both inside and outside the city didn't seem to be a big problem for the rebels—but their cries of oppression rang hollow. Werrdun had even allowed Kurrethi candidates to run in city ward elections, presumably to prove that the battle of reason versus faith was a fair one. But when the Kurrethi were soundly thrashed, as they had been repeatedly, they simply claimed the votes were rigged and bombed another public building. It seemed a lose-lose situation for Werrdun.

Recently, though, the terrorist threat had declined. It was rumoured the rebels had gone to ground somewhere in the Hurrun Peaks, using the jungle to hide their location and movements. But rumour also had it that post-Year Zero the Kurrethi had a new leader, a shadowy guru called Ven Dazarus, a dangerous, war-hardened man. Worried by the prospect of a genuine soldier leading the Kurrethi, the Hurrundan authorities had tried to flush them out of the mountains, but to no avail. Whatever was going on, the Kurrethi had suddenly gone very quiet.

This was all amazing to Nicco. Religious unrest was unheard of in Turith, where the state religion had long ago been supplanted by secularism. Nicco didn't know a single person who still attended church—though given his social circle, that probably wasn't much of a surprise—and the Turithian gods were relegated to being used as curses and turns of phrase. The idea of fighting a rebellion over gods was completely alien to Nicco.

But to Hurrundans the threat was very real, and decades of religious terrorism had honed Hurrundan security practices to a keen edge. Nicco saw for himself the discipline it enforced in Werrdun's security as he shadowed the governor. After the first couple of days, though, it was clear the besuited heavies were relaxing a little. Azbathan politicians were in more danger of being hit by the mob than a disenfranchised electorate, and Werrdun's schedule generally kept him to low-risk areas like industrial districts, tours of technology plants and dinner receptions at City Hall. But Nicco had seen men like Werrdun's security guards before, usually working as mercenaries for gang bosses. Ex-military, born to fight and trained to kill. No amount of relaxation would suppress their instincts if something serious kicked off, and it was pointless making any plan that relied on them letting their guard down. Instead, Nicco had to find some way to use their zeal to his advantage.

That was why he posed as an engineer and planted the bomb under the stage, the morning before Werrdun made his speech outside City Hall, so he could see Werddun's security in action.

As Nicco expected, Werrdun's own men were the first and fastest to react to the explosion. Two of them threw themselves at the governor, driving him to the ground and shielding him with their own bodies. Another two ran to the back of the stage, clearing an exit path for the governor and his entourage. The remaining pair drew blasters—entropy guns, typical bloody Varnians—and guarded Werrdun, scanning the crowd for signs of any further trouble.

Nicco followed Werrdun through the binoculars. Thick, black smoke billowed out from under the stage and filled the air, threatening to block his vision, but the binoculars automatically switched to infra-red motion sensing. The guards shielding Werrdun covered him completely. They weren't looking at the governor, they weren't even looking around for the source of the explosion. They just lay on top of Werrdun and didn't move. That wasn't what Nicco had wanted to see.

By contrast, the Azbathan police panicked. Two of them had their guns out, waving them around at the crowd and looking more dangerous than any potential assassin. One of them was cowering on the stage floor. The last—a tall, thin sergeant with long white hair—actually had the presence of mind to bundle the mayor, his wife (her silly hat had fallen off) and Werrdun's personal assistant backstage. Whoever he was, the man was wasted in the Azbathan force. Nicco made a mental note to avoid him.

As the people forty-eight floors below waited for something bad to happen, Nicco packed his equipment into a kit bag and left the room, leaving no trace he'd ever been there. Out in the corridor he headed for the nearest grav tube, stepped into it and slowly floated down to street level. The tube was packed, full of people above and below him, all shouting and screaming that there had been a huge explosion in the square.

But the people waiting for bad things to happen never got their climax. The explosion had just been a smoke bomb, a test to see what kind of security Nicco could expect if he went straight for Werrdun. And the answer was: a lot. This was the last in a series of recces Nicco had made on the governor's security and it was the final straw. He'd hoped to use their security routines against them somehow, to twist their efficiency and tactics to his advantage. But Werrdun's security simply didn't leave the man alone. They were loyal and attentive, and now Nicco knew they were also willing to die to protect him. How on earth could he get past that kind of commitment?

To make matters worse, it also seemed that Werrdun never took that damn necklace off. The only pictures Nicco had found showing Werrdun without the necklace were thirty years old. Not that Nicco could tell at first—the governor's appearance hadn't changed a bit in the intervening time, apart from the necklace. Nor had Nicco seen him without it since his arrival in Azbatha. For all he knew, the governor slept with it. Nicco had to conclude that Xandus was right—it really *was* magical in some way. Why else would he be so attached to it?

Nicco had to figure out some way to get Werrdun alone. It was the only possible answer. But the mayor had given his own official residence over to the governor for the duration of his visit, and security there was tight as a bug's arse. No chance of sneaking in and lifting the necklace from Werrdun while he slept. And even if there were, Nicco wasn't convinced Werrdun's security men didn't sleep in the same room. He probably didn't even go to the bathroom alone.

He joined the confused throng outside, racking his brains for an answer. Werrdun was only here for another two days, and after this little stunt his guards would be twice as vigilant as before. Tomorrow, the governor toured the Azbathaero Industries plant—that was what the sole surviving company down at the docks was called, Nicco had learned—to see their new prototype engine. In the evening he had another official dinner, this time with leading West Turithian fatcats. The day after that, the mayor had arranged a dinner cruise on Azbathaero's prototype airship to see the engine in action. Perhaps the mayor was hoping the trade agreement would encourage Hurrunda to invest in a few good cargo vessels. That evening was the final dinner reception, this time to sign the trade agreement itself, before Werrdun flew home again.

All of the events would be crawling with press, business moguls and hangers-on. There was no way Nicco would be able to get anywhere near Werrdun without being seen, and to get the governor alone would take a miracle. It was enough to make Nicco regret taking the job, and he felt his stomach knotting with worry and drugs. Sleep hadn't come easy the past couple of days, and Nicco had resorted to doping himself each night to help him rest. It worked a treat, but too much would give a man the cramps from hell, along with a nauseous fever. He feared he'd overdone it last night.

Nicco felt his forehead, but it was cool. No fever. He was just worrying too much. Think clearly, man! How could he get Werrdun alone long enough to take the necklace and make sure he didn't raise the alarm before Nicco slipped away? His security were with him everywhere, but Werrdun himself looked three hundred years old. How difficult could it be? There must be some way of getting to him, even past the police and the security goons and the press and the legion of doctors that must be necessary just to keep a man of his age alive...

Nicco smiled. Things always turned out be simple when you looked at them from a different angle.

CHAPTER SIX

THE *AZBATHAERO ASTRA* waited on the launch platform, gleaming and proud in the bright midday sun. The flagship of Azbathaero Industries, its sleek lines and smooth ovoid shape belied the power and efficiency of its prototype magnapulse engine. It was this engine that the company had shown off to Werrdun the day before, the same engine the mayor was hoping would win over the notoriously technophobic Varnians and persuade them to inject a much-needed booster into Azbatha's economy.

The congenital Turithian antipathy toward magic had cost the country dearly in some respects. Comul, its Archmage, was barely above Wegnak of Kyas in power; and Wegnak was a joke. Sure, by definition every Archmage had enough power to destroy the planet, but even at the top of the heap there was a hierarchy. The Institute at Turilum, Turith's capital, faced perpetual funding cuts and neglect by the state, who saw Archmages and their wizards as a foolish drain on the economy. Turith had been one of the last countries to adopt charm-enhanced power sources such as the engines that kept the ubiquitous airships running. Even then, most native Turithians would still choose a locally-built, all-tech vessel over something with a charm engine. A vessel like the *Astra*.

But if magic was mistrusted and largely ignored by Turithians, they more than made up for it with their faith in technology. From holovids to smartphones to grav tubes, from the world's only 500-storey tower to the lowly vacpac meal, it had all been invented right here and exported across the globe. For five centuries the global war had been a perfect testing ground for new technology. Azbathaero was just one of the country's many technological success stories, designing and building airships using both pure tech and magical engines. And now the company claimed its magnapulse prototype was as efficient and powerful as any charm engine on the planet. The company was poised to make a fortune.

At least that's what Nicco had read in a holozine when he was researching in the library. Frankly, he didn't much care. This maiden voyage was his best chance to steal Werrdun's necklace, and that was all that mattered to him.

Nicco stood in the VIP lounge and watched Werrdun's party board the *Astra*, led on board by the mayor, his wife and the CEO of Azbathaero. The mayor's wife seemed incensed that the boarding door wasn't big enough to fit through without removing her outrageously large hat. Then the wind snatched it out of her hand and propelled it straight into the Nissal Straits, and he had to fake a coughing fit to keep from laughing out loud.

Nicco took the opportunity to check out his fellow VIPs. Most of them were businessmen and -women, the same CEOs, CFOs, MDs and SOBs who'd been trailing Werrdun's tail since he arrived, all hoping for a juicy export contract to swell their bottom line. Another dozen or more were press, and the remainder was a large assortment of personalities and celebrities—rock stars, holovid presenters, lifestyle gurus, models and actors. At first they struck Nicco as a random selection, possibly invited just because they happened to be in Azbatha at the time. But then he recognised a few, and realised there was a very real connection: they weren't just *in* the city, they were all from Azbatha.

Most of them didn't live here any more, of course. It was a standing Azbathan joke that the second you made a million, a computer somewhere in Shalumar transferred the money directly to a realtor in Turilum. The only people still in Azbatha with any real money were corrupt politicians and merchants, and the crooks who corrupted them. But all of these celebrities had been born here, in the Pit-on-Stilts. Nicco had even seen some of them mention it on holovid interviews, normally to the horror and sympathetic noises of an interviewer whose idea of hardship was only having enough money to buy half a crate of Varnian wine.

The mayor must have pulled a lot of strings to set this up, another all-out attempt to impress the governor. Well, he'd get that, all right; Nicco would make sure this was one media event none of them would ever forget.

Nicco's own name-tag identified him as 'Durrun Karth,' a Varnian doctor of medicine. He wore a false beard, old-fashioned eye-glasses to disguise his face and an equally old-fashioned trouser suit. Strapped tight around his stomach was a fake paunch, and he bent his back a little and spoke with a heavy accent, inserting the occasional Varnian word or phrase into his conversation. Nicco's Varnian wasn't great, but like most of the criminal community in Azbatha a few choice words and phrases proved useful from time to time. He'd be in trouble if anyone tried to talk directly to him in Varnian, but Nicco was here to rob the governor, not strike up a polite conversation with him.

Nicco had squeezed his, or rather Dr Karth's, way onto the VIP list with a simple bribe in a shadowy bar. Come war or peace, some things would never change, and the corruptibility of Azbathan officials was one of them. If this plan was going to work, Nicco had to count on it.

Two security guards re-opened the exit and the guests slowly shuffled their way onto the launch pad toward the *Astra*. Nicco joined them, sauntering through the boarding checklist with a quick "Hurrka"—*thank you* in Varnian—and then he was through, heading to the boarding door, keeping to the centre of the crowd. He walked through the airlock at the same time as an ageing rock star accompanied by three nubile women. Nicco struggled to remember his name, but it wouldn't come. Some long-faded, big-haired synth-rocker, anyway. Nicco didn't recognise any of the girls, but he had no doubt they were earning a packet for this little sortie. The rock star winked at him. Nicco stayed in character and turned his head as if embarrassed.

They had ten minutes until take-off. Nicco put the time to good use.

First, he headed for the onboard storage locker area. After a quick check that nobody was watching, he took a keycard from the pocket of his trouser suit and slotted it into the lockpod of 72A. Nicco's examination of the *Astra*'s blueprints (chalk another one up for bribery) had shown him the most suitable place for his plans, and 72A was it. The locker was close to a set of stairs leading down to the emergency escape pods, very near a bathroom and positioned at the end of a corridor that couldn't be seen from any of the main rooms without turning a corner. It was perfect.

The lockpod illuminated green and the door slowly swung open. It should have been empty. No-one on board was actually going anywhere, after all. The flight plan consisted of four hours circling over the northern reach of the Nissal Straits. Enough time for Werrdun to see the magnapulse engine in action, conduct a dinner reception, listen to some formal music and get back down to earth again. But the locker wasn't empty, and Nicco thanked the watery saints under his breath. He closed the door and locked it.

Next he made his way to the galley. He could hear the chef bawling out his cooks all the way from the top of the stairs outside the main lounge, barking orders and insults with equal aplomb. Presumably the chef was having some problems with the mainly Varnian menu, served in honour of the visitor. From the way he shouted, Nicco wondered if he'd been a Turithian army chef during the war. And now here he was, cooking Varnian dishes for a Varnian dignitary. Nicco could only imagine how many bodily fluids the governor would be ingesting today.

Bold as he could muster, Nicco walked through the door and looked around to get his bearings. The chef had his back to him, berating two of his cooks by the main dish counter. The starter cook was at his station, stirring a large pot. According to the manifest Nicco had read, the starter was a broth of boiled tanglefish, a Turithian dish, with root vegetables from the Hurrun Peaks and spices from Praal. Being an archipelago, most of Turith's native dishes were seafood of one kind or another, and the tangy smell from the steaming fish made Nicco salivate. But this was one meal he wouldn't be eating.

Nicco walked over to the starter cook, gesticulating wildly. "Hey, you!" he shouted in a thick Varnian accent. The cook looked up, startled. "This is tentacle fish, yes? Tentacle fish soup for the governor?" Nicco stood close to the cook, almost touching him, and pointed furiously at the pot of boiling tanglefish.

"It's, erm... tanglefish... kind of like tentacles, yeah... sorry, who are you?"

Nicco ignored the question. "Tanglefish, yes! Now listen, it's very important you cook this properly! The governor is not from this country and his stomach is delicate—very delicate! If not cooked properly, this fish could poison him, do you understand? I am a doctor from Varn, and you must listen! What instructions have you been given to cook this... tanglefish?"

The cook trembled, bewildered and caught off guard by Nicco's ranting. "Well, we—that is—hang on, I'd better get the chef..."

The cook turned away from the pot and called over to the chef. The chef looked over his shoulder to respond, saw Nicco and almost ran to the starter counter. Evidently, he wasn't used to people just walking into his galley.

Equally evidently, he wasn't Turithian. The chef's skin was the deep brown colour of a born and bred Varnian.

"Ekklorn's hooves, what's going on here? Get out of my galley!"

"He was asking about the tanglefish broth, sir," said the cook. "Said it might make the governor sick. Does it really give Varnians the squits, sir? I think..."

"Be quiet, boy!" roared the chef. He loomed over Nicco and jabbed a finger at his chest. "Now look here, you! I spent twenty years cooking out of a damn *tent*, and never had a single man sick! Not one! So shut your trap and get out of my galley before I have you thrown off this ship, Mr—" He peered at Nicco's name badge, but Nicco didn't give him a chance to finish.

"Doctor Karth," said Nicco, dropping the strength of his fake accent a little, hoping the Chef wouldn't spot it. "Very well, Mr Chef. I am only concerned for the health of our illustrious guest and I can see you have the situation under control. I will leave you now. Sorry to trouble you!" Nicco turned and strode to the galley door. Behind him, the cook said something about the good doctor being Varnian to the chef. Nicco opened the galley door...

"Hold on!" the chef shouted.

Nicco stopped in the doorway, sweating.

"Thought you had an accent, but I couldn't place it... Whereabouts in Varn are you from, Doctor?"

"Tykkas," said Nicco, perhaps a touch too quickly. He'd selected the good Doctor's home with care, a university town halfway across the continent from Hurrunda in the northern province of Haslandia, to account for his half-coloured skin.

"Really!" said the chef. And then he said something in pure Varnian.

Nicco made out the words *cousin*, *over there* and something that might have been *school*, but he couldn't be sure. This was getting out of hand. He looked around nervously as the chef, smiling now, waited for a reply.

There was nothing else for it. Nicco would have to run for it and ditch the disguise. He hunched his shoulders slightly, ready to push the chef backwards...

"*Staff announcement: three minutes to lift-off, three minutes. Lock down and secure, I repeat, lock down and secure. Three minutes.*"

The chef's smile vanished, replaced by the hassled expression of a man up against the clock. He gently pushed Nicco out the galley door, and spoke again in Varnian. This time Nicco made out the words *go*, *now*, *talk* and *later*. Nicco said "Hurrka" and "Felishe"—*goodbye*—then hurried up the stairs as the chef pulled the galley door closed.

Only when he reached the top of the stairs did Nicco breath again. That was close, and risky. He couldn't risk running into that chef again. But he'd pulled it off. It was all going according to plan.

Nicco hurried to the VIP launch lounge to find his seat ready for lift-off. He was worried that he might arrive to find everyone else already seated, and that would be bad. His job here was to be as bland and inconspicuous as possible.

He needn't have worried. To ease the pressure of lift-off, the launch lounges of all modern Turithian airships were fully grav-enabled, and the units automatically activated two minutes before lift-off. A small bunch of the celebrities were having way too much fun with this, taking giant leaps across the floor and vaulting over rows of chairs with ease. The stewards, wearing omnimag-soled shoes to keep them firmly on the floor, were frantically herding everyone into their seats.

Nicco recognised the rock star from earlier among those jumping around in the semi-gravity. When a steward bodily pulled him back down to the floor, he started demanding to know why they had to sit here when the governor and mayor's entourage got their own private launch lounge and what sort of stupid rule barred them from drinking during lift-off. He added some speculations as to the stewards' parentage.

Nicco took advantage of the chaos and slipped into the first available seat he could find, hitting the 'secure' button to activate the locking straps as he sat down. The straps whirred into action and snaked across his lap and chest, holding him tightly. There was no going back now. The stewards' determination appeared to have won the day, and all the passengers were now seated—even the drink-deprived rock star, who quietly sulked. The stewards took their own seats at the side of the lounge.

The base thrusters fired up, sending tremors through the floor. Nicco took a deep breath.

Lift-off.

THE NEXT TWO minutes, like any airship ascent, were very exciting.

The ship launched vertically at a tremendous velocity. Even in the pressurised grav-controlled environment of the launch lounge Nicco felt G-forces pushing against him, trying to compress his spine. After thirty seconds the airship slowed its ascent, switching from base thrusters to the main engines, and the G-forces eased off.

The automatic locking straps fell open, freeing the passengers to move. Nicco saw the ageing rock star across the room stand

and simultaneously thrust himself up out of his chair, expecting to float into the air. He didn't—the grav had automatically deactivated as the locking straps opened. He fell, face first, onto the floor, and the rock star's entourage gasped. Everyone else laughed, none louder than the stewards.

As was customary on any airship journey, everyone hurried through to the lower viewing pod to catch a glimpse of the distant earth below. The pod was hemispherical, criss-crossed by ladders and gantries to enable views from every possible angle under the ship. There was one on the upper deck too, for stargazers.

Everyone had seen it before, of course. There wasn't a man on board who didn't regularly travel on airships. But they went to the pod to 'ooh' and 'aah' all the same. It was a tradition.

The hour after that was very dull.

Nicco found the bar and ensconced himself in it, hunched over a non-alcoholic drink. He had no desire or need to speak to any of the other VIPs, and certainly not the ageing rock star currently drinking himself and his girls into a daze a few tables over. Right about now, the MD of Azbathaero would be conducting Werrdun's tour of the engine with the mayor and entourage in tow. In the meantime, all Nicco could do was wait.

Finally, the tannoy announcement came for dinner and Nicco joined the wave of people moving from the bar to the restaurant. His nerves were on edge as he took a seat. His dinner companions were two holovid presenters he vaguely recognised, a man and a woman, and two other men he didn't know at all. One of them was loud and slick, a holokino producer in trademark all-black, the other a middle-aged corporate type in a dark blue suit. Nicco wondered who in the fifty-nine hells had organised the seating arrangements.

Werrdun, the mayor and their companions were already seated at the head table. When everyone was seated, the mayor stood up and called for quiet. Time for a speech. "Ladies and gentlemen," he said, "It is my great honour to welcome you all aboard the *Astra* for her maiden voyage. And it gives me even greater pleasure to welcome Governor Werrdun aboard, to see superior Azbathan technology in action." There was a smattering of applause. The press crowded around the top table, recording the event for their streams, taking notes and snapping holopics. "And now, ladies and gentlemen... Governor Werrdun."

The mayor led the applause himself this time, and Werrdun stood up to deliver his own speech. As he began, thanking everyone involved for their time and hospitality etc., etc., Nicco cast a glance at the tables of suits. How many times must they have already heard this speech, with slight variations, during Werrdun's visit? Didn't they *ever* get bored? He was zoning out already; all he cared about was the food.

And finally, it came. Nicco sniffed at the tanglefish broth. It smelled pretty good. Any other time, he would have tucked in. But not today.

"Doctor," said the young woman on his table, "are you not eating?" She was a kids' holovid presenter Nicco had seen while channel-hopping in the mornings. She was apparently something of a lust object for teenage boys, but Nicco didn't see the attraction himself; the woman was bone-thin and wore enough make-up to make Xandus think twice. Nicco preferred his women natural, like Tabby. Not that he'd ever tell Tabby that, of course.

"I am from the mainland of Varn," he replied in his fake accent. "I am unused to seafood, and find it does not sit well with my digestion."

"Have you ever tried tanglefish?"

"Once. I was sick for many days."

"Where did you try it?"

By the watery saints, thought Nicco, take a bloody hint. "In the Lighthouse Tower restaurant, miss. I am sure it was very good, but..."

"No, no, that was your mistake," said the holokino producer. From his incessant pre-food anecdotes and egotism, Nicco had him marked as some kind of bigshot. "Tea For Turith's a right hole. Overpriced rubbish, and their chefs don't know one end of a fish from the other. You should try Marakide's, at the Hotel Azbatha in downtown. Now *there's* a chef who knows his fish."

"I've never been to Marakide's," said the other presenter, a sports commentator Nicco had seen once or twice on late night shows. "Is it really that good? I mean, you say the Tower's expensive, but Marakide's is positively extortionate."

"Is it?" said the producer. "I hadn't noticed, I don't really look at the bill. But I don't care what they charge, it's worth every lira. Palluk Marakide's a good friend of mine, actually."

"Really?" The woman's eyes lit up.

"Sure," said the producer. "We go way back..."

The corporate, who'd barely spoken a word, looked over at Nicco and raised an amused eyebrow as the three media darlings began to yap. Nicco's issues with the fish had been forgotten, and by the looks of it so had Nicco himself. He smiled back at the man and shrugged.

"So, Doctor," said the businessman as he tucked into his tanglefish broth, "if you're Varnian, what's your purpose on board? Trying to broker your own deals under Werrdun's nose, perhaps?"

He was sharp-eyed and well-kept for his age, and Nicco couldn't help but wonder if there was more to him than met the eye. He decided to play it safe, and shook his head. "No, no," he said, "I am attending in the place of a colleague from the Turith, who is indisposed today."

"Ah. Medicine without borders, is it? Nations working together for the common good?"

"Yes... yes, something like that."

"Very admirable, old boy." He raised his glass and smiled. "I'm all for a bit of international co-operation."

Nicco glanced at the other guests on his table. They were swapping yuppie restaurant tips and swooning at the producer's tales of his fat expense account, eating their broth between snatches of gossip and resolutely ignoring the foreign doctor. That was all fine by Nicco.

He glanced at the top table. Werrdun—and, Nicco noted, half of his security—were eating the broth, too. Excellent.

It happened as the waiters retrieved the diners' bowls. The children's presenter groaned and rubbed her stomach. The sports presenter made concerned noises and asked if she was all right. She nodded, and said it was just a bit of cramp.

Then she vomited in the producer's lap.

Nicco forced himself not to laugh. The producer yelped in horror and called for a waiter. But the waiter was distracted by one of the fatcat CEOs falling out of his chair and moaning in pain. Then another, another and another... Nicco looked to the top table and saw the mayor's wife doubled up in her chair, trying to hide the fact she was throwing up all over her husband's expensive shoes. Not that he cared, as he was busy clutching his stomach and roaring about cramp.

Governor Jarrand L. Werrdun, meanwhile, had collapsed on the floor.

CHAPTER SEVEN

MOVING ALMOST AS fast as the governor's security team, Nicco sprinted to the top table and made a beeline for Werrdun.

A meaty hand slamming against his chest stopped him in his tracks, but he'd been expecting that. Nicco looked up into the stern eyes of a dark-skinned, narrow-eyed Hurrundan security man. "Where do you imagine you go?" he said with a thick accent.

"I am a doctor," said Nicco. "Let me through, I can help!"

The guard narrowed his eyes. "What is this? Poison of the food?"

"Yes and no. We call it Aberrant Intestinal Haematomic Occlusion Syndrome. It is common with certain foods at high altitudes, yes. What did the governor eat this morning?"

The guard had to think about that for a second. Finally he said, "Roast tallus hearts. With the pepper sauce."

"Ah!" Nicco exclaimed as if he'd discovered a cure for cancer. "Pepper with tanglefish, at this altitude—I feared something like this might happen! Let me through, I can help him!"

The guard hesitated, watching dozens of people around the room vomiting and moaning. "Is it could threaten his life?" he asked. But before Nicco could answer, a fresh bout of retching from Werrdun persuaded the guard that, life-threatening or not, his boss needed help. "All right. Go forward. You do Werrdun first."

"Hurrka," said Nicco, and bent over the governor. He was curled up on the floor in a fetal position, moaning softly. Nicco put his ear to the man's back and tapped it in several places. Then he pulled Werrdun's shirt up and prodded his stomach, looking for something. Werrdun whimpered with every jab.

At least, Nicco hoped that's what it looked like he was doing. The truth was he knew exactly what was wrong with Werrdun, and everyone else currently expelling the contents of their stomach over the restaurant floor.

He had doped the starter pot back in the galley, when the cook turned his back to fetch the chef. It had been given plenty of time to ferment in the soup, and right now it would be coursing through the digestive system of practically everyone in the room. Nicco had no doubt they were all in immense pain. They probably all thought they were going to die.

Nicco looked up to see the guard who'd questioned him watching his impression of a doctor. He leaned back as if in thought, and across the room he spotted what looked alarmingly like a ship's doctor approaching. He couldn't have that. Nicco leapt to his feet and shouted at the guard.

"It is as I feared! Quickly, to his quarters!"

The guard looked around. "What of the others?"

"Who is the most important man here?" Nicco hissed at the bodyguard, hoping his Varnian impersonation would give his patriotism some weight. "The proud governor of a Varnian state, or a bunch of Turithian fools?"

"Is true, exactly. This way."

The guard lifted Werrdun onto his broad shoulders and carried the governor out of the room, followed quickly by Nicco. He didn't have much time.

The guard led him through the corridors to the VIP guest suite. Still carrying the governor, he pulled a card from his jacket and slotted it into the room's entry lockpod. The door slid open with a quiet hiss and the guard led the way inside.

Two Hurrundan security men leapt to their feet from the couch. One of them dropped the holovid remote. They shouted what looked like a formal salutation at the bodyguard, but he just snarled at them and continued through to the suite's rest chambers. Nicco stifled a smirk and followed. Once inside, he placed Werrdun on the bed and looked at Nicco. The governor was already drifting in and out of consciousness, which suited Nicco perfectly.

"Will governor die?" asked the guard.

"Not if we act fast," said Nicco. "I must administer certain medicines. You must fetch for me. Go, to the ship's doctor!" Nicco reeled off a list of medicines, just ordinary antibiotics and bowel remedies that would speed up the natural process of the dope wearing off.

But to Nicco's chagrin, the guard didn't leave the room. He just poked his head out the door and relayed the instructions to one of the guards, then stepped back inside and closed the door.

"Is there no magic for this to him?"

Nicco shook his head. "I am a doctor of medicine and science, not a wizard." He reached inside his suit jacket and pulled out three things: a vial, a hypodermic needle and a small metal box. It was a last resort, but the guard's reluctance to leave the room had tipped Nicco's hand.

"Ekklorn's hooves!" said the guard, staring aghast at the hypodermic. "What is this?"

"A sedative," said Nicco. "I carry it for air sickness, as a precaution." Unseen by the guard, he pressed a button on the metal box.

"No," said the guard, approaching Nicco and holding out his hand. "You will not, it is forbid. Give to me!"

Nicco obliged, giving him all fifty mills straight into his upper arm.

He staggered back, eyes wide with surprise. "What...?" he croaked. Then he collapsed.

Nicco caught the guard before he hit the ground, then gently lowered him to the floor. He couldn't chance any other guards in the suite hearing the sound and coming to investigate. He knew no-one would see what was going on—the metal box was a miniature black noise generator, a smaller version of the one in Allad's stock room that the fence had loaned him, no questions asked. According to the ship blueprints, there was both a day/night camera and a sensing mic in this room. The black noise would block them completely, giving Nicco some time to work, safe from prying eyes. But not much.

Werrdun tried to sit up and shout in protest, but he was too weak to make a sound. Nicco pulled another vial from his jacket and smiled at the frightened governor.

"Relax," he said. "You'll live." Then he plunged the hypodermic into Werrdun's shoulder. The governor was unconscious before Nicco removed the needle.

Nicco took Werrdun's necklace in both hands and pulled it from around his neck. It was lighter than its size suggested, and once again Nicco wondered if it really was magical, but there was no time for philosophy.

Nicco opened his shirt, exposing the fake paunch, pulled a small zipper on its side and pulled out a small canvas bag. Inside the bag were two small omnimag grips. He removed the grips, put the necklace in their place and fastened the bag, then attached the grips securely to the bag's straps. He creeped over to the door to check it was fully closed, then moved across the room to the single small window looking out across the sky.

Nicco pulled open a small panel underneath the window. Set

into the hull wall was an emergency opening lever. This was risky, as the *Astra* was cruising at several thousand feet. The pressure differential between the room and outside would be enormous. And pulling this lever would normally sound an immediate alarm on the bridge. Nicco hoped the black noise generator would take care of that.

He pulled the lever. The window seal popped with a loud hiss, opening just a crack. But already the suction was fierce, raising up the bed sheets like a snake charmer. Nicco steadied himself. He had to be quick, very quick, to avoid getting sucked out and dropped into the Nissal Straits below.

Deep breath...

He opened the window with one hand, shoved the canvas bag through it with the other and slammed it back against the outside of the hull. The omnimag grips hit the surface with a metallic *clang*. Nicco pushed the sealing button and let go, hoping they would work quickly enough. He pulled his arm back in, slowly, fighting against the suction that threatened to throw him into the clear sky. A pillow flew past his head and through the window. He pushed against the interior wall with his free hand, using it as leverage, twisting his body to pull the other arm back in...

It was in. Nicco pulled the window closed again, then raised the emergency lever. The window seal closed with a satisfying slurping sound.

He'd done it. He'd stolen Werrdun's necklace.

Now came the hard part.

CHAPTER EIGHT

"He's resting. Your colleague is watching over him, and I have given him instructions for when those medicines arrive." Nicco closed the bedroom door behind him and headed for the suite door. He talked fast, hoping to distract the guards from his suddenly appearing several kilos lighter than when he first entered.

One of the room guards moved to block his exit and said something in Varnian. Nicco didn't understand it, but it was clear enough that the guard didn't want him to leave. He looked the guard in the eye. His nerves were jangling like a brass band, but he maintained his composure and sounded deadly serious.

"Young man, right now there are more than a hundred other people on this ship who need my help." Nicco glared at the guard. Could this man even understand him? He didn't know, and he wasn't about to try his own rusty Varnian on him. Nicco just tried to sound as ominous as possible. "There is nothing more I can do for Governor Werrdun—he is safe, and sleeping through the pain. Now stand aside and let me do my job."

Whether or not the guard had understood what Nicco had said, it seemed to work. The guard reluctantly stood aside and let Nicco past.

Nicco walked through the door, briskly but not so fast he gave his nerves away. When it closed behind him he finally allowed himself to breathe out, then started to jog down the corridor, retracing his steps back toward the restaurant. He checked his watch. By his reckoning, he had about two minutes before the room guards went to check on Werrdun. They'd see their unconscious colleague, of course, and immediately start looking for 'Dr Karth.' How long from that point until they noticed Werrdun's necklace was missing? No more than another minute, Nicco reckoned. He'd tucked the old man under his bed sheets before leaving, but as soon as the guards checked the governor was still alive they'd pull back the covers and notice. So that gave him two, maybe three...

Nicco turned a corner and collided with someone coming from the opposite direction. Stumbling to keep his balance, he looked down and saw a dark-haired woman, green to the gills and leaning on the wall for support. Sweat beads peppered her forehead, but she was upright, just about, and looked determined to stay that way. And with her was a doctor. A real one.

The woman looked up at Nicco from under heavy eyelids and spoke with a heavy Varnian accent. "How... is he?"

Nicco realised who she was and why she was headed toward the guest suite. Mirrla Werrdun, the governor's daughter. He slipped back into the role of Dr Karth, calm and reassuring.

"He is resting, miss, but stable. He will be all right."

"Who in the fifty-nine hells are you?" said the doctor, with no accent. He was the local medical support, probably the ship's doctor.

"I am Dr Karth, of Varn," said Nicco. "I attended the governor immediately after his collapse. He is in his suite."

"So you know what this is? Because if it's ordinary food poisoning, I'm a bloody Praali adept."

Nicco shuffled from foot to foot. He didn't have time to try and con a doctor about symptoms and made-up disorders, but to just up and leave would raise suspicion.

"Indeed, no. It may be some kind of allergic reaction, I am not sure. Please, I must now attend to others."

But the doctor didn't budge. Nicco wondered if the man was playing for time until security came by. "Allergy? I hadn't thought of that. But what kind—"

"Aaaaaah!" Mirrla Werrdun grimaced and doubled up in pain. "Never mind... your bloody theories... just get me to a bed!"

Nicco took that as his cue. "She is right, she needs rest." He set off down the corridor at a fast pace. "I will check on the other passengers!" He didn't look back, hoping Mirrla's distress would keep them both engaged.

It seemed to. He rounded the next corner and broke into a run. That little exchange had cost him thirty seconds. He had maybe a minute and a half at most to reach Locker 72A.

Turn left, forward fifty yards. Turn right, pass two more corridors. Turn left. Ignore the heaving passenger on the right...

Finally Nicco stood at the end of the back corridor he'd visited before take-off, along with locker 72A. He ran to the end, pulled the locker card from his trousers and shoved it in the lockpod, which showed green and slowly opened. Nicco yanked it open, grabbed a medium-sized cardboard box, slammed the locker door shut, retrieved the card and made it to the nearby bathroom in two long strides.

The bathroom was occupied.

Nicco froze, unsure of his next move. He cursed himself for not slipping the hastily scrawled *OUT OF ORDER* note on the bathroom door. By the watery saints, what a stupid oversight!

He hammered on the door with his fist. "Hey, hurry up in there!"

A muffled giggle, a woman's laugh, came from inside. Then a man's voice, also muffled: "Find another one man! I'm busy!"

Nicco recognised the voice: the ageing rock star, the one with the escorts. He sighed.

He couldn't wait. He'd been lucky to get this far without the alarm being raised. There was no sense in pushing it. He'd just have to get changed right here in the corridor.

Nicco opened the box. The steward he bribed to stash the bag for him before the passengers boarded had thought he was secreting a present for the governor, from one Varnian abroad to another. And sure enough, at the top of the box was a Turithian fish carving, a common souvenir from the island nation. But underneath the carving, under the packing materials holding it, were a skyfall suit, a pair of goggles, a pair of omnimag boots, two handheld omnimag grips and a grav belt.

Nicco laid them on the floor and began to undress. He pulled off his suit jacket and shirt, then unstrapped the empty paunchbag. Next were the shoes and trousers. All the clothes were fitted with quick-release fastenings, a trick he'd learnt as a child from the girls at Madame Zentra's, and within ten seconds Nicco was naked except for his underwear.

The bathroom door opened.

The rock star and his girls—all three of them, Nicco noted with surprise—fell out of the bathroom and onto the carpet, laughing all the way down. When they looked up and saw Nicco standing there in his underwear, they laughed some more.

The rocker picked himself up and leant against the wall. "Bathroom's free," he laughed. His words were slurred, and Nicco remembered he hadn't seen any of them at dinner. They must have spent the entire trip up till now in the bar. "Here, if you're that desperate, I could always lend you one of the girls. Sharla...?" He looked around hazily.

Sharla, if that really was her name, looked Nicco up and down and smiled. "No, sorry... Nice bod, but I can't stand beards." They all laughed and staggered away.

The beard! Nicco had forgotten about it. He ripped it off, followed by the eye glasses, then threw everything he'd removed into the box. He scooped up the new gear and leapt into the bathroom.

The skyfall suit was pro-quality: fully padded and insulated, with integral gloves and socks and a lined fabric hood to protect his ears from the high altitude winds. Nicco slipped the goggles on before pulling up the hood. Next came the boots, more military than pro, with secured fastenings and one-touch omnimag activation. He pulled the grav belt around his waist, then clipped the handheld omnimag grips to it. He was ready.

Nicco opened the bathroom door and poked his head out just a little to check the coast was clear. No-one around, but he could hear running footsteps from elsewhere around the ship. Maybe they'd found the unconscious guard. What about the missing necklace?

It didn't matter. Nicco only needed another twenty seconds.

He stepped out of the bathroom and kicked the box a couple of feet across the floor. There was one more item inside, taped to the lid—a cigarette lighter. He lit it and held it to the packing materials inside the box, igniting them immediately. The fire spread quickly. Nicco dropped the burner inside the box and ran down the nearby stairs.

The floor below housed the ship's emergency escape pods, non-steering grav vehicles that would drop anyone escaping the ship safely onto dry ground or sea. As Nicco sprinted along the corridor to the nearest pod, he counted in his head. The fire should destroy his disguise, more or less, but more importantly, burning the fish carving would produce thick smoke, smoke that would hit the ceiling of the corridor any second now.

Five. Four. Three. Two. One...

Sirens blared. Emergency lights flashed. Ceiling water extinguishers sprayed.

And the doors to the emergency escape pods automatically unsealed with a satisfying *hiss*.

THIS SHIP HAD forty escape pods. Each pod was accessed by a double-skin door that led directly from the main ship interior to the pressurised pod cabin, and which was normally fully locked down. Only a few things could unlock these doors: direct activation by the captain from the bridge, an emergency activation by two senior crew members on the floors above this one... or a fire alarm, which automatically opened the locks.

The system was simple. Once the pod was full and everyone had locking straps on, the escapee nearest the door pressed a big red button helpfully marked *LAUNCH*, which closed and sealed the pod door, then ejected it from the airship to float gently down to earth.

But there was also an override, a manual switch on this side of the door that could be used to seal and launch a pod in case of unconscious escapees.

Nicco hit the switch.

The pod door closed silently. Magnetic repulsor rings around the pod bay housing powered up with a hum, glowed sky blue, then pulsed three times. The pod shot from the bay in silence.

Nicco smiled. Tracking that would keep them occupied for a while.

He bent down and pressed the button to activate his omnimag-soled boots. They attached to the floor with a deep thud. Nicco braced himself, then pulled open the door to the now-empty pod bay. The pressure differential hit him again, but this time the boots kept him safely inside.

Not for long. Nicco walked into the bay as quickly as he dared. If he lost his grip now, he'd be sucked into thin air; but if someone came down to check on the pod and saw him still here, he may as well throw himself off anyway.

He reached the end of the bay and took the omnimag grips from his belt. Holding one firmly in each hand, he leaned forward and reached around, clamping them to the external hull. He hit the seals with his thumbs. It was too noisy to hear the grips' activation hum or the oddly wet sound of the seals coupling against the surface. And it was too bright to tell whether the soft green light was on or not.

Oh well, thought Nicco. Here goes nothing.

CHAPTER NINE

THE GRIPS WORKED. That was the good news.

The bad news was that holding onto them at an altitude of ten thousand feet was a lot more difficult than Nicco had expected. As he crawled around the *Astra*'s hull on all fours, he lost his grip several times. Only his other hand and the omnimag boots kept him in place each time, a tiny, unnoticed figure clinging to the ship's exterior like an ant traversing a balloon.

Struggling against the rushing wind, he made his way round the ship, careful to remain unseen. There was a six-yard region around the hull's equator that couldn't be seen by either the upper or lower viewing platforms, and Nicco stayed within it as much as possible.

Finally, he neared his destination. He'd lost all track of time. Had it taken him five minutes, or fifty? His arms and legs ached like never before. Nicco had scaled hundred-storey buildings in storms using omnimag grips, but this was a whole different kettle of tanglefish. With a grunt he crawled the last few feet upward, over the equator of the ship, toward his goal, Werrdun's bedroom window, where Nicco had left the bag.

It was gone, along with the omnimag grips that should have been holding it to the hull.

Nicco's mind raced. Had the grips failed? Had he let go of them too soon? Had he been discovered? Were the security guards patiently waiting for him inside, laughing at his amateurism?

Nicco's thoughts were interrupted when his hand came away again, losing his grip on the hull...

He stared at the omnimag grip in disbelief.

Then his boots came away too.

As Nicco plummeted to earth, he found himself smiling serenely.

He'd read the *Astra* brochure when planning the job, and it made a big deal about the ship's security measures. The war may be over, but people were still nervous about air travel. What if some extremist nutters in the middle of nowhere decided to take potshots at a commercial flight? What about all those floating magnamines still up here in the sky, waiting for a passing ship to attach themselves to?

That was what Nicco had overlooked. Azbathaero claimed that the *Astra* was completely immune to magnamines. Of course, it hadn't gone into detail; but now that he was falling to earth at terminal velocity, Nicco could hazard a guess. The boffins on Turilum had been making great strides in active surface coatings: holovid displays as hard as steel, for instance, and waterproof digital smartcloth.

A recent breakthrough he'd read about reconfigured its molecular structure when it sensed nanomagnets. They were supposedly still at the prototype stage, but maybe Azbathaero had got hold of some before official production began. Or perhaps they'd developed their own. Maybe this one just changed constantly, cycling through different molecular formations.

However it worked, the bag had fallen afoul of it, probably dropping into the Nissal Straits after just a few seconds. Nicco guessed he'd only stayed on the hull as long as he had because he was constantly moving. As soon as he'd stopped, the grips had failed.

He was halfway down, five thousand feet above the ocean and facing the Azbathan skyline. In front of him lay the docks, the industrial ghost town and longtime thorn in the city council's side. To his right the steel needle of Azbatha's famous Lighthouse Tower pierced the sky, gleaming in the pink afternoon sunlight. To his left, the whole of Turith stretched out across the ocean, and directly below him the Nissal Straits beckoned, black and cold. He did his best to push through the air, skyswimming to get closer to land, but it was too far and Nicco was falling too fast. He'd just have to swim.

Five hundred feet above the ocean, Nicco activated his grav belt. It kicked in almost instantly, resisting his terminal velocity and slowing his 160-feet-a-second freefall to a slow, gentle drop within a few seconds. He floated the last couple of hundred feet and landed in the water feet first.

The grav belt would keep him afloat during the swim to shore, and Nicco was a natural swimmer. He just hoped the skyfall suit would keep him warm for long enough. Out here in the sea there was a good chance you'd die of exposure long before you drowned.

As he began the long breaststroke to shore, Nicco felt that, overall, the job had gone well. Despite the omnimag problems, he'd stolen the necklace and got away scot-free. Now all he had to do was lay low for a couple of days.

He wondered if he'd make the top story on tonight's news stream.

CHAPTER TEN

HE WASN'T THE top story so much as the entire stream for the next twelve hours.

Nicco finally returned to his apartment, damp and shivering, a couple of hours before sundown. He undressed as soon as he got through the door and threw the wet clothes over the back of a chair. He hadn't dared take the monorail to get back—he would have stood out too much, and all it would take is some wiseass cop to notice, think about what had happened on the *Astra* and put two and two together—but on the bright side, the walk back to his apartment had given him time to dry off a little.

He picked up the remote and flicked on the holovid, setting the stream to autosurf.

"*Political outrage and an embarrassed mayor this evening, as an unknown thief steals visiting Varnian Governor Jarrand Werrdun's priceless necklace...*"

Not bad, short and to the point. Nicco walked into the bathroom and took a long, hot shower.

"*In a daring theft today, a gang of thieves stole a necklace belonging to the governor of Hurrunda, who is visiting Azbatha to sign a new trade negotiation between Turith and Varn...*"

'Daring,' he liked that. But 'gang of thieves'? They made him sound like a bunch of dim-witted bank robbers. He dressed and cooked himself a meal.

"*It just goes to show, some things never change. What in the fifty-nine hells did he expect, coming to Azbatha and waving his priceless magic necklace around? Is he senile?*"

Not the most sensitive wording, but Nicco couldn't argue with the logic... He sat on his couch, barefoot and relaxed, flicking from stream to stream with equal parts amusement and amazement that it was such a big story. Slow news day?

"*The mayor tonight expressed his anger at what he called a 'blatant act of sabotage against the trade agreement between Turith and Varn,' which remains unsigned after Governor Werrdun's sudden illness and the theft of his chain of office. The mayor promised to direct every available resource to finding the necklace and punishing the culprits...*"

Sabotage against the trade agreement? Nicco laughed, almost choking on his roast tallus.

"*Mirrla Werrdun, the governor's daughter and personal assistant, told reporters tonight that Mr Werrdun is still unwell after what now appears to have been an outbreak of food poisoning during his dinner reception on the* Azbathaero Astra, *a prototype airship belonging to the local engineering company. The governor, who is... erm...*" The anchor suddenly looked confused. He looked angrily at someone off-camera and hissed, "*What do you mean, 'check and confirm age'? Never mind...*" He turned back to the camera. "*Excuse me. Miss Werrdun said the governor, who is staying at the mayoral palace, will now remain in Azbatha until he is well enough to return home to Hurrunda.*"

Nicco felt a brief pang of worry. Whatever the official line, and sprightly as he'd been, there was no denying Werrdun was an old man. Had the dope been too much for him? An average man would be over the worst of it by now: the vomiting should have stopped after an hour at most, and the stomach cramps would fade by the evening. But Werrdun wasn't an ordinary man, he must have been ninety years old. By the watery saints, thought Nicco, don't let him die of a bloody ulcer or something.

"The thieves have not yet been identified, but sources close to the mayor tell us one of them may have been disguised as a doctor. Whether this is connected to the outbreak of food poisoning is..."

That hit a little close to home. 'Sources close to the mayor'? What in the fifty-nine hells did that mean, anyway? Nicco doubted any of the Hurrundan security men would be talking to the Azbathan police. Who else might have pegged him as a fraud? The ship's own doctor, perhaps? Nicco thought he handled that one rather well, but it had been touch and go...

Regardless, there was nothing solid to tie Nicco to the theft. The only person who'd seen him out of his Dr Karth disguise had been the rock star and his escorts. The rocker was too drunk to recall anything clearly and the escorts would never give it up to the police. At least, he hoped not. Xandus wouldn't even be a suspect and of course wouldn't give himself up, but even if he did, the wizard couldn't prove a thing. And the necklace itself was currently lying somewhere at the bottom of the Nissal Straits. All that could tie Nicco to the crime was a skyfall suit and some omnimag grips, which were easy enough to explain away. If that was all the police could pin on Nicco, they'd be laughed out of court and they knew it.

Someone hammered on the door.

"Police! Open up, Salarum! We know you're in there!"

* * *

"WHAT IN THE fifty-nine hells are you doing in my elevator? Ballasar, couldn't you just ring the bloody bell downstairs?"

"Frankly, sir, no."

There were two of them, Azbathan plainclothes cops. Nicco knew Detective Ballasar from his days as a teenage tearaway. Ballasar was a street cop, with family of his own living in the city. If he could solve a problem without actually bringing something messy like the law into it, Ballasar would do it. He was that kind of cop.

The other, the one who spoke and shoved his way into the apartment, Nicco didn't know. He was tall and thin, with a mop of long white hair, and he looked vaguely familiar...

Ah, yes. It was the officer he'd seen during the bomb hoax in City Plaza, the sergeant he'd marked as one to avoid.

Too late.

Ballasar looked faintly embarrassed. "Sorry, Nicco, we got a tip-off..."

"Pretty ballsy, nicking it in broad daylight," said the tall cop. "But the game's up. Now where have you stashed it? Is it in here? You're probably stupid enough." He walked around Nicco's apartment, lifting up printzines and holovids in a cursory way.

"Tip-off, my arse!" said Nicco. "Ballasar, who *is* this clown? Have you even got a bloody warrant?"

"My name is Sergeant Patulam," said the thin cop. "Remember the name, because you'll be hearing it a lot more during the trial. And here's your warrant." He shoved a folded sheaf of papers into Nicco's hand and turned back to the apartment.

Ballasar hadn't moved from the doorway, evidently keen to let the sergeant get it out of his system. He took a pack of cigarettes from his pocket, lit one and watched.

"Oh-ho, what's this?" Patulam held up the damp skyfall suit.

"I sometimes go skyfalling," said Nicco. "But I'm not very good at positioning. I ended up in the drink instead of on land."

Patulam smiled. "Oh, no you didn't, lad. Not today. The

north end of town was an exclusionary zone from sunrise to sunset. The *Astra* was the only ship within ten miles."

Nicco hadn't known that. The more this guy talked, the less he liked him. But if Nicco clammed up now, he and Ballasar would whip him down the station for sure. He had to maintain his front. Then he realised what the cop had just said, and smiled. "I didn't say I was at the north end. Actually, I was down southside. The water's not so choppy."

Patulam narrowed his eyes at Nicco. "And your card records will back that up, will they?"

"Ooh, I'm not sure. Do you know, now that I think about it, I may have paid with cash."

Ballasar coughed on his cigarette and tried not to laugh. Patulam shot him a hard stare. Nicco smiled to himself and opened the warrant, to see what on earth this joker thought he had on him.

It was a menu from the fried fish café down the road.

Nicco's sense of humour abandoned him, and he threw the fake warrant at Patulam.

"Get out! Get out of my apartment right now, before I call the city attorney's office and tell them how well you follow procedure."

Patulam let the menu drop and slowly walked to the exit. Ballasar dropped his butt and ground it into the elevator floor.

"We'll be back," said Patulam.

"I doubt it," said Nicco. "You haven't got a clue who did this, have you? You never had any bloody tip-off, you're just fishing around blindly. Get out!"

Ballasar gave Nicco a sheepish look and started to apologise, but Nicco slammed the door to the elevator so hard he almost whacked Patulam in the back.

Well, he thought, that could have gone better.

Time to call Xandus.

CHAPTER ELEVEN

Tea For Turith was almost full. The one good thing about the freezing Azbathan winter was the ocean winds cleared the usually smog-ridden air for three solid months. In the clear air, the view from the restaurant situated atop the 500-storey Lighthouse Tower was stunning. On a good day you could look south-east and see fully half the archipelago stretched out across the water, right the way to Shalumar.

Nicco entered the restaurant and scanned the room for Xandus. The wizard was sitting on his own at a small table, nursing a glass of purple wine and gazing out over the city. Nicco nodded at the maitre d' and strode past, leaving the man no chance to ask his name or check his coat. He walked straight to Xandus' table and sat down opposite him.

Once again the wizard was dressed in drab, dark clothes and unaccompanied by his thinmen, though the make-up was still there. It struck Nicco, then, that perhaps he was being too harsh on the wizard. With everything that had happened in the past year, the Turithian attitude to magic had probably become the norm rather than the exception. Not that Archmages like Ramus-Bey or Comul would care, but perhaps ordinary wizards like Xandus no longer felt safe wandering the streets in outfits that advertised their calling to all and sundry. He imagined Xandus donning his silk finery in that stone-walled lair, admiring himself in the mirror but unable to go outside. Not an image Nicco particularly wanted in his head, but he couldn't deny he may have judged the wizard too soon.

"Good afternoon, Mr—"

Nicco shushed him. "Keep your bloody voice down, and call me Mr Millurat." It was the most common name in Turith.

"Exactly, Mr Millurat. Is it with you?"

Nicco slowly reached a hand into his coat, but the sudden appearance of a waiter stopped him removing it.

"Good afternoon, sir, and welcome to Tea For Turith, the highest restaurant in the country. You are now on the northern most point of the entire archipelago, and from this unique vantage point the view—"

Nicco cut the waiter off. "Cut the spiel, and just get me a glass of whatever he's drinking." He gestured at Xandus' wine.

The waiter's smile faltered for a moment, then returned as if nothing had happened. "The Hurrundan '75, sir, certainly. An excellent choice."

Nicco watched the waiter retreat, then looked over at Xandus and laughed. "You ordered Hurrundan wine?"

Xandus smiled and raised the glass to his lips. "It seemed appropriate."

Nicco shook his head and quietly laughed. Yeah, this wizard wasn't so bad. At least he had a sense of humour.

The waiter returned with Nicco's wine. When he'd left, Xandus leaned across the table. "You were saying. It is with you, yes?"

Nicco reached back into his coat.

* * *

SILVER MOONLIGHT LAY on the water like a knifeblade. The moon hung low on the horizon, bright and full, bringing light to the otherwise dark sky over Azbatha.

Not the best night to remain unseen while out in a dinghy.

But Nicco couldn't wait any longer. It had been two days since the police called round at his apartment, and Xandus was becoming impatient. So was Nicco—he wanted this over and done with, and the money to pay off Bazhanka. He was sure another twenty-five grand would persuade the mob boss to forego the balance. And then Nicco would be a free agent once again.

He let the oars rest for a moment and pulled a cheap smartphone out of his pocket.

Every phone could be set to display its own location on a map; people used them in navigation all the time. More usefully, though, every phone could display the location of any *other* phone. You had to know both the number and an access code—nobody wanted stalkers tracking them—but that wasn't a problem for Nicco. After all, it was his own phone he wanted to find.

He opened the tracker software. A white point in the centre gave his current location, and a small red point showed the location of his other phone. He released the breath he hadn't known he'd been holding.

Nicco picked up the oars and resumed rowing. According to the tracker, it was another couple of hundred yards north. The water lapped quietly against the dinghy as Nicco worked the oars, back and forth, steady and slow. He checked his watch. Just gone two in the morning. Three hours until sun-up. He'd waited until the sky whale ferries finished running for the night, back and forth across the Nissal Straits. Nicco was a couple of miles away from the nearest ferry route, but there was still a chance he might be seen, and he couldn't take that risk. Not right now.

He let the dinghy come to a stop close to the location of the phone signal. In the bottom of the boat was an oxygen tank and mask, all black—as were the boat itself and the wetsuit Nicco wore under his jacket. He strapped on the tank and picked up the final piece of kit, a powerful waterproof torch.

Turith called itself the 'Nation of a Thousand Islands,' but in truth there were probably many more. No-one had ever bothered to count them all, not least because politicians, scientists and cartographers could never agree on what exactly should be classed as an 'island.' The entire archipelago sat on its own tectonic plate, the Tur Shelf, crushed on all sides by the larger plates making up Varn, Praal and Hirvan, forcing up the islands and peaks marking the region. Swarming around a handful of large islands up to 40,000 square miles in size—like Turilum itself—were hundreds of city-sized islands like Azbatha and *thousands* of tiny skerries that thrust out of the water like the fingers of drowning men, some barely more than ten yards wide. Many of the 'islands' disappeared or merged with the changing tides.

Turith was a cartographer's nightmare. In the age before airships, Turithian sailors who could navigate the waters had been rare and highly prized.

And the seas were shallow. Under pressure from its neighbours, the Tur Shelf had risen nearly to sea level; here on the northern edge of Turith, where the Nissal Straits fed into the Demirvan Sea, the water was deeper than in the centre of Turith, but still shallow enough for a man to dive down and retrieve something from the seabed without having to spend twelve hours in a compression chamber.

Nicco wrapped his smartphone in a vacpac bag and sealed it tight. Then, with the phone in one hand and torch in the other, he rolled backwards over the side of the dinghy and disappeared under the surface.

He kicked out and descended a few feet in darkness before switching on the torch, to minimise the chance of someone seeing it from the surface. The red target on the display almost overlapped the white dot marking his own position. Nicco continued straight down. As he descended, nearing the signal, the resolution of the display changed, the scale dropping from hundreds of yards to tens.

He looked up from the screen to see the translucent bell of a tanglefish in his path, its tentacles shimmering behind it. Nicco kicked sideways and watched it float past and upwards. The light from his torch refracted as it passed through the tanglefish's ghostly body, illuminating the surrounding water in a rainbow of dancing colours.

It was quite beautiful, but he wasn't here to admire the marine life. He kicked again, and reached the seabed two minutes later.

At the bottom he turned, rotating in the water until the signal was directly ahead: just twenty feet away, according to his phone. He moved forward, skimming the black coral that covered the sea-bed in this area. Bottom feeder fish, pale and blind, flapped lazily across his path as he swam toward the signal.

The torch beam passed over the black coral. He should have remembered it would be colourless down here. A more brightly coloured bag would have been easier to see. Too late for that now. He'd just have to—

There. A strap, poking out from under a flatfish. And nearby, an omnimag grip.

Nicco batted the flatfish out of the way and checked the bag. Still sealed. Should he open it down here, to double check? What if someone had found the bag before he did, removed the necklace and thrown it out of the *Astra*? His phone was stitched into a waterproof section of the lining, anyone looking through the bag would probably miss it completely.

On the other hand, exposure to water might damage the

necklace. Or worse, it might already be damaged and opening the bag could dislodge a fragment into the murky water. Nicco didn't fancy searching around down here for a single chain link.

Bugger it. He had to check. He let the tracker fall to the bed and carefully opened the bag.

The necklace was fine. Complete, as far as he could see, and unharmed by the water. Nicco exhaled with relief and refastened the bag. Now for the ascent back to the surface, but first he had to destroy the burner phone. The vacpac bag containing it was bloated with surface air. Nicco took it in both hands and pressed it hard against a jagged outcrop of black coral. The bag burst, spewing forth a cloud of air bubbles, and water rushed into the bag in its place. The unit was submerged immediately, destroying the electronics inside and hopefully taking care of any errant fingerprints. Nicco dropped it back to the sea-bed.

Then he kicked out—disturbing the flatfish, which had just gotten settled again—and slowly floated up.

NICCO DREW A brown paper package from his coat, unmarked and tightly wrapped, and pushed it across the table toward the wizard.

"Don't even think of opening it here. You'll just have to trust me."

"Exactly, yes. I believe you right." Xandus reached under the table and pushed a briefcase over to Nicco's side.

"More cash?"

Xandus nodded. "Another twenty-five again, all it is."

Nicco nodded. The wizard had been good for his advance; he had no reason to think he'd rip him off for the rest.

Nicco looked closely at Xandus, wondering again about the wizard's motives. "You've seen the chaos this has caused? This could turn out to be a major international incident. So much for the peace, you know?" He didn't mention that, actually, another outbreak of war could be good news, in Nicco's line of business.

Xandus placed the package inside a shoulder bag and stood up. "Then is good we shall not see again, yes? I was not ever here. Exactly." He turned and walked away without finishing his wine.

Nicco watched him go, then turned to look out the window. Pink sunlight reflected off the Nissal Straits and the wide ocean beyond. They caught the polished hulls of skycars and airships overhead, steel and chrome and pink light dancing though the air like fairy dust. The light poured down on distant trees and hills across the water, bringing a warm, inviting glow to the countless islands occupying the hundred-mile stretch of water between Azbatha and Rilok. Hype aside, the view from Tea For Turith really was spectacular.

Nicco ignored his Hurrundan wine and patted the briefcase happily. First he had to stash the cash, but then he'd call on Tabby and celebrate.

It was only as he stood that he realised Xandus had stuck him with the bill.

CHAPTER TWELVE

"I've got twenty *holovid units for you. Jalakumi Corp, top of the line... Yeah, original boxes, all the paperwork. You interested? I can show you... What? Ignore it, it's nothing. I'm... Look, never mind where I am, just meet me at the lockup in two hours. All right.*"

Nicco closed his phone and sighed. He hardly noticed the grunting and yelping from next door any more, but evidently it was loud enough to be heard over the the line. The sooner he could get out and find a place of his own, the better. Not that there was much chance of that; even in Azbatha, not many people would rent a place to a ten-year-old boy.

He dialled a number. It rang three times—it always rang three times—then picked up.

"Razhko Investigations." said the voice on the other end of the line.

"Mr Razhko, it's Nicco Salarum. I'm just calling to see..."

"Kid, every day for the past three weeks you've called me 'just to see.' You don't have to explain yourself. But today's no

different. I've got nothing for you. Look..." Razhko paused. Nicco wondered if maybe he did have something after all. Anything.

"Look, kid, it's your money and I'm not going to tell you how to spend it. But are you sure you want me to carry on? I mean, this is a real dead end. I've been doing this a long time and it's not looking good. I don't have anything. Are you sure you can't just ask your mom?"

Nicco sighed. "No. I already tried, and she won't tell me anything. Please, Mr Razhko. Just keep trying."

"All right, kid. But really, you've got to stop stressing about it, you know? I promise, I'll call you the minute I get anything."

"You promise?"

"I swear on my mother."

Nicco wondered just how much that actually meant, coming from a grizzled muckraker like Razhko. He ended the call.

"Razhko? Birrum Razhko?"

Nicco was so startled he dropped his phone. He turned to see his mother standing in the doorway, cinching a gown around her waist.

"Um..." Nicco considered his options, but couldn't see any, beyond confession and outright denial. Neither would go down especially well with his mother. So he said nothing.

"What in the fifty-nine hells are you doing talking to that lowlife? And exactly what is it I won't tell you?"

"I... I wasn't talking about you."

"Don't lie to me, Nicco." She stepped into the room, then sighed. "By the watery saints, this is about your father, isn't it? Oh, Nicco." She sat down on the edge of his bed, and patted the space beside her. "Come here."

Nicco didn't move. "You said he was a soldier."

"I know."

"You said he was from Varn."

"Nicco, listen..."

"You said his name was Cheradd. But there weren't any soldiers called that here in Azbatha, mum! Not when I was born! Mr Razhko checked!"

His mother took a deep breath and invited him to sit beside her again.

"Nicco, I didn't know you'd be so... insistent about it. Not yet. You're only ten years old. Not that anyone would know it, to look at you... Come here, please, and I'll tell you the truth. I promise."

Nicco shuffled over to the bed and sat down, staring at the floor.

"Your father was... nobody. He was just a sailor, a man who passed through one night and dropped in. I never saw him before or after that one night. He was just a mark." She put her hand under Nicco's chin and turned him to face her. She smiled. *"He was a handsome man, I remember that. Just like you'll be."*

Nicco pulled his face away. *"So he was nobody. Not important."*

"I didn't mean that..."

Nicco felt tears welling up behind his eyes, but fought them back. *"Why did you say he was a soldier?"*

"I thought you'd like that. That he was brave and macho, and all that stuff. I thought you'd be pleased."

"When were you going to tell me the truth? Were you ever going to tell me?"

"Yes, I swear. I..."

"Lilla, I've got someone waiting downstairs for you. Are you done?" Madame Zentra stood in the open doorway. She smiled at Nicco. *"Hello, Nicco. I thought you were out."*

He stood up. *"I was just leaving."*

"Wait!" Nicco's mother got up, *"Just wait here one second, okay? I have something for you."*

His mother went next door, to her working room. Madame Zentra shrugged. She seemed as confused as Nicco.

Lilla returned quickly and held out a clenched hand. "This is for you." It was a pendant necklace, a teardrop of golden glass engraved with interlocking lines. Nicco took it and stared. He'd never seen anything like it.

"It was his," said his mother. "He took it off and forgot to take it with him... I was going to give it to you on your thirteenth birthday. The same day I wanted to tell you about him."

Nicco felt the tears coming again, but he bit his lip and closed his eyes. He wouldn't let himself cry in front of his mother, not over this. "What does it mean?" he asked.

"I don't know," said his mother. "I think it's a good luck charm."

Nicco opened his eyes and looked at the pendant. It was nothing, just a bit of scratched glass. His mother could have bought it herself in any market, just to appease him. But he didn't let himself think such thoughts. Instead, he closed his hand around the pendant and thought of a handsome man, sailing somewhere on the Demirvan Sea, laughing as he told his shipmates about the night he spent in Azbatha ten years ago and the brothel that was so good he accidentally forgot to pick up his good luck charm when he left.

It was all Nicco had. It was better than nothing.

"Nicco?" Tabby stood over him, eyes wide. "I said, what do you want to drink?"

"Get..." Nicco hesitated. "Oh, just get us a couple of bottles of sparkling amber. I'm buying, remember?"

"I remember," said Tabby as she walked away. "But I worry about you sometimes."

They were in the White Fatty. It was early evening and the place was starting to fill up with clients, drinkers and assorted ne'er-do-wells. As Nicco looked around, he realised he was rubbing his father's pendant through his shirt. He stopped, suddenly feeling very self-conscious. Why was he thinking about that? Xandus had been interested in his pendant, and Nicco couldn't help thinking it wasn't just an aesthetic interest. Something about the wizard's eyes, the tiniest hint of surprise, when he'd first seen it. Nicco was too disorientated at the time to notice, but thinking back... He should have asked him, pushed Xandus for an answer. Was it Shalithi? Had his father gone the entire length of Turith? Was it something in the pattern? Could it mean something? Or had Xandus thought perhaps it was a magical charm? If only. A silly little good luck charm was one thing, but if it had actually had some sort of power he might never have gotten into this mess with Bazhanka. And sadly, that wasn't the case.

But that look in the wizard's eye still bothered him.

Xandus' number was still written on that scrap of paper in his apartment. He could go home and call the wizard right now. It was a simple question. It was probably nothing, after all. Xandus probably just liked the look of it. His clothes had been odd enough, perhaps he thought a glass pendant was all he needed to top off the ensemble. Yes, it was probably nothing. Just a vain wizard—weren't they all?—admiring a bauble. Besides, contacting Xandus right now would be a mistake. It was too soon after the hand-off, after the theft. Nicco couldn't afford to do anything that might further connect him to the wizard.

No. Best to leave it. It was nothing.

"I said, I'm thinking of becoming a man."

Nicco blinked at Tabby as she poured his glass of amber, a deep and rich golden wine that fizzed and sparkled.

"Oh, you're listening now, are you? Honestly, Nicco, it's like you're on a different planet. You haven't even told me what we're celebrating yet."

Nicco took his glass and raised it, smiling.

"I'm sorry, love. I've just been thinking a lot about... the past.

But don't worry about it, we're here to celebrate the future. Things are looking up."

He chinked her glass with his and drank. The wine sent a warm glow down his throat and across his body. It was the first drink he'd allowed himself since that night in the businessman's apartment. It felt good.

Tabby smiled at him and leant forward, speaking quietly. "Have you got a big job?"

It was already done and paid for, but he couldn't tell her that. She'd guess it was him who stole the necklace if he did, and until Governor Werrdun scurried back to Hurrunda and the police moved on to something else, Nicco couldn't risk her gossiping to one of the girls. Nicco had learnt that early on, when the slightest thing he told his mother would suddenly find its way around every girl in the brothel.

He smiled back at Tabby. "I might have."

"Is that what you've been working on? I haven't seen you for almost two weeks."

"Yeah. You know, research and all that."

Tabby downed her drink. "Poor baby, all work and no play. I know what you need, though. Come on, let's take this bottle upstairs."

Best idea she'd had in weeks, as far as Nicco was concerned. He followed her to the elevator.

All of Zentra's girls lived on the premises, another legal tangle and a lucrative tax dodge to boot. Tabby's room was on the fifth floor, the same floor where Nicco and his mother had lived before he moved out. But he'd been coming back to see Tabby for so long, and the memories of his mother were so far in the past, that Nicco hadn't felt sentimental about it in years.

For some reason he couldn't place, tonight was different. As he stepped into the thickly carpeted elevator with Tabby on one arm and two bottles of sparkling amber under the other, he couldn't help thinking about it. Tabby's mother had been a working girl too, two floors down from Nicco and his mother. Tabby was four years younger than him, but that hadn't mattered when they were growing up, the only two kids of their generation living at Madame Zentra's. They'd played together, fought together, watched holovids together. Until Nicco moved out, when he was just thirteen, they were inseparable. But as Nicco carved out his career in burglary, the short, gawky young girl he used to play with faded into the background. He had work to do, jobs to pull off, a name to make. He didn't even visit his mother—they'd fought over the move—so why on earth would he go back to see some girl he used to sit and play childrens' holovid games with?

Then Nicco's mother contracted cancer five years ago, and everything changed. For the next two years he made weekly visits to the brothel. His mother had stopped working, but Madame Zentra was a job-for-life kind of woman and Lilla Salarum had worked for her since the age of sixteen. She'd earned a sickbed for as long as she needed it.

They exited the elevator and walked along the corridor, passing his mother's old room.

Nicco hadn't even thought about Tabby during his first few visits to his mother. He'd seen her around, the very first day, but didn't realise it until two months later, when a beautiful young woman with long, black hair stepped into the elevator with him and giggled. Her name was Tabathianna—Tabby for short. She was working here herself now, and had watched him come and go for the past two months as he fretted over his mother. She knew he didn't recognise her, and why should he? The awkward, skinny, messy-haired girl with freckles that Nicco knew had blossomed into a confident, curvy woman with sparkling eyes and an easy smile. She introduced herself, and Nicco almost missed his floor in surprise.

They slept together for the first time that night. Five years and countless nights later, here they were again.

Tabby skipped through the doorway and jumped onto her bed. Nicco entered, closed the door behind him with a kick and held up the wine bottles and glasses. Enough navel-gazing. It was time for some good old-fashioned fun.

She sat up against the pillows, her long legs stretched out, and gently pulled the hem of her dress up with her fingertips. "Forget the wine," she breathed. "Strip for me."

Nicco grinned and put the bottles and glasses down on a table beside the door. "Right you are." He pulled his sweater over his head and threw it at her. She caught it and laughed, smoothing it out over her chest and sighing. Nicco unbuckled his belt, never taking his eyes off Tabby.

Dimly, he was aware of muffled noises from the corridor. A woman's voice, shouting in protest. Nicco barely registered it. It was nothing to do with him.

He was forced to quickly reconsider that thought when the door burst open behind him and two of Wallus Bazhanka's faceless thinmen dragged him, half-naked and yelling, out of the brothel and into a skycar.

CHAPTER THIRTEEN

"NICCO, MY DEAR boy. What trouble and anguish you cause me."

Wallus Bazhanka sat behind his desk, his massive bulk framed by an equally giant chair. The dark leather squeaked under his weight as he shifted from one elbow to the other.

"I've got the bloody money!" said Nicco. "You could at least have had the decency to pick up the phone and call me yourself. These creepy sods dragged me out of bed!" The thinmen flanked Nicco, one on either side of him—just like his first encounter with Xandus. The comparison wasn't lost on him, and he almost laughed.

Bazhanka raised a hand for quiet.

"I am no longer interested in the money you owe me. In fact, we are going to make a deal, you and I. For my part, I will release you of all debts owed to me."

Nicco's face must have been a picture, because Bazhanka smiled.

"Almost too good to be true, isn't it? An enormous weight off your shoulders, I'm sure. And the task you shall perform for me, in return for this favour, is so small and simple that it is barely a thing at all. Such a trivial act, to secure a man's freedom from obligation."

Here it comes, thought Nicco. What did he want for it this time? Another trailer full of skycars? A bank job? Corporate espionage? All of the above? Nicco cleared his throat. "So what is it? What do I have to do?"

"You must return Governor Werrdun's necklace."

THEY HADN'T EVEN waited for him to button his trousers back up. Bazhanka's thinmen grabbed an arm each and dragged Nicco along the corridor in Madame Zentra's, back into the elevator.

"I've got the bloody money!" he protested. "And it's not even due till tomorrow!"

They ignored him.

They continued ignoring him as he was taken through the lobby, past a very displeased Madame Zentra, and bundled into the back of a skycar parked outside. In fact, they ignored him all the way across town. He tried reasoning with them, but it was useless. He tried telling them to call Bazhanka, but they were deaf to his pleas. He tried asking them if he could call Bazhanka, to no avail.

The skycar sped through the aerial highways of Azbatha's skyscrapers, crossing flight paths and cutting off anyone who dared get in its way. Nicco had never been driven in a skycar by thinmen before, and he was pretty sure this'd be the last time.

They were heading south, which confused him. Downtown, and Bazhanka's club, was a couple of miles west from Madame Zentra's place. Where were they going? After a few minutes he saw Riverside up ahead, and the skycar slowed to make a descent. Nicco finally realised where they were taking him.

They landed in a palatial estate on the edge of the Nissal

Straits, on a skypad big enough to accommodate an airship. The central figure of the estate was a grand, baroque mansion in green-black sea stone, an antiquated building material that hadn't been used for two hundred years. The house extended over the Nissal Straits on stilts, with a boating jetty running the width of the mansion. A hundred yards of garden, edged by high walls infested with security cameras, surrounded all three sides of the dwelling on the land side. Nicco counted at least twenty men patrolling the grounds as the skycar made its descent.

It was the single biggest estate Nicco had ever seen in Azbatha. You could have built four skyscrapers housing thousands of people on the footprint, and anywhere else in the city they would have. But this was Riverside, exclusive home to the rich and famous, where land was a status symbol.

And only one man in the city could afford a place this big.

The thinmen hauled Nicco from the skycar and frogmarched him into the house, past half a dozen armed guards who seemed to be as wary of the golems as Nicco was. They took him in the main doors, through a large reception hall and along two corridors, stopping in front of a solid door. One of them knocked, and Nicco heard Bazhanka's voice on the other side shout a curt, "Come!"

The office was long and wide, a cavernous room that could comfortably hold a large crowd. But there was only Bazhanka, sitting behind a heavy wooden desk at the far end of the room, his hands folded across his outsize belly. The mob boss watched, motionless, as his thinmen pushed Nicco down the room toward the desk.

NICCO HAD ASSUMED Bazhanka wanted the money a day early. That the urgency with which his thinmen dragged Nicco from Tabby's room was just their usual brand of overzealous obedience. But he'd assumed wrong. And now, for some unfathomable reason, Bazhanka wanted the necklace.

Did he know for sure that Nicco had taken it? How could he? It was tempting to lie and say he still had it, just to wipe out his debt to Bazhanka. But he'd be found out soon enough, and Bazhanka would probably double what Nicco owed him once he discovered the bluff. Or offer the same for Nicco's head.

"What in the fifty-nine hells do you care about some ambassador's baubles?" Nicco said.

"I care a great deal about the welfare of Governor Werrdun, as it happens. Where is the necklace?"

"I don't have it. I never did. You've got the wrong man, Bazhanka. Now let me go."

Bazhanka shifted his weight and the high-backed chair's leather seat creaked in protest. "Ah, Nicco. You should know by now that I am not in the habit of being wrong. Wallus Bazhanka does not grope around in the dark."

Nicco grimaced at the image that came into his head.

"You say you have the money to settle your debt? Should I be surprised if it is once again in *cash?*" He shivered visibly as the word passed his fat lips. "I wonder how you might have come by such a sum so quickly."

"None of your business."

"Oh, I think it is. I think it is very much my business. And not just mine..."

A short, dark-haired women with tanned olive skin stepped out from behind Bazhanka's high-backed chair to stand beside the mob boss. She fixed Nicco with an angry scowl, and his stomach suddenly felt very tight.

"Of course," smiled Bazhanka, "You've met Mirrla Werrdun, the governor's daughter. When the necklace was stolen, she came to me. One of the things she remembers very clearly is the doctor who treated her father's illness, a doctor who seemed to have magically disappeared when the *Astra* landed."

"Maybe it *was* magic," said Nicco nervously. "You can't trust those wizards, you know."

"Perhaps, perhaps. Of course, had he been a wizard, this doctor would almost certainly not have needed to drug one of Werrdun's own bodyguards before leaving the governor's suite in such a hurry. And yet, despite pleas, he has not come forward to our esteemed police. What a mystery it is!"

Nicco felt sick. What on earth connected Bazhanka to Werrdun? He was sure Bazhanka hadn't been on the *Astra* himself.

"I don't have it," he said again.

"A mysterious doctor, whom no-one recalls ever meeting before. A thief who suddenly comes by a large amount of money. And library logs that show various terminals made an exceptional number of searches for information on Hurrunda, and Governor Werrdun himself, scant days before the theft."

Nicco knew Bazhanka was trying to provoke him, surprise him with his connections to the police and city officials. But it was a bluff. The doctor could have been anyone; Mirrla Werrdun was very ill when she saw him on the *Astra*; the money could have come from anywhere; and the citi-card he'd used at the library was stolen. Nicco couldn't resist a smirk as he imagined that stupid cop Patulam eagerly chasing down the citi-card's real owner, only to lead a squadron of armed police through the door of an 87-year-old retired fisherman with one leg.

"You find this amusing, dear boy?"

Nicco suppressed the smirk. "No, of course not. A terrible crime has been committed."

Bazhanka snorted. "I wish to complete this puzzle, Nicco, and I don't care what it takes. I don't even care how or why you stole the necklace. All I require is the loot itself, returned to the governor through me. And then we shall consider the jigsaw complete, and this silly game concluded."

Nicco sighed. "You're not listening to me, Bazhanka. Even

assuming I stole it in the first place, I don't have it. You can turn me and my entire place upside-down, but you won't find any bloody necklace! And you still haven't told me why you care. What in the fifty-nine hells is she doing here? Why not go to the police?"

Bazhanka chuckled. "Ah, sometimes you can be so naïve... Very well, Nicco. To understand, you must know that my family tree is very large and very complex. I myself have six brothers, eighteen half-brothers, forty-five cousins... no, excuse me, forty-six... and too many uncles, aunts, great uncles, great aunts, second, third and fourth cousins to count. Our clan is spread far and wide, and we are an ambitious family. Most of its members are, of course, in the family business. Many of us run entire cities, behind the scenes... including Hurrunda."

Nicco groaned. "Oh, no."

Bazhanka smiled. "Oh, yes."

"But still, so what? Why does your brother or whatever give a flying squid about Werrdun?"

"This theft, this one thoughtless action, could destabilise the city. Many are concerned that the Kurrethi—do you know anything about Hurrundan politics?"

Nicco nodded.

"The Kurrethi may be able to take advantage of this situation, to stir up unrest and religious fervour. Without Werrdun to calm the waters, Hurrunda may face revolution."

"All because he hasn't got his necklace? Rubbish. You're having me on."

"Without the necklace, there is no Governor Werrdun." It was Mirrla who spoke, for the first time since stepping out from behind Bazhanka's chair. "Haven't you seen the news streams, you idiot? Don't you know how unwell he is?"

"Look, it was just dope, he'll be fine..."

Nicco stopped. Why couldn't he just keep his big bloody mouth shut for once?

Bazhanka leant back in his chair and pursed his lips. "Ah, dear boy. So we come to the truth at last."

Mirrla Werrdun continued. "He will not be fine, you fool. You've heard the rumours that the necklace is magical? Well, they're true. Not completely true, of course—all that nonsense about him consorting with Ekklorn—but the necklace is enchanted."

Bazhanka held up a hand for Mirrla to stop, and leaned forward. "Nicco... I know you better than you may suppose, and one thing I am sure of is that you are no killer. That is, after all, the very reason you were in my debt."

Nicco didn't like where this was going. "I don't see the connection."

"In a week—perhaps a day more, perhaps a day less—you will. Jarrand Werrdun is ninety-three years old. Do you suppose he looks so well for his age because he takes long walks on the beach and eats plenty of seafood?"

"Without the necklace, my father will die," said Mirrla. "You have not just stolen his necklace. You have stolen his life."

Bazhanka leaned forward to fix Nicco with a hard stare. "And that, dear boy, is murder."

Nicco reeled. Murder? But he wasn't to blame, it was Xandus who wanted the necklace stolen. He should be the one standing here now. But even if Nicco called Xandus right now, what would he care? Nicco didn't even care all that much.

But he wasn't about to take the rap for it. He had no choice—he'd have to get the necklace back. Except he'd already given Bazhanka half the money, which removed the possibility of simply buying it back from the equation. And even if he had the money, Nicco had a feeling Xandus wouldn't be too enthusiastic about a refund.

"I see the gravity of the situation is not lost on you," said Bazhanka. "Now. Where is the necklace? And don't say you don't have it."

"I really don't. It's already been delivered."

"Ah." Bazhanka tutted and shook his head. "Then you will have to get it back, dear boy."

"Don't be stupid. The client's not just going to give it back because I ask nicely. He doesn't care about Werrdun."

"Then we will persuade your client that the governor's well-being is in his best interests." Bazhanka pressed a button on his desk phone. "Clarrum, please come in now."

Nicco looked over his shoulder as the door opened and the big bodyguard stepped into the office.

"You will leave immediately, and take Clarrum with you. Let him do the talking." Bazhanka chuckled. "Not that I imagine much conversation will take place."

CHAPTER FOURTEEN

NICCO HADN'T HAD the nerve to tell Bazhanka that the only contact information he had for Xandus was a phone number. Or that Xandus had made it quite clear he expected never to see Nicco again. Nicco had a strange fondness for life, and at that moment he figured admitting to any obstacles was tantamount to suicide.

So he stayed quiet and sat very still as Clarrum guided the skycar through the city's towering avenues of steel and glass, past blaring neon holovid signs now in full flow as night fell across the island. They were heading North to Nicco's apartment so he could get some clothes on and call Xandus. Bazhanka didn't have any clothes that would fit him, not that Nicco would have accepted them if he did, and Nicco had deliberately not stored Xandus' number on his own phone. But he still had the scrap of paper the wizard's thinmen had left in his backpack, and that was back at his place.

Clarrum was a big man—Nicco wasn't sure how he crammed himself into the small driver's cabin—and he didn't speak much.

Nicco wasn't really in the mood for talking either and, apart from the occasional mumbled direction, they soared over the city in silence.

Nicco didn't want to talk because he was desperately running through his options. What could he say to Xandus? What possible reason could he concoct to arrange a meet that wouldn't arouse the wizard's suspicion? He had to think fast, but his apartment was approaching faster than he could formulate a plan.

The roof of Nicco's building wasn't strong enough to hold a skycar, but there was a public landing pad just a couple of blocks away. Clarrum found a space and landed. Nicco hopped out, shivering from the sudden cold outside the air-conditioned skycar. Clarrum killed the engine, unfolded his bulk from the interior and took Nicco's arm.

"Lead on, and don't even think about running."

His apartment was freezing. It required constant heating to stay warm in the winter, and the system was so old that Nicco didn't dare leave it running when he was out for fear he'd come back to a tepid lake where his lounge used to be. He told Clarrum to stay by the elevator door while he found some clothes and made the call, then took a fresh shirt and trousers from his wardrobe and changed in the bathroom cubicle.

The scrap of paper with Xandus' number on it was still in his backpack. Nicco sat on his couch and made the call. Listening to the ring at the other end of the line, he ran through what he would say to the wizard one last time. He couldn't tell the truth—that would scupper any chance of Xandus meeting him. He decided to bluff instead. Tell the wizard he'd found something else that might suit his collection, that Nicco wanted to discuss it and maybe make a deal to steal it for the wizard. It wasn't a great plan, he knew. It could very easily make Xandus suspicious. But it was all he had.

The line kept ringing. And ringing. *Great*, thought Nicco, *it's going to go to voicemail. That's all I need.*

But it didn't. It just kept ringing. And ringing.

Nicco cut the call and dialled again. Same thing. Did Xandus recognise Nicco's number? Was he deliberately ignoring the call? Were his suspicions already roused?

"Well?" Clarrum said.

Nicco jumped, startled by the bodyguard's sudden appearance over his shoulder.

"I told you to wait by the door."

"And Mr Bazhanka told me to make sure you didn't pull a fast one. So what's going on?"

"He's not answering, is what. It's just ringing out."

"Then we'll just have to pay him a visit, won't we?"

"But I don't..."

"What?"

Nicco hesitated. Should he admit he didn't know where Xandus lived? Plead with Bazhanka to wait a while, until the wizard decided to answer his phone?

No. Bazhanka wouldn't like it, and Nicco could find himself in even worse trouble with the mob boss than he already was. More than that, he needed to find Xandus for his own peace of mind. He couldn't sleep with another man's imminent death on his conscience.

"I don't understand why he's not picking up, that's all. He normally answers really quickly."

"Maybe he's on the toilet. Maybe he's getting laid. Whatever. I'm sure he'll be more attentive once I break his legs."

"You've got a one-track mind, Clarrum, you know that?"

Clarrum grunted in response.

Nicco stood, picked up a jacket and slung the phone in one of the pockets. "Come on, then, hardman. We'll need to go by my lockup first, though."

* * *

THE NISSAL RIVER ran from the north-east of Azbatha to the south-west, dividing the city into two unequally sized islands. The north side had everything; downtown, Riverside, Azbatha International airship port, the seaport and docks, the Lighthouse Tower, the central shopping area, even the red light district. South of the river there was nothing but residential ghettos, run-down malls overtaken by armies of squatters and enormous storage and warehousing districts. Nicco's lockup was in one such district, well away from his own apartment, Madame Zentra's place and anywhere else he might be known to hang out. Secured with both electronic and mechanical locks, it was an ideal stowaway location.

"You won't find a landing pad anywhere around here," said Nicco as Clarrum swung the skycar over the warehouse district. "You'll have to land on the street."

Clarrum slowly turned to face him with a level gaze that made Nicco regret speaking.

"Do I look like I grew up northside?" said the bodyguard.

Nicco mumbled a quiet apology and sank into his seat.

The sun had set completely by the time they left Nicco's apartment. By now the streets round here were populated mainly by pushers and streetwalkers, all of them hollering and calling to colleagues, rivals and the addicts and marks that made up the remainder of the street traffic. Compared to the north side of Azabatha it was practically empty, but the room to move with ease came at a social price. Nicco didn't associate himself with street criminals like these. He was a better class of crook. But they were one more element to draw attention away from his lockup.

Clarrum took the skycar down to ground level. He found a space on the kerbside between two wrecked groundcars and lowered the skycar down expertly. As soon as they landed, the car was mobbed by streetwalkers, pushers and at least one probable carjacker, but the sight of Clarrum—and the large blaster under his shoulder, which he deliberately exposed as he exited the car—gave them all second thoughts.

Then Nicco climbed out and one of the streetwalkers said, "Hey, Grissul! Fancy ride! You stepped up in the world, or what?"

Nicco smiled back at the emaciated, pale-skinned hooker and nodded. "Yeah, Nurra. Bought myself a batman. And you should see his brother."

The streetwalker looked Clarrum up and down and whistled. "I'd see 'em both. I do group discounts, you know..."

Nicco laughed and walked to his lockup entrance. Clarrum locked the skycar, grunted at Nurra and followed him. "Grissul?"

"Because I'm really going to rent a lockup full of tools and use my real name. I thought you said you grew up around here?"

The big man grunted. "Time was a man could use his real name without fear."

"Time was a man could steal jewellery without having the mob breathing down his neck," snorted Nicco as he opened the locks. "But that's progress for you."

He slotted a security card into the last lockpod and pushed the door open. "You should probably stay here and keep an eye on your car."

"Nice try."

"Have it your way."

They entered a small, non-descript vestibule. Nicco had built it himself out of sheet metal, to keep prying eyes out of his store-room when the main door was open. He waited till Clarrum pulled the door closed behind them, and heard it lock again automatically. Then Nicco flicked a switch and opened a makeshift door into the lockup proper.

The store room was a treasure trove of burglar's kit; grav units, omnimag grips, monofilament wire, black noise generators, traditional lock picks, infrared visors, radio snoopers and more. Unlike his apartment, it was also well organised. Steel shelves, wooden workbenches and wall hooks held everything in its place. Easy location and quick retrieval were vital to Nicco's working methods, with nothing left to chance.

He moved quickly to a metal shelf holding deep glass trays. The trays were unlabelled, but Nicco didn't need labels. He knew the location of everything in this lockup, down to the last diode or lock pick. He could find a tool with his eyes closed. Which was just as well, because what he was about to do had the same feel of floundering around in the dark.

He pulled one of the trays off the shelf and rummaged through it, hoping he had a spare. He did, and pulled it out of the tray with a smile.

"What's that?" Clarrum said.

Nicco took a deep breath. Xandus' refusal to answer his phone had left him with no choice. He had to explain.

"It's a burner phone. I'm not using my own phone for this."

"You're heading for a smack, Salarum."

"All right, listen to me. I don't know where the client lives. I was blindfolded the whole time. But I do have his phone number, and that means I can locate him."

Clarrum was already pulling out his own phone. "You lying sneak," he said. "Come on, back in the car. We're going home to Mr Bazhanka."

"You can't call him from here," said Nicco. "No signal."

Clarrum checked his phone, but Nicco wasn't lying. The switch he hit on the way in wasn't to open the door, or switch on a light—it fired up an omniscrambler loop embedded in the walls, just like the one at Allad's place. Black noise prevented anyone from calling in or out. Clarrum stomped through the door into the vestibule and pulled on the outer door.

"You can't get out, either," said Nicco. "The door locks itself automatically."

Clarrum stormed back into the lockup. "So give me the cards."

"No. Besides, you need the codes as well, and I'm not telling."

"Oh, you'll tell me." The big man advanced on Nicco, fury in his eyes.

"Watery saints, grow up and listen to me, you big oaf. It might be my neck on the line here, but think about yourself for a second. If I'm wrong, if I can't find the client, what have you lost? A few hours of your time, that's all. But if I'm right—if we find him, and get the necklace back—then Mr Bazhanka will be very grateful to you for a job well done. Think of the trust you'll earn from him. Who knows, he might even promote you." Nicco could see Clarrum was considering it. "I'm the one with everything to lose, here. It doesn't matter if we go back right now, or first thing in the morning. Either way, it's my arse Bazhanka will burn if we don't have the necklace, not yours."

It was all Nicco had, all he could bargain with. "Come on, at least let me try. I'm doing my best, here."

Clarrum pursed his lips. Nicco could see he wanted nothing more than to smack the thief in the mouth, but if there was any kind of functioning brain in that thick skull he should see the truth in what Nicco said.

"All right," said Clarrum finally. "But you're still a lying son of a squid."

Nicco exhaled with relief. Now all he had to do was get Xandus' access code.

"THIS IS SERGEANT Patulam calling from the Police Department. Get me someone in your secure records department."

BEEP

"*Records and customer security, how can I help you?*"

"Patulam, Police, major crimes. I need the security access code for a cell phone, and I need it right now!"

"*Sir, are you the registered owner?*"

"If I was, I wouldn't need to call you idiots for the bloody code, would I? The number is..."

"*Sir, we can only give out access codes to the registered owner, or...*"

"Or the bloody police! Now just give me the code, the number's 207212-578707!"

"*Sir, you'll need a warrant issued by the court, I can't just...*"

"And where in the fifty-nine hells am I going to find a judge sober and awake at this time of night? Listen to me! There is a smuggling operation going on *right now*, and I need that code to locate the drop, do you understand? The unit is owned by a major importer of drugs from Varn, and if you do not give me the code I will personally see to it that your face is splashed all over the news streams as the man responsible for letting eight million lire's worth of purple creeper loose on the streets of our fair city!"

The operator said nothing. Nicco worried he might have over-egged the hard cop act.

"*Sir... Sir, I have an idea. Why don't I track it for you?*"

"What?"

"*Well, you see, that way I don't have to give you the access code. But you can still get this smuggler. I'll... I'll be fired if I give you the code. I have two kids in school...*"

Nicco considered the option. He could push it, try to reassure the operator that he could protect him from the wrath of his boss. But of course he'd be lying. In all probability, he really would be fired. And maybe he really did have two kids in school.

"All right," said Nicco. "But by the watery saints, hurry up about it! The number's..."

"*I got it the first time, sir. I have the location for you. Would you like it now?*"

Nicco nearly exploded. "No, I've changed my mind after all! Of course I want the bloody location now!"

"Sir, there's no need to shout. I'm doing everything I can."

"All right, all right. Please, just give me the location."

"It's on the dockside, sir. The signal is weak, but it's definitely there. The address is 873 Gutter's Walk."

Nicco cut the line and turned to Clarrum. "Did you hear that?"

Clarrum banked the skycar to the right, then hit the accelerator and sped north. "Loud and clear."

IT ALL MADE sense now that Nicco knew where he was going. The ocean scent had been strong, even over the assault of waxy golem flesh as they'd bundled him out of the groundvan. You could hear the sea just about everywhere in Azbatha, but it had been louder than usual because the sounds of daily life were muted; Xandus' place was downstairs from the street, and that meant a basement. Plenty of those in the dockside warehouses. And of course, the docks themselves were all but deserted, the last eyesore of a dying industry. It was the perfect haven for a wizard who wanted his privacy.

Nicco looked for the groundvan as they landed, but the street was empty. It had probably been a rental job anyway, especially as the wizard had used it to kidnap a man off the streets. Building 873 was just a few yards from a rusting dockside jetty and looked completely deserted, a dark, abandoned five-storey building of green-black sea stone, steel and shattered windows. Clearly, Xandus' quarters didn't extend above ground.

"You sure this is the place?" Clarrum said as they exited the skycar, looking doubtfully at the derelict.

Nicco looked around to get his bearings. He remembered his short journey from the back of the van, onto the street, through the heavy metal door and down the flight of steps. Outside, at least, everything matched. He even caught a faint whiff of wax.

He nodded. "Yeah. Definitely. He's in the basement, through that door."

"Then that's where we go. You first."

Nicco approached the door. There was no control pad, and it was locked with a heavy steel padlock. "And how am I supposed to open this?"

"Try knocking."

Nicco shrugged and did as Clarrum suggested. The metal rang, deep and hollow, as he rapped it with his knuckles. But no-one answered.

"All right," said Clarrum from behind him, "Stand aside."

"I doubt your blaster's going to break this lock. That's pretty thick steel."

"Who said anything about a gun?"

Nicco turned to see Clarrum holding a metal construction pole, one of several lying abandoned at the base of the building from previous renovation efforts. The burly man grinned and shoved the pole between the latch and the door, then pulled down. Nicco watched, impressed, as the hasp slowly bent outward, levered away from the door by sheer brute force.

It took a couple of minutes and as many breathers, but finally the hinges of the latch sprang apart. The door recoiled and creaked open. Clarrum dropped the pole with a loud clatter and wiped his forehead with the back of his hand. "After you."

Nicco pulled the door open and waited, listening for signs of movement or activity. All that greeted him was a stony silence.

He entered the short corridor behind the door. It turned a couple of yards ahead, then turned again before opening out into a stone staircase. The torches that had illuminated Xandus' room weren't present here in the entrance—and only a dim light emanated from the steps. Nicco turned back to call Clarrum, but the big man was already standing behind him.

"Something's not right," said Nicco. "I can't see a thing."

The bodyguard grunted, and a small beam of light shone

directly in Nicco's face. Nicco looked down and saw a small keyring light in Clarrum's hand.

"Get moving, Salarum. We've wasted enough time already."

As Nicco reached the foot of the steps the thin beam of light from Clarrum's keyring torch shone past him, moving over the wall at the far end of the room. A dim light emanated from the large fireplace in the back wall, filled with ashes and embers that glowed weakly. Something was definitely wrong, here.

"Wait," he said, and put a hand out to stop Clarrum moving forward. Nicco took out his phone and dialled Xandus' number again.

A high-pitched beep sounded somewhere in the room, echoing off the stone walls, the echoes and repeating tone merging into one high-pitched wail. And there, at the far end of the room, a small blue light on the floor. Nicco walked over to it, feeling a sinking sensation in his stomach.

He bent down and picked up Xandus' phone.

"Clarrum, shine your torch around the walls."

Nicco heard Clarrum's footsteps as he walked into the centre of the room. "What's going on? Are you sure you've got the right place?"

"Just do it!"

Nicco watched in horror as the beam of light moved over the basement's bare stone walls. No torches. No tables, no display cabinets, no rugs or ornaments or curious. No arcane symbols on the walls. Where he stood right now should have been a set of stone steps leading to Xandus' makeshift throne. But there was nothing.

The glow from the fire's embers threw faint, shifting shadows across the walls. Clarrum's torch beam moved slowly across the floor, around the walls, up and down the fireplace. Empty.

Except...

"What in the fifty-nine hells was that?" Clarrum shouted. He swept the torch beam back to one of the far corners, past Nicco.

"What?"

"Thought I saw something..."

Nicco's fear rose as he realised what had happened. Xandus didn't live here. He'd never lived here. It was an elaborate set-up, a façade for Nicco's benefit. That was why he'd been blindfolded and knocked out—not because the wizard didn't want Nicco to know where he lived, but because he was taking Nicco somewhere *no-one* lived, and Nicco would have figured it out if he'd been able to see the location properly.

It had all been a lie. A big fat lie.

"He left his phone here deliberately... it's a trap of some kind!" Nicco pushed at the bodyguard, urging him to the exit. "Clarrum, get out!"

"What's going on? What on earth are you talking about?"

He left the big man standing in the centre of the room and broke into a run. "Come on! Just get..."

Nicco skidded to a halt on the grey flagstones. His path was blocked by a pale man with thick black hair, a neat black beard and piercing blue eyes. He peered through the gloom.

"Xandus? Is that you?"

The man said nothing. And then Nicco saw a second man approach. They could have been twins, but for the fact that this one had a gun pointed straight at Nicco.

"Oh, no," said Nicco. "Thinmen."

CHAPTER FIFTEEN

NICCO BACKED AWAY from the thinmen, collided with someone and yelped in surprise. He spun round and found himself face-to-face with Clarrum. Bazhanka's man shone his torch beam past Nicco and peered at the thinmen blocking their exit.

"They belong to this client of yours?"

"Yes."

"All right," Clarrum said, addressing the golems. "Where's your owner? We need to see him."

"I don't think these thinmen speak, Clarrum. And one of them has a blaster..."

The torch beam suddenly went haywire, moving erratically over the walls. Clarrum had dropped the torch. At the same time he lunged forward, twisting inside the reach of the thinman holding the blaster. He brought one open hand up into the golem's face, pushing it back, then wrapped his other hand around its wrist, before delivering a sharp blow to its stomach with his knee. As the golem lost its balance, Clarrum stripped the gun from its hand.

"Not any more," he said, drawing his own blaster. "Here."
He tossed the thinman's blaster to Nicco.

Nicco had never liked blasters. He looked down at the weapon
in his hands. "*I* don't want it, why—?"

Two shots rang out, the reports echoing off the stone walls.
Nicco looked up to see the unarmed thinman fall to the ground
with a ragged burn hole in its chest. Then Clarrum turned to the
one he had just disarmed and shot it in the head.

"Come on, let's go. There's nothing useful here." Clarrum
picked up his keyring torch and began walking to the steps.
"Did you get his phone?"

"Yes, but I don't think it'll tell us anything we haven't already
worked out. It's a dead end..."

Nicco stopped walking. At the base of the steps stood
another two thinmen, their pale flesh glowing in the beam from
Clarrum's torch. Neither of them appeared to be carrying a gun.

"Just shoot the buggers," said Clarrum, raising his own
weapon.

Nicco looked down at the blaster again, feeling its weight in
his hands. But before he could shoot, Clarrum let out a muffled
groan.

Startled, Nicco raised the gun and whipped around. "What's
going on? Who's there?"

He just had time to see a ghostly face, the features marred
by a hole in its forehead, before he felt a heavy blow to his
stomach. He doubled over, confused and gasping for breath.
Then the face leered over him as he felt clammy hands lift him
off the ground.

The thinmen were still alive. Or whatever passed for life in a
golem.

It threw Nicco back. He sailed through the air and landed
badly, his hip slamming into the hard flagstones. He cried out
in pain and dropped the gun reflexively. Not that it mattered, if
blasters didn't stop them.

Four of them. Xandus had four thinmen, Nicco remembered that now. He cursed himself for not remembering sooner, before they hit Clarrum. Where was he? The big bodyguard hadn't made a sound after getting hit from behind. What had they done to him?

Nicco scrambled back on his heels, scratching his palms on the cold, rough floor. Clarrum's torch had fallen facing the back of the room, silhouetting the thinmen as they advanced toward him. Nicco's head collided with the back wall, but the pain barely registered. He crawled sideways, heading for what he thought was the corner, but instead came up against the side of the fireplace. The thinmen surrounded him, slowly approaching from all sides. There was nowhere to run.

So this was how it would end. Killed by mindless golems in the basement of a broken-down warehouse. Not quite the debonair death Nicco had hoped for.

THE THINMEN STOPPED.

They were about ten feet away. In seconds they could be on him, tearing Nicco's head off. But they just stood there.

Were they about to die? Had they reached their expiry date? If so, Nicco made a silent vow to start attending church, even if he had to go Turilum to find one that hadn't been bulldozed to make way for a mall. But after a few seconds he realised the thinmen weren't slowing down, or frozen. They just wouldn't come any closer. Why not?

Nicco slowly turned his head. Glowing embers in the fireplace warmed his cheek, and he smiled.

He rummaged through his pockets for the scrap of paper with Xandus' number on it. He was sure he'd put it back in his pocket after reading it to that security operator on the way here... Yes, there it was. He didn't need the number any more. But the paper could still be useful.

Nicco folded the paper and thrust it into the dying embers. Disturbed ash tumbled onto the hearth, exposing brighter remnants of the fire that had been left to burn itself out. Some of the embers fell onto his hand and scorched his palm, but Nicco gritted his teeth and held the paper against the ashes.

With a tiny rush of air, the paper lit.

Behind him, Nicco heard the thinmen grunt. He climbed to his feet and waved the makeshift brand at them. They backed away, staring at the small flame with fear in their inhuman eyes.

Exhilaration overtook him. He laughed and walked forward, turning in a small circle to keep the golems away as he crossed the floor. They might have had orders to kill him—for all he knew, Xandus left them with orders to kill anyone who found the basement—but evidently, they had a fear of fire that couldn't be overcome. Nicco told himself to remember this, to maybe start carrying a lighter everywhere in case Bazhanka's thinmen ever got too close for comfort.

He'd walked three steps when the paper burned out. Nicco and the thinmen both stopped dead in their tracks.

Then Nicco leapt forward, starting a sprint toward the exit. Out the corner of his eye, a shadow flitted across the static torch beam—then came a muffled grunt as Clarrum slammed into one of the thinmen, tackling him to the ground. Man and golem both landed on the hearth with a dull thud.

"The fire!" Nicco shouted. "They're scared of the fire!"

"I saw, thank you!" Clarrum grunted in response, before shoving the thinman's face into the smouldering embers. It shrieked, a guttural sound that made Nicco wince, and desperately tried to crawl back out of the fireplace. Clarrum kept its struggling body down for a second or two before it threw him off with an inhuman roar and staggered back.

Its head was on fire. The other thinmen shrieked and backed away as their brother floundered, spinning and stumbling around the room in panic.

Clarrum scrambled to his feet and pulled Nicco toward the steps. "Come on!" he shouted. Dazed, Nicco let himself be dragged across the room.

When they reached the base of the steps, Nicco suddenly remembered the gun. "Wait!" he said. But the big man had let go of his arm and was already taking the steps two at a time, heading for freedom.

The first thinman was now fully engulfed in flames. It collided with one of the others, and the fire spread to it instantly. Both golems shrieked and careered round the room while the other two backed away, trying to avoid them. It was like a perverse waltz, lighting up the room and making shadow plays even as they burned to death. Nicco saw the blaster lying on the floor where he'd dropped it. He ran to it, dodging between the erratic thinmen to avoid getting burned himself.

He reached the gun and scooped it off the floor. But as he stood back up, one of the uninjured golems loomed towards him, some glimmer of its master's instructions still driving its magical mind. Nicco raised the blaster, ready to shoot—it would slow the thinman down, at least—but before he could pull the trigger, a flaming golem smacked into the back of the other and knocked it to the ground, fire already licking its face.

Nicco ran for his life.

CLARRUM WAS WAITING by the skycar, breathing heavily and clutching his chest.

"Are you all right?" Nicco said as he staggered to the car.

The big man winced. "Think one of them... broke something."

"I got the gun they had, it might give us a lead on Xandus. You want me to drive?"

Clarrum shook his head. "No... chance," he said. "This is a Soarus... Bullet. Brand new. Just... give me a minute..."

"I thought you worked with Bazhanka's thinmen? I can't

believe you didn't know they're immune to assault blasters!"

"Did you know?"

"Well, no, but..."

"So shut up." Clarrum grimaced and held his chest again. "You think we... use them for target practice... or something? I never tried... shooting one before!"

A metallic clang and guttural shriek interrupted Clarrum's protests. Nicco turned to see one of the thinmen, flaming from head to toe, stagger out of the warehouse and head directly for them.

"Watery saints!" Nicco shouted. He and Clarrum both struggled into the skycar as fast as they could.

Clarrum fired up the engine, gripped the joystick that controlled the launch thrusters and slowly pulled back. The thinman was almost upon them. "Come on, come on..."

The thrusters blasted, lifting the skycar off the ground.

"Where in the fifty-nine hells...?" A hollow clang sounded from the front of the car. Clarrum looked over at Nicco.

"Was that you?"

"No! The engine?"

"I told you, this car's brand new. If the engine's gone already, I'll be having stern words with... do you smell burning?"

Clang.

"Oh, no," said Nicco.

A flaming hand slapped down on the hood. Paint blistered at its touch. Nicco and Clarrum watched, stunned, as the thinman they thought they'd left on the street clambered up onto the skycar's hood and roared with fury.

Nicco reached into his pocket and pulled out the blaster he'd retrieved from Xandus' basement. He aimed it at the thinman's head.

"No, wait!" Clarrum shouted. With a firm hand, he lowered the weapon. "You're not shooting through my bloody windshield! It'll cost me a fortune!"

Nicco gaped. "That thing is going to kill us if we don't get rid of it! What do you suggest, a *stern word?*"

Clarrum jammed the joystick hard to the right. Caught unawares, Nicco smacked his head against the passenger window and yelped in pain. Before he could recover, Clarrum swung back to the left. Nicco almost fell into the bodyguard's lap.

"Blast!" Clarrum hissed through clenched teeth.

Nicco looked up. The thinman was still there, grimly hanging on to the hood. But it was almost over—the golem was literally coming apart, losing flesh and muscle to the relentless fire that burned through it. Surely it couldn't hang on for much longer.

It didn't need to. The thinman pulled back one hand, roared and smashed its fist through the windshield. Clarrum shouted in surprise, struggling to keep control of the skycar as the golem stuck its blazing head through the shattered glass. The skycar's nose dipped.

"Shoot it! Shoot it!" Clarrum yelled.

Nicco still had the blaster in his hand. He held it against the thinman's burning face. The stench of its false flesh burning made him retch, and the heat from the fire seared his hand, but he held the barrel steady and pulled the trigger.

The golem's head snapped back and smacked against the windshield, shattering what glass remained. It had one hand wrapped around the joystick, its fiery skin melting and fusing with the plastic. Clarrum wrestled with it, burning his own skin as he struggled to prise the golem off the controls and stop the skycar's dive.

Nicco looked out the windshield and knew it was too late. They were over the Nissal Straits, and losing height much too quickly. Even if Clarrum regained control, he'd never pull up in time. And now there was no time to escape with the fitted grav belts.

There was barely time for Nicco to take a breath before they hit the water at full speed.

The skycar ploughed into the ocean, driven deep under the surface by its own momentum. Nicco felt the impact like a hammer to his chest, forcing air out of his lungs. The sudden water pressure made his ears pop, and he clamped his mouth shut reflexively to prevent inhaling any water. He kept his eyes closed, knowing that even if they were open all he would see would be a cloud of escaping bubbles.

Nicco waited for the water's inertia to push back against the vehicle's momentum and slow the skycar, then opened his eyes. The thinman was gone, probably ripped away from the car's hood on impact. Clarrum was hunched over the joystick, unconscious. Nicco tried pulling on his arm, but the big man didn't move. He wanted to take him up with him, to drag the bodyguard to the surface, but he was growing more light-headed with every second. Bright lights began to dance in front of his eyes. He needed air.

Nicco kicked out through the hole where the windshield had been and aimed for the surface. He had no strength left, no air remaining. He had to trust his own buoyancy to get him there.

He broke the surface with a long gasp, then floundered as the tide covered his head again. He kicked out his legs and pumped his arms to maintain his level, then took another deep breath when the wave subsided. After twenty seconds the lights in front of his eyes had gone out. He took one last breath and dived back under the surface.

He went straight down, kicking upwards. It took him fifteen seconds to reach the top of the car, now sinking slowly through the water. He grabbed the windshield frame and pulled himself down with one hand, bracing himself to wrench Clarrum free of the wreckage.

But Clarrum wasn't there.

Nicco spun round in the water. There was no sign of the bodyguard.

He must have woken up and surfaced. Nicco shoved against

the car, thrusting himself back up through the water. He broke the surface, gasped for breath and shouted.

"Clarrum!"

No answer.

"Clarrum!"

But the big man was nowhere to be seen.

AZBATHANS WEREN'T ESPECIALLY predisposed to calling the police, but gunshots, a burning basement, shrieking thinmen on fire and a skycar crashing into the Straits—all in the space of about five minutes—was probably enough to rouse even a hardened local from his practised nonchalance.

Nicco couldn't risk that. He didn't have the time, energy or inclination even to tell the truth to a cop, much less make up a plausible story. So he swam a mile downcoast, to the mouth of the Nissal River, and dragged himself out of the water there.

He still had the blaster in his pocket. That was something; if Xandus had bought it himself, even if he paid in cash, there might be a record somewhere. An address, even.

It was better than nothing. Which was precisely what he had to show Bazhanka for his efforts.

CHAPTER SIXTEEN

"How did he die?"

Nicco shifted uncomfortably from foot to foot. "I can't be sure he's actually dead, but it seems pretty likely. It was a trap. Xandus—that's his name, the wizard who hired me—has moved out of his quarters. I'm not sure he ever really lived there."

During his long walk back to Riverside, Nicco had thought a lot about Xandus' motives. He didn't like it, but the most likely explanation was that he'd been used as a tool in some kind of political game. The war might be over, but the messy business of Ramus-Bey and Year Zero proved there were still plenty of people vying for some kind of power. He just couldn't see what the ploy was, and that bugged Nicco as much as not knowing Xandus' whereabouts. "And he left his thinmen guarding the place. We walked straight into it. We tried to escape in Clarrum's skycar but... well, turns out golems are pretty hard to kill."

"Any witnesses?"

Bazhanka's question caught Nicco unawares. He had been expecting the mob boss to be furious at Nicco for losing one of his personal bodyguards, but Bazhanka was taking it all in his stride.

"I don't think so, no. Not on the street, anyway. Someone may have seen us ditch the car in the drink. I think you'd tend to notice a burning skycar crashing into the Straits."

Mirrla Werrdun was still with Bazhanka, sitting by his side. "Fire and explosives is about all you can do to a thinman," she said to the mob boss. "If they weren't prepared, it's surprising either of them got out alive."

Bazhanka snorted. "Nicco is full of surprises, my dear. He has a knack for narrow escapes."

"This wizard," said Mirrla. "'Xandus,' you called him? How did you come to know him?"

Nicco shook his head, wishing there was somewhere for him to sit down. Bazhanka presumably kept this side of his desk clear of seats for precisely this reason. "I didn't. He came to me and asked me to do the job. Xandus said he was a collector, that he wanted Werrdun's—your father's—necklace for his collection."

"Do you think he is still in Azbatha?"

"No idea. He's from Shalith, originally, on the other side of the archipelago. He may have gone back there. I can get an airship over there tomorrow morning, try and find him—"

"You will do no such thing," Bazhanka interrupted. "You're in deep trouble, Nicco, such deep trouble. If you so much as book an airship ticket, I'll be sending my own thinmen to pay you a visit. No, I want you here in Azbatha, looking for this wizard. I have contacts in Shalith who can cover that area."

"And how am I supposed to find him now? There are four million people on this island, and I don't have anything to track him with! What in the fifty-nine hells should I *do*, put an ad in the free printzines?"

"How you go about the search is of no consequence whatsoever, dear boy. All that counts in this grave matter is your results, and the consequences if you fail."

After his brush with death, Nicco was all but past caring. He sighed. "If you're going to kill me, just get it over with and start looking yourself. I'm too tired to care."

"Dear boy, who said anything about killing you?"

Nicco breathed a sigh of relief.

"That whore whose bed I dragged you from, on the other hand... well. She seems such a fragile thing."

Nicco glared at Bazhanka. "You wouldn't dare. She's under Madame Zentra's protection, you wouldn't get within half a mile of the place once I tell her what's going on."

Bazhanka curled his fat lips into a smile. "Don't underestimate me, dear Nicco. My reach is long. And if you utter a single word to your whore, or the good Madame, I shall have your tongue mounted on my wall. Now get out. Time is short."

"REMIND ME WHY we're here again? This place gives me the creeps."

The campus was an oasis of quiet and greenery in the Azbathan desert of steel, concrete and glass. A stone path divided the walled garden in two. On either side, as they walked through the campus, were carefully tended lawns dotted with trees and shrubs. Herbs and flowers brought colour to the swathe of green, but the whole was marred by occasional, random patches of burnt grass.

Half a dozen students in grey robes walked around the garden, speaking in hushed tones. They stopped and turned to stare at Nicco and Allad as they walked through the stone arch into the college compound.

"You can't just hack into a wizard's college infosite," Nicco replied.

"Why not? I know a really good hacker who owes me a favour. We could..."

"Because they don't *have* an infosite, dummy. It's all paper and ink, here. You know what wizards are like."

"I try to stay away from them as much as possible, actually. Can't you just come back at night and break in?"

Nicco gestured to one of the burnt patches on the lawn. "And end up like that? Now come on." They stepped up into a single-sided cloister at the front of the main building. A young man wearing the same grey robes approached and nodded at them in greeting.

"My name is Darro. Can I help you?"

"We're looking for a wizard—" said Nicco.

"Then you've come to the right place," said Darro with a smile.

"—called Xandus. I'm not sure if he attended this college, but he lives in Azbatha now, so we were hoping someone here would know him."

The young adept stroked his chin. "Doesn't ring any bells," he said. "Is he a friend of yours?"

"Acquaintance. Do you have records we could look at?"

The adept smiled. "Yes, of course we have records. But I'm afraid you can't look at them."

Nicco knew that look. It was the kind of look that said *by the saints, what a pair of non-magical simpletons I have here.*

"It's very important we find him. We have something of his that must be returned."

"Oh, really? And what would that be?"

Nicco nodded to Allad, who unwrapped a small bundle of cloth he was carrying to reveal a metal box. He opened it slowly, and Darro leant forward to examine the contents.

The adept gasped. "That... that... um, perhaps I should fetch the chancellor..."

Nicco smiled. "You do that."

Darro hurried inside the building, and Nicco and Allad followed him in. Nicco had never seen the campus before. It all seemed very out of place in Azbatha. It was only a fraction of the size of the main Archmage's Institute in Turilum, but stepping into it still felt like crossing a boundary. A nation unto itself. The building was remarkable for being only three stories tall—a dwarf in this city of steel titans—and made entirely from sea stone. Nicco guessed they simply couldn't make it any taller than that without reinforcement of some kind. Or perhaps wizards just preferred rubbish old buildings.

The reception hall had the same feel: wood and stone that smelled of mould and rot. As Darro scurried away to find the chancellor, Nicco looked up to see a stone tablet embedded in one wall, engraved with the names of the college's graduates. He nudged Allad.

"Check it out. Engraved stone."

Allad gave a low whistle. "It must be worth a fortune. You'd never sell it, though. Well, maybe to a bunch of Varnian students for a prank, but they'd pay bugger all."

Nicco scanned the list. He didn't see anyone called Xandus on it, but he'd expected that. If Xandus was from Shalith, he would have graduated there. Or, if Shalith didn't have its own college—Nicco had no idea—then maybe he would have gone to Promith, the next major island. Either way, it had always been unlikely that he'd graduated from Azbatha, if for no other reason than his accent.

But perhaps someone who had graduated here knew him. Nicco figured that in a place like Turith, where magic was considered impolite at best and insulting at worst, wizards stuck together for security. Even if Xandus didn't seek out the college himself on arrival, it wouldn't take long for a visitor to become known to them.

Allad had read the list as well. "He's not there. Right, can we go now? I don't want to start making enemies of—"

"Gentlemen."

An elderly woman approached them, treading softly across

the bare wooden floor of the reception hall. She wore a robe of the same style and cut as the adepts but in plain, bright white.

"I am Sarathin, chancellor of this college. Young Darro tells me you have something with you that I should see... is this it?"

The woman gestured at Nicco's chest. He raised his hand to it, confused, then felt his father's pendant through his shirt and shook his head.

Allad coughed. "No," he said. "It's this." He opened the metal box again, and Sarathin peered inside with surprise in her eyes.

She looked up at Allad. "May I?"

"Sure."

The chancellor reached into the box and lifted out a small silver brooch. It was a sky whale, fat and smooth like the creatures used to pull ferries back and forth across the Nissal River—and much of Turith—all day long. Its single eye was a tiny crimson jewel. It was exquisitely carved, and beautiful.

Sarathin didn't care about any of that. She held it in her thin, pale hands, taking shallow breaths as she turned it around and examined it. It was enchanted. Very heavily enchanted, in fact.

Slowly, the old woman began to rise into the air. Nicco grabbed her by the arms, gently pulling down to keep her on the ground.

"Steady, now. Don't want you floating off into the rafters."

The brooch was Allad's, or rather it had been stolen by someone and sold to Allad. What Allad hadn't known when he bought it was how much of a burden it would become. The brooch was very powerful, there was no doubt about that. Its natural—or rather magical—state was to be rising into the air. Constantly. After he'd bought it, Allad left it untethered in his store-room and had to pick it down from the ceiling on his return. Shenny had once taken it from the heavily-anchored container Allad stored it in, thinking she might wear it to a society function. Allad had returned home to find his wife lying on the floor in pain, and the brooch floating up on the ceiling.

Shenny had panicked, let go at ceiling height and sprained her ankle.

Allad's problem was that the brooch did nothing else. It just floated. It couldn't be steered, it couldn't be used to slow a fall like a grav unit, it didn't have any kind of speed control. It just kept rising, slow but unstoppable, and took anything up to about a human being's weight with it.

None of which made it an easy sell. In fact, he'd been lumbered with it for almost six years now. In truth, he'd stopped trying to sell it after the first two. But still the brooch kept rising. The enchantment didn't seem to need any kind of topping up.

That didn't half impress wizards.

Sarathin put the brooch back into the box and Allad snapped the lid shut. When Nicco had asked to borrow it, Allad insisted he accompany him to the wizard's compound. Useless it might be, but deep down Allad still knew it was worth a packet to someone, somewhere. And he didn't trust anyone else not to mishandle it and end up thousands of feet above the city.

"It's a beautiful piece of work," said Sarathin. "The enchantment is most impressive."

"Yeah," said Nicco, "And it belongs to a friend of ours, a wizard called Xandus. He's from Shalith originally, but now he lives in Azbatha. Do you know him?"

Sarathin frowned. "Xandus... I can't say I do. He's in Azbatha, you say?"

"Well, he was until a few days ago. Now we can't find him, and we want to return this brooch to him."

"I don't think I've ever met someone of that name, wizard or not. And as far as I know..." She closed her eyes and took a deep breath, then began humming softly.

Nicco and Allad looked at one another. What in the fifty-nine hells was she doing?

Sarathin stopped humming as abruptly as she started and opened her eyes. "No. There are no wizards on this island except my students, and... one other, who is most *definitely* not your friend."

Nicco smiled. "Bindol." The old wizard was an outcast, thrown out of the Turilum Institute after he was found fencing minor artifacts from the Institute's library to the highest bidder—who just happened to be Wallus Bazhanka. Bindol's concerns were more material than spiritual. Since his exile he'd adopted the title 'magus,' hired himself out to crooks and gangsters, and rapidly become a rich and powerful man.

Sarathin almost spat in disgust. "Please, don't speak his name. It makes me ill just to think of him. Darro!"

The young adept had stood patiently by the door all this time. Now he approached the woman, his head bowed. "Chancellor?"

"I did feel a quiet stirring somewhere around 4th Avenue. In the Crolling Heights area, I think. Not a strong signal, but perhaps there is potential. Go and find out, would you? If I am right, bring the child to me."

Darro bowed even lower. "Chancellor," he said, and walked out the door.

Nicco's mouth dropped open. "Potential? You're just going to snatch some wizard-to-be off the street?"

Sarathin scowled at Nicco. "And if I were to ask you to attend this college, would you come voluntarily? Would your parents allow you to, here in Azbatha?"

Nicco backed away a little and shook his head.

"I didn't think so," said Sarathin. "Now, there is nothing more I can help you with. Please go."

Nicco and Allad hurried back through the garden, toward the arch and a return to civilisation, in silence. When they were finally outside the compound walls, Allad was the first to speak.

"Oh, brilliant. Just get on the wrong side of a wizard, why don't you? You'd have us turned into flatfish or something!"

"Yeah, sorry about that. I just couldn't believe what I was hearing."

"Me neither, but by the watery saints..." Allad shook his head. "Anyway, no luck there. What's next?"

"Nothing I need you for. Thanks anyway, Allad. I owe you one."

"I think by now you owe me about five."

Nicco laughed. "Probably."

FREEZING AIR BLASTED down the street, funnelled by the towering skyscrapers. Nicco shivered against the cold, hunched his shoulders and thrust his hands into the deep pockets of his overcoat. The moon was full and bright, the silver disc blurred by the sodium haze of streetlights. Neon spilled out from the forest of holo billboards, blocking all but the brightest stars from view.

Nicco checked his watch. Almost midnight. The street was thinning as most of Azbatha's population made its way home for the night, leaving just the nighthawks, crooks, dealers and cops. On any other night, Nicco would have felt very much at home. But tonight he had other things on his mind.

He checked his watch again. Still almost midnight.

Skycars zipped high overhead, mainly cops and cabs. Groundcars rumbled by down on the street, more cops and cabs with the occasional groundtruck or freight car pulling a graveyard shift.

He checked his watch. Midnight.

"Salarum!"

Nicco looked up. A sleek black groundcar, long and low, sat idling by the kerbside. Nicco hadn't noticed it a moment ago, and didn't see it drive up. A tall, muscular man with very pale skin stood by the passenger door, gesturing for Nicco to approach. As he did, dodging his way through the oblivious crowd, he noticed that the man wore an expensive suit and shoes. The shoes positively gleamed, reflecting the streetlights like a mirror. The goon opened the back door of the groundcar and nodded at Nicco.

"Get in."

Nicco ducked into the car. The goon slammed the door behind him and returned to the passenger seat. He'd barely closed the door when the driver moved off, pulling the groundcar into the main flow of traffic.

The back of the car was separated from the front by a semi-opaque screen of glass, with a speaker grille inset into the centre of the screen. Nicco turned to observe his companion in the back.

The man was past middle age, with a spreading belly and several chins on his clean-shaven face. His skin was pale, his eyes deep and dark. He wore a black suit, crisp and well-fitted. His fingers were adorned with ornate rings, silver and steel carvings of fish and birds with inset jewels. The fingers rested on a black cane, topped with a silver head in the shape of a bird.

"Hello, Bindol," said Nicco.

"Salarum," said the 'magus' in greeting. His voice was calm and low, a steadiness that belied his seeming infirmity. "The last time we met, you told me to take my magic and stuff it up my backside. I did not take your advice, much to the delight of my delicate regions, but I remember the incident well."

Nicco winced. He had hoped Bindol would have forgotten by now, but it had always been a long shot.

"And now, on this night, I receive a message. A message that Nicco Salarum, whose skills as a thief are matched only by his contempt for my own talents, wants to see me. No—that he *needs* to see me. Witness the generosity of my character, that I deigned to hear his plea."

Nicco hesitated. One wrong word here could see him wearing a tanglefish's head for the rest of his life. Finally he said, "I'm very grateful, Bindol. I only disturbed you because this matter's very urgent. And very important, possibly to everyone in Azbatha."

The magus snorted. "I doubt that very much. What do you require?"

"Do you know a wizard called Xandus? He says he's from Shalith, but living in Azbatha at the moment. Or at least, he was. He's disappeared."

"We are very good at that." Bindol chuckled. "What more can you tell me about this wizard?"

"He's tall, dark-haired... blue eyes, small beard. Long, thin face."

"You misunderstand. What more can you tell me about his magic?"

Nicco sighed. "Not much. I know he didn't go to the Azbathan college. I know he had four thinmen bodyguards, all with his face." A thought struck Nicco. "Did you...?"

Bindol turned to face Nicco for the first time, his dark eyes narrowing.

"I make golems for civilians, Salarum. Men like Bazhanka, who barely have the wit to wipe their own arse, let alone create works of magic. Men like you. Why would a wizard need me to make his golems?"

"That doesn't exactly answer my question."

Bindol tutted. "Foolish child. No, I did not create this wizard's guards. Now tell me more."

"There isn't much more to tell. He's a collector, or so he said. He didn't want me knowing where he lived. He left his thinmen to guard the place. When I found it, they nearly killed me."

"Ah." The magus pursed his lips and turned to look out the window, watching the streets roll past.

He was silent for a long time. Nicco rubbed his hands. In contrast to the streets outside, Bindol's groundcar was warm. But that wasn't the only reason his palms were sweating.

The magus spoke without looking at him. "You have nothing more to tell me?"

"Not really."

"Why do you wish so urgently to find this man?"

"It's... complicated. But he has something I need."

"And you are here at your own behest?"

"Absolutely."

Bindol sighed. "Salarum, your dishonesty disappoints me almost as much as your lack of faith in my talents. Consider: I am the foremost magus in Turith. Do you think Bazhanka has not already called on my talents to answer these questions?"

Nicco closed his eyes and sank into the soft leather seat. "You don't know where he is, do you?"

"I do not. I have never even heard of this man, and cannot locate him. Perhaps he is even more powerful than I. Though that is, of course, absurd."

"Why didn't you just tell me that straight away?"

"I am still human," smiled Bindol. "At my age, humour is in short supply." He lifted his cane and tapped it on the back of the dividing screen. The groundcar pulled into a space by the kerbside, and the muscle-bound goon opened the door for Nicco.

"Goodbye," said Bindol as Nicco stepped out. "Give my regards to Bazhanka before he kills you."

Nicco pulled a face at Bindol before the goon closed the door. He watched the muscle-bound man hop back in his own seat and pull the passenger door closed. Then the groundcar vanished.

We are very good at disappearing. No kidding, thought Nicco.

The cold bit at his hands and face as he began the walk back to his apartment. He could have taken a cab, but he needed time to think. He needed a plan.

CHAPTER SEVENTEEN

Nicco whacked his knee against a bolt sticking out from the drainpipe's fastenings and cursed. It had all been a lot easier when he was a teenager.

Of course, back then he didn't normally have a large kit bag slung over his shoulder. He'd climbed this side of Madame Zentra's place almost every night, sneaking out to steal gear to fence while his mother went about her working day. His spoils would then be stashed at Allad's house, in the basement. Allad's parents only used it to store their own clutter, so never noticed the growing collection of hot potatoes under their roof. That had been the start of Nicco and Allad's working relationship, and the friendship that followed. Nicco's *only* friendship for many years in fact, until he came back here and met Tabby.

He reached the window of Tabby's room and peered inside. She was just finishing with a client, waiting on the bed while the mark dressed and made his awkward excuses. When he'd finally gone, Nicco tapped on the window.

Tabby spun round, startled, and he waved at her with an

embarrassed smile. She sighed and opened the window.

"What in the fifty-nine hells are you doing?" said Tabby.

Nicco heaved the kit bag over his shoulder and tossed it inside. "Nice to see you too, my love. And I seem to recall it was you asked me to come here."

"I was trying to call you all day yesterday, too. Where have you been?"

Nicco swung his feet over the windowsill and dusted himself off. This conversation was always the same. "I've been working."

"You should get voicemail. I can't believe you won't pay for it."

"If it's that urgent, people call me back. You did."

Tabby huffed and walked back to the bed. "Well, I've got something important to tell you. And I've got another client in ten minutes."

"I know. You can get ready while I'm here. Just listen to me for a minute."

"What's in the bag?"

"That's what I need to tell you."

Tabby stopped plumping up pillows and turned to face him. "What's going on? Are you in some sort of trouble?" Her expression was suddenly quite serious. "You are, you're in more trouble with Bazhanka, aren't you? I recognised those thinmen that took you away, I knew they were trouble."

Nicco walked over to the bed and sat down beside her. It was time for the truth. "Do you remember that big job we were celebrating?"

"Before those monsters dragged you from my bedroom screaming? It rings a bell, now that you mention it."

Nicco took a deep breath. "I was hired by a wizard to steal... something. Something big. And I did, and he paid me, and it was all fine. But it turns out that he didn't tell me everything. Or maybe he didn't know, I'm not sure..."

"Nicco, you're not making any sense. What did you steal?"

He looked into her big brown eyes and grimaced. If he told her, he'd put her in direct danger. He didn't want that. But she needed to understand how much danger he was in, too.

He was still wrestling with his conscience when Tabby's eyes grew wider. "It was you, wasn't it? You stole that necklace!"

Nicco exhaled. It was almost a relief that she'd worked it out for herself. "Yeah. Yeah, and it turns out it's a lot more valuable than I thought. Trust me, love, you don't want to know the details. But if I don't get it back, Bazhanka's going to kill me."

"Oh come on, how bad can it be? You already owe him thousands of lire, tell him to put it on your tab."

"I'm not being metaphorical, Tabby. He's going to kill me."

What little colour remained in her pale cheeks drained away. "Then we'll hide you away somewhere," she said, talking as fast as she could think. "We could go to Turilum, or Jalakum, he'll never find us somewhere big like that. Or we could get an airship, go to Praal until it all blows over. We can go anywhere, I've got money..." She trailed off.

Nicco hung his head. "No, we can't. This is Bazhanka. He'll find us, one way or the other. And he won't forget, either. We'd never be able to come back."

Tabby threw her arms around him. "I don't care. As long as I'm with you, we could go to Hirvan and I wouldn't mind."

Nicco put his arms around her and kissed the top of her head. "I wish it was that simple, I really do, but I don't have a choice. I have to find this guy who hired me. And I have to go alone. When Bazhanka realises I've skipped town, it'll be bad enough. If you're with me, he'll think I'm not coming back, either. He'll go mental."

"You are coming back, aren't you?"

"Of course I am." It wasn't quite a lie. If he did find Xandus then Nicco could take the necklace from him and return a hero, or at least free of his obligations to Bazhanka. But if he didn't find the wizard, or couldn't locate him before Werrdun croaked, then he may as well be dead himself. Nicco was sure that Bindol hadn't been joking about that part.

"So where are you going?"

Shalith. About as far away as I can go without falling into the ocean. But he couldn't tell her. Bazhanka had already threatened Tabby. When the mob boss discovered Nicco's disappearing act, she was the first person he'd interrogate. But Nicco needed a head start, at least, to track down Xandus. He had to find the wizard, to redeem himself in Bazhanka's eyes.

"It's safer if you don't know." Nicco leaned back and took Tabby's face in his hands. "Now what do you need to tell me?"

She looked at him blankly. "What?"

"You said you had something important to tell me. That's why you called me in the first place?"

"Oh, that. It's not important. Never mind."

Somebody knocked at the door. "Tabathianna! Are you in there?"

Only Zentra ever called Tabby by her full name. Tabby leapt to her feet and began straightening the bed sheets. "The time! You have to go, I've got an important client waiting..."

Nicco stood and picked up his kit bag. "No problem. Look, as soon as this is all sorted I'll call you, okay? Don't worry about me, I'll be fine."

Madame Zentra opened the door and stepped into the room, aghast that Tabby was only just now tidying up. "What are you doing, girl? Your last client left ten minutes ago, and you don't want to keep your—oh, Nicco!" She noticed him for the first time and frowned. "By all the watery saints, what are you up to?"

Nicco had one leg over the windowsill, ready to climb back down the wall of the building. He felt like a naughty child, caught in the act. He often felt like that around Madame Zentra.

"I'm, um, just leaving. It's a long story."

"Wait, child! Don't be silly. Come inside with me. I'm just relieved to see you're all right after those ghastly golems came for you."

There was no love lost between Madame Zentra and Bazhanka. The mob boss had tried time and time again to buy Zentra out, to enforce protection rackets on her, even just to threaten her, but all to no avail. The Madame was old, cantankerous and stubborn to a fault, but just like Bazhanka, she also had connections. Half the Azbathan police force was on her client list, from street cops to chiefs, and that was just the ones Nicco knew about. He had no doubt the brothel's clientele stretched even further up the chain of city office, and with clients like that, any hostility—criminal or legit—was laughable.

Nicco had a feeling that in his situation, it wouldn't hurt to stay on the Madame's good side. If his plan went badly, he might need to call in a favour or three. He climbed back into the room, kissed Tabby on the cheek and followed Madame Zentra into the corridor.

She led him away from the door then looked over to a couple of usher girls waiting by the elevator. She nodded at them, and one of the girls took Tabby's next client by the arm and led him to her room. Madame Zentra walked in the opposite direction along the corridor, gesturing for Nicco to follow her. "I do hope she hasn't ruined her chances by keeping him waiting," she said. "You know she'll only blame you if she has."

"Chances? Of what?"

"Didn't she tell you? She's been bursting about it since yesterday."

Nicco looked back over his shoulder at the client. He was just opening Tabby's door. Nicco thought he looked vaguely familiar, but couldn't place him...

"What is he, a holokino star or something?"

Madame Zentra smiled. "Nothing so mundane. He's a holovid producer, and he wants Tabby to... audition. He saw her shopping downtown yesterday and followed her here."

The client glanced over his shoulder at Nicco. And now, Nicco recognised him. It was the producer from his table at the *Astra* dinner, the one the kids' presenter had vomited all over. What a small world, thought Nicco. Of all the people...

The producer smiled at him. A knowing smile. "Hello, Mr Salarum."

Nicco's mind raced. How did he know Nicco's name? How on earth could he possibly know who Nicco was, or what he looked like?

My reach is long...

Bazhanka. It was the only explanation. The mob boss must have set this up, told the producer what had happened and who was responsible. Did Bazhanka already know the producer? Did he have some dirt on him, blackmail material maybe? Or had the producer simply relished the thought of getting back at Nicco?

He had no idea. But he couldn't keep the producer away from Tabby without telling her what was going on, and that would just make the danger even more immediate, both to himself and Tabby.

"Are you all right?" Madame Zentra asked.

"I'm... I'm fine, yes. Sorry, I just thought I recognised that client."

"Well, that wouldn't surprise me. He's a top man in holovids. Tabathianna could do quite well out of him."

"Aren't you concerned?"

"She's not an innocent, Nicco. You of all people should know that." She smiled. "Now, come and have a drink with me." She led him to the stairs at the other end of the corridor, up two flights and through a door into her office. As Nicco took a seat, the Madame poured two glasses of wine. "So what did those thinmen want with you? I'm concerned I might have caused you some trouble."

"You? No, they were Bazhanka's. I owe him some money, that's all. They were a day early, mind."

She sat down behind the desk and sipped at her wine. "Nicco, I've known you since you were born. I watched you grow, and even when your mother had no idea you were off learning your trade, I knew what you were up to. You can't lie to me."

"I'm not lying, I swear. But why would you think it was your fault?"

"I thought perhaps the wizard I sent your way was working for Bazhanka. If so, I apologise. I never intended to get you mixed up with *that man*." She grimaced, as if she could barely bring herself to talk about him.

"Wait a minute. What wizard?"

"The one you were in the Silver Sky Whale with, last week. Didn't he tell you?"

Nicco was speechless. What was it Xandus had said? *You are recommended to me by an associate... of your skills they speak very highly*. "He never mentioned you by name. So it was you who recommended me to him?"

"Yes, he visited us a couple of weeks ago. Just another client, until he came to see me before he left. First he asked me who in Azbatha he should see to arrange a job, and naturally I put myself forward. Then, when he told me he needed an skilled burglar, someone who could be trusted to do a sensitive job, I told him you were the best. Of course, I took a commission, but I hadn't seen you since to ask you if he got in touch. He didn't tell you any of this?"

"No," Nicco mumbled. "He... he had my number all along?"

"Yes. I told him you were in and out of here quite often, but he insisted it was urgent, so I gave him your number. Nicco, you look quite pale. Is something the matter?"

"Had you ever seen him before? Did you recognise him?"

"No, I assumed he was from out of town. His accent was quite strong, but of course you'll have noticed that yourself."

"How did he pay? For his girl, I mean?"

"Cash. Another reason I suspected he was from out of town, though I don't know what backward part of the country he must be from not to have a Shalumari card."

Nicco sank into the chair. For a moment his hopes had been lifted, the hope that maybe, just maybe, Xandus had left a trail or some details. Anything that might give Nicco a clue as to his whereabouts. Now those hopes were dashed.

"Wait! Which girl did you give him?"

"Gurinama. Why?"

"Can I see her?"

As THEY WALKED to Gurinama's room, Nicco told Zentra everything, on the condition that she didn't repeat it to Tabby. Not quite everything, of course—he didn't tell her about Bazhanka's threats against Tabby, or why the holovid producer was really here—but by the time they reached the room on the second floor, she knew everything else.

At Gurinama's room, the indicator light next to the door frame was green. She was between clients. Zentra knocked on the door. "Gurinama! Are you there, girl?"

A muffled shout of "Yes" came from inside the room, followed by the sound of a hasty tidying up session. Zentra smiled and rolled her eyes, but dropped any sign of amusement when Gurinama opened the door.

"What is it, Madame? Oh... Hello, Nicco."

"May we come in, child?"

"Of course, Madame, of course." Gurinama stood back to let Nicco and the Madame inside, then closed the door behind them and stroked her thumb across a small plate underneath the light switch. The plate controlled the door locking mechanism; as it read Gurinama's thumbprint a quiet clicking sounded. The door was locked, and the indicator light outside would now show red.

"Cast your mind back," said Zentra. "I need you to remember a client from two weeks ago. He was..." She looked to Nicco.

He took up the description. "His name was Xandus. Black hair, a neat little black beard. Very strong Eastern accent. He has blue eyes, he's quite tall and thin..." Nicco racked his brains, trying to remember Xandus' features. "He probably wore a lot of make-up to give him a very pale face."

Gurinama sat on her bed, trying to remember.

"He paid in cash," prompted Zentra.

"Oh!" Gurinama smiled. "Yes, I remember him now. He was a funny one, actually. Wanted me to take the lead, if you know what I mean." She winked at Nicco.

Nicco sat down on the bed beside her. "Can you remember anything else about him? Anything at all. I can't stress how important this is, Guri. It's literally a matter of life and death." A muffled shout sounded from the corridor outside. Nicco ignored it, concentrating on Gurinama. The girl held his life in her hands. "Did he mention where he lived? Any family details, perhaps? He might have mentioned a brother, or sister, even his parents? Or which college he attended?"

She pulled a puzzled face at Nicco. "College?"

"He was a wizard, remember?"

"He didn't look like one. And he didn't do any bloody magic with me, more's the pity. An enlargening spell wouldn't have gone amiss..." The shouts from outside were becoming louder. Gurinama looked up at Madame Zentra. "What's going on out there? Is it a fight?"

Nicco tried to contain his frustration. "Please, Guri, concentrate. Try and remember..."

"I can't, Nicco, I'm sorry. He didn't say much at all, really. And I couldn't understand much of what he did say, with his accent. I'm really sorry."

Another yell sounded from outside, even louder this time, and now female voices joined in the shouting match. Madame

Zentra ran her thumb across the locking plate—her print was a skeleton key for every door in the building—and pulled the door open. "What in the fifty-nine hells is going on here?" she shouted.

A dark-skinned man stood in the corridor, his shirt missing and his trousers flapping around his ankles, leaving just his underwear to cover his modesty. He held a small knife in one hand, brandishing it at anyone who came near. His other hand gripped one of the girls by the arm. She screamed in fear as his fingers squeezed hard into her flesh. Nicco recognised the girl. Her name was Lullu; she was a couple of years younger than Tabby.

"Has anyone called security?" shouted Madame Zentra to the girls. They all nodded. She turned to the man with the knife. "Are you *insane?* What on earth do you think you're doing?"

The man shouted through clenched teeth. "My purse! The whore, she has my purse within her! Will not to me return it!"

The elevator at the end of the corridor pinged, and two of the brothel's resident security men stepped out. All of the girls' rooms had panic buttons by the bed—one press transmitted the room number to all internal security guards. Nicco guessed the client had caught Lullu unawares and grabbed her before she had chance to hit the button.

One of the guards drew his blaster and took up a covering position halfway down the corridor. The other slowly approached the man and his hostage, calling out to him.

"Sir!"

The client spun round, pressing the knife to Lullu's throat. "Do not step any more, no! My purse will you return, or to the whore is death!"

The unarmed guard stopped, but Madame Zentra took another step forward. "Whatever the problem is, we can sort it out. Put down your knife, and we'll find your purse."

"The whore she takes it!" the man screamed at Madame Zentra. "Much cash is there, she sees it!"

Another cash freak, thought Nicco. What the hell was wrong with these people?

Lullu whimpered. "I didn't take anything, Madame, I didn't. I don't know where his purse is, he's turned my room upside-down..."

"It's all right, child," said Madame Zentra. "Just stay calm. Now, sir—where did you put your purse after you paid downstairs? Are you sure you had it when you went into Lullu's room?"

Nicco had a sudden thought. He broke into a run, heading for the elevator. "Hold those doors!" he shouted. The armed security guard stared at Nicco as he ran past, and he wasn't the only one. They all probably thought he'd flipped his lid. The doors were almost closed...

Nicco leapt the last few feet and jammed his outstretched arm between the doors. The inbuilt safety sensors kept the doors open, and the whole elevator juddered. Nicco stood up and pushed the doors open. He stepped inside and jabbed the *EMERGENCY HOLD* button, then got down on his hands and knees.

The elevator carpet was thick, a deep, red, woollen pile, in imitation of the Praali style. Deep enough that you could drop something in it and, in all probability, not even hear it hit the ground. Something like a purse...

There it was, in the corner. Small, fashioned out of brown, scaled leather. Nicco picked it out of the carpet and shook it. It jingled with the sound of cash. He held the purse above his head and shouted down the corridor. "Found it!"

He needn't have shouted. Everyone was watching him anyway, wondering what he was playing at. As he walked back down the corridor, holding the purse above his head, their puzzlement was replaced by groans and tuts.

Madame Zentra gaped at Nicco. "It was in the elevator?"

"Must have dropped out of his pocket on the way up. Easy to miss, with that carpet." He held the purse out to the dark-skinned man. "Is this yours? You're lucky it was still there," he said, though he wasn't all that surprised. A brothel, even a classy joint like Madame Zentra's, operated under an unspoken social contract between clients—don't look, don't acknowledge, don't talk, eyes front. The mayor himself could walk through the place, and nobody would try to greet him. It just wasn't the done thing. The odds of someone using the elevator and looking anywhere but straight ahead, so as to avoid eye contact with the person standing next to them, were so slim as to make no odds. That purse could have been there an hour or more.

The client stuttered and stammered, staring at the purse.

Lullu scowled over her shoulder at him. "I told you I didn't take it, you bloody idiot!" She reached up and pulled his arm away from her neck. "Now let me go!"

"I... I apologies, the purse I thought... Oh, dear."

With Lullu free, the security guards rushed the man and restrained him. Nicco opened the purse and whistled. There was a fair amount of cash in there. He snapped it shut and handed it to one of the guards.

"Somebody pull his trousers up," said Madame Zentra. "Then get him out of here."

"You want him dealt with?" said one of the guards.

Language barrier or not, the client seemed to understand the tone of the guard's voice well enough. "No, no! I am make the mistake, exactly!"

Nicco stared at the man.

"Hang on," he said to the guards. "Give me that purse for a minute."

The guard shrugged and handed the purse back to Nicco. He looked closely at it. The brown scales... Nicco had assumed it was seasnake skin, or something like it, from the eastern side of Turith. But now he wasn't so sure.

"What is this?" he asked the man. "This isn't seasnake, is it?"

"Leather," said the man. "Groak skin, exactly."

Nicco stared at him. "Where are you from?"

"I am of the Hurrunda, from Varn."

IT HAD BEEN bugging him since the man first spoke. His accent was stronger, his speech more broken than Xandus', but similar enough to grab Nicco's attention. His use of cash instead of a Shalumari payment card. His dark skin... skin that could have been obscured by heavy make-up, had he so wished.

Sitting in Madame Zentra's office, Nicco felt like slapping himself. What a fool he'd been! Shalith, indeed.

"He was from Varn. Probably Hurrunda itself. No wonder nobody around here knew him... even assuming Xandus was his real name."

"Do you think that's how he knew about the governor's necklace?"

"Maybe. I don't know, I suppose any wizard might keep track of magical items and whatnot. I just don't understand why he did it. Why go to all this trouble? Why use someone he's never met before? Surely there must be thieves in Hurrunda, they'd know Werrdun and his people better than I do."

"And they might also know the thief."

"Yeah." Nicco sighed. "Perhaps that's why he waited till Werrdun was in Azbatha. He knew the security wouldn't be as tight as back home, where they have to deal with bombs and fanatics every other week. But why all the secrecy? He basically tricked me into doing this job, but I would have done it anyway. Why would a wizard need to worry about what a thief like me knows? And now he's gone into hiding, but... yesterday I saw a wizard sniff out every other magic user here in Azbatha in a few seconds. So where in the fifty-nine hells does he think he can hide without another wizard finding him?"

Madame Zentra leaned back in her chair and pondered the conundrum. "Perhaps he's more worried about someone else finding him... or perhaps he's not as powerful as you think. What sort of magic did he do?"

"Well, he had thinmen..."

"Nicco, much as it might make me vomit, I could visit Bindol and get myself an army of golems. Even Wallus Bazhanka has thinmen, and he doesn't have an ounce of magic in his soul. What else did this wizard show you? Anything spectacular or powerful?"

Nicco blinked. "I didn't see..."

"What didn't you see?"

Nicco gaped. Like the village beyond a burst dam, his mind drowned in a sudden wave of realisation. "Watery saints. The lying son of a squid!"

Madame Zentra looked puzzled. "I don't understand. What?"

"I didn't see anything. I never saw him cast any spells or use any magic, apart from his thinmen." Nicco's mind raced as he replayed his meetings with Xandus over in his mind. He didn't cast any enchantments. He wore oddly matched clothing, part wizard and part faux countryman. And outside of his sanctum, he didn't wear any wizard's clothes at all. Nicco had thought it was because Xandus feared hostility in a post-Year Zero world, but Nicco was wrong. He didn't wear wizard's clothes, because...

"He wasn't a wizard at all!"

CHAPTER EIGHTEEN

NICCO HAULED HIS kit bag off the security scanner and made his way through the crowded concourse toward the waiting lounge. Like the city it served, Azbatha International was always crowded with foot traffic vastly disproportionate to its size, and Nicco was glad to get out of the crush into the lounge. He'd spent so little time in the heave-ho of Azbathan street life the past couple of weeks that dodging and weaving his way through people, normally something he barely even noticed doing, was starting to grate on his nerves. It was a sure sign this whole business was stressing him out.

The lounge was three-quarters full, split roughly evenly between business travellers and holidaymakers. Of the latter, Nicco counted a few dozen with dark skin. That was good. He wouldn't stand out quite so much if vacation travel was becoming more common.

He found a seat and began waiting. He'd left Azbatha plenty of times before; financial trips to Shalumar, vacations with Allad to Turilum, hops across the Straits to do a quick job on

Rilok or Kesam. If he'd been of a more legal bent, Nicco would have racked up an impressive frequent flyer account by now. But he wasn't of a legal bent.

"All aboard! Now boarding for flight 517! Citi-cards and flight passes ready, please!"

He approached the desk and handed his forged papers to the airline clerk.

NICCO HAD LEFT Madame Zentra's through the back door. There was a chance Bazhanka had posted someone to watch the place to look out for Nicco, or just accompanying the holovid producer. Either way, he didn't want to risk the mob boss following him.

He contemplated asking Tabby to come with him, but it was too risky. It would be hard enough for Nicco to leave Azbatha incognito, twice as hard if he had to keep her unseen as well. He was already taking a risk just leaving her here. The set-up with the producer had to be Bazhanka's way of letting Nicco know his threat to Tabby was serious. Madame Zentra could afford her a certain amount of protection, especially now that she knew about Nicco's predicament, and would keep a watchful eye on the girl. But there was only so much the Madame could do.

Besides, Tabby didn't speak any Varnian.

Nicco's planned trip to Shalith was a non-starter, of that he was sure. Xandus had lied about everything else, and now Nicco knew he'd lied about where he came from as well. The wizard (not a wizard, Nicco had to stop thinking of him like that—the con man, more like) had probably chosen Shalith because it was so far away, so foreign to Azbathans, that it may as well be a different country—and Nicco had fallen for it. All the mannerisms, the odd syntax, the layers of white make-up to hide his true skin colour... Nicco should have seen through it from the start. His need for money had betrayed his better judgement. To think, he'd almost come to *like* the son of a squid!

No, Nicco wouldn't find Xandus—if that was even his real name—in Shalith. He wouldn't find him in all of Turith, Nicco was sure of that much. But his bag was already packed. He had to find the con man, for the sake of both himself and Tabby.

There was only one place left to search that made any sense.

"Hurrunda, is it, Mr Millurat?" said the desk clerk. He took Nicco's citi-card and flight pass and slotted them both into a scanpod.

"Yes," said Nicco. The pod's amber light winked as his cards were checked. That citi-card had cost him an arm and a leg, or at least an IOU of his major limbs, from Allad. Nicco needed a forgery for two reasons. The first being the cops were almost certainly watching for him leaving the island, and putting his real name in the airship port system would be like paying for an *I'M SKIPPING TOWN* holo billboard.

The second reason was that despite his extensive travelling across Turith, Nicco had never actually left the country before. Local airship flights within the archipelago weren't monitored; like taking a sky whale ferry, you just turned up, bought a ticket and hopped on board. Nobody cared who you were or whether you were even Turithian. But foreign travel was a different matter, closely monitored and verified. It was a habit formed during centuries of war, and five-hundred-year-old habits died hard. To travel abroad Nicco needed a citi-card, at both ends of the trip.

Nicco only hoped there wasn't some kind of magical augmentation to the immigration process in Varn. Allad's cards were always flawless, but even he couldn't fake Nicco's brainwaves, or magical aura, or whatever other outlandish method they might use to verify your identity in a place like Varn.

The pod's light flashed green. The desk clerk handed Nicco's forged cards back and smiled. "Hurrunda's the first stop, sir." He waved Nicco on.

Nicco walked through the double doors behind the desk, smiled at the attending hostesses and proceeded to the launchpad. When he was outside he exhaled with relief and put the papers back in his carry-on kit bag. It was a bright, crisp morning, and Nicco saw his breath mist in the cool air.

What he didn't see was an elderly maintenance worker cleaning the window to the waiting lounge. As Nicco stepped onto the launchpad, the worker put down his sponge, took out a phone and dialled a number. When the other line picked up, he spoke just six words.

"Got him. He's going to Hurrunda."

CHAPTER NINETEEN

NICCO STOOD ON a gantry in the lower viewing pod and watched Azbatha recede into the distance. Unlike the day he'd flown on the *Astra*, the sky below was full of air traffic. He sighed, wishing none of this had ever happened. But what could he have done differently? He'd taken the job from Xandus because he owed Bazhanka money; and he'd only been in debt in the first place because he refused to kill an innocent man. And he wouldn't have had to make *that* choice if he didn't owe the mob boss for getting him off the robbery charge. Which he wouldn't have been facing if he'd been more careful to start with.

In the final analysis, Nicco only had himself to blame.

"Bit more impressive than your place, don't you think?"

A middle-aged Turithian suit stood next to Nicco on the gantry.

"I'm sorry?" Nicco said, confused.

"I said it's a bit more impressive than Hurrunda. That's Turithian technology at work, old boy. None of your mumbo-jumbo magician rubbish."

Nicco felt like his stomach was trying to escape via his throat. It was the same corporate type who'd sat at his table on the *Astra*. What on earth was he doing here? Was he following Nicco?

"Actually," said the merchant, "have we met before? You must forgive me—I'm good with faces but terrible with names. I'm Sothus Lubburon."

Nicco froze. *He recognised me. He knows who I am, he's probably got that son of a squid Patulam waiting outside the pod...* But he'd been wearing a full body disguise on the *Astra*, not to mention a fake beard. *There was no way this Sothus guy could really recognise Nicco. And if he thought he did, he couldn't prove it. He's just some middle manager, not a cop. Relax.*

Nicco regained his composure and shook his head. "No, I don't think so," he said. "And I'm afraid you're mistaken. I'm an Azbathan, born and bred." He held out his hand. "Nicco Millurat."

"Oh. Well, then I'm sorry. And pleased to meet you." The businessman shook Nicco's hand and looked him up and down. "Thought you were Varnian, see. You're a bit..."

"Dark? Yeah, I know. Blame my father."

"Ah! Going back to visit the old country, is that it? In touch with your roots!"

"Something like that." Nicco turned away and watched the view. The airship was rising through the cloud layer, obscuring islands and ocean alike. In another minute there would be nothing to see but a carpet of cotton wool.

"First time? You picked a squid of a month to visit."

Nicco had hoped Sothus would take the hint and leave him alone, but that remark made him reconsider. Perhaps this man could be useful. "What do you mean?"

"You didn't hear? Have you been living in the ocean for the past week? Governor Werrdun's necklace of office was stolen. He's stuck in Azbatha trying to find it."

Nicco finally let himself relax. Evidently Sothus didn't recognise him at all. He'd been panicking over nothing. "Oh, that. Yeah... I heard something about it. I don't watch the news streams much."

The man snorted. "I don't know how you could have missed it. I think it was the Kurrethi, myself."

"What makes you say that? I thought the Kurrethi were lying low at the moment."

"Ha!" Sothus laughed. "Not since Werrdun lost his necklace, which is another reason I think they're connected." He leaned back on the railing, giving Nicco the impression this was a story he'd told more than once that day. "I was on the *Astra* that day. Special guest, and all that. Now, the whole ship got food poisoning—never felt so ill in all my life—and then the very same trip, the governor's necklace goes missing and the Kurrethi start bombing Hurrunda again? You can't tell me that's coincidence."

Nicco nodded. "I didn't know they were bombing again. Do you think they infiltrated the airship? Maybe they were the caterers."

Sothus snorted. "Or the waiters, or the flight staff, or anyone. I didn't see much in the way of security. But Hurrunda's up in arms about it, calling it a plot to destabilise the city, so clearly they're thinking on the same lines."

I bloody wish, thought Nicco. That must have been the official line. They probably didn't want to admit a lone thief had punched a hole in their security, at least not until Nicco got the necklace back. Assuming he could actually find Xandus, of course.

"Have the Kurrethi said why they're bombing the city?"

"Maybe they think they can take over the city while Werrdun recovers. Who bloody knows? They haven't said anything yet, just set a couple of bombs. And they've been coming down from the mountains, too. Carrying out guerrilla raids on the edges of the city. The local police are gearing up for another big crackdown in the mountains, but they're up against it. Mind you, there's a big pro-Kurrethi rally scheduled for this evening. Rumour mill says Ven Dazarus himself is going to be there. Maybe he's going to announce something."

Nicco whistled. This wasn't what he wanted to hear. If Hurrunda was in chaos, it would make finding Xandus even more difficult.

Sothus clapped Nicco on the shoulder. "Anyway, enough doom and gloom. I'm off to the bar. Fancy a drink?"

"No thanks." Nicco shook his head.

"Suit yourself," said Sothus. "Nice yakking with you. Come find me in the bar if you feel the urge." He turned away and began climbing the stairs back to the main belly of the airship.

"Wait!" Nicco called out. "If Hurrunda's so dangerous at the moment, why are you going?"

Sothus winked back over his shoulder. "I'm in armaments, my boy. And if there's one thing the Hurrundan police need plenty of right now, it's firepower."

IT WAS RAINING in Hurrunda, a warm rain that hung in the air long after it hit the ground. The landing pad was slick with it, and Nicco almost slipped twice on his way inside. His view of the city had been obscured by clouds as they headed into landing. All Nicco could make out before being called back to his seat in the launch lounge was a sprawl of buildings, all much lower than the Turithian skyscrapers he was used to, spread over every inch of space within the natural enclosure of the horseshoe-shaped Hurrun Peaks. The mountains themselves were lush and impressive, their steep-sided peaks thick with vegetation.

Now that he was on the ground, it seemed his first impressions weren't far off. Looking around from the launchpad, he was unable to see anything beyond the airship port's buildings except the distant mountains. No towers rose into the sky, no holovid billboards shouted their wares high up in the air above the port's low-rise structures. It felt like a strange dream.

It felt pretty backward, frankly.

Nicco walked through to the immigration area, which consisted of just one desk, and waited in line. The desk clerk looked hassled and overworked. Nicco guessed that until the wars ended, Hurrunda hadn't received a lot of foreign visitors. And by the looks of things, they hadn't yet expanded the area to accommodate the rekindled interest in global travel.

He watched the clerk processing people, looking for signs of any magical procedures that could jeopardise his entry to Varn, but saw nothing. Of more concern was the armed policeman who stood a little apart from the desk, scanning the faces of the Turithians waltzing into his country like the war had never happened. At least, that was what Nicco assumed he was thinking by the way he caressed his entropy rifle.

When his turn came, Nicco walked up to the desk and handed over his citi-card. The clerk slotted the card into a scanning pod without looking up.

"Business or pleasure?" said the clerk in heavily accented Turithian, preparing to tick off the checkboxes on his screen.

"Pleasure," said Nicco, smiling. "I'm on vacation."

"How long are you to stay for in Hurrunda?"

"Oh, just a week."

"Where are you staying?"

That caught Nicco by surprise. He hadn't sought out accommodation, figuring he could just find a cheap hotel if needed.

"Um... in a hotel," said Nicco. He glanced down at the scanning pod. It seemed to have been stuck on amber for much longer than was necessary.

"Which one? Address, please."

Nicco winced. He hadn't had the time to research this properly. Was he really expected to tell this bureaucrat exactly where he was going to sleep?

"The Varnian Star, 720 First Avenue."

Nicco turned to see who had spoken. It was Sothus, the arms dealer. Nicco hadn't seen him, next in the line. Sothus took a step forward, but the armed policeman blocked his path and glared at him. Nicco looked at Sothus, then nervously at the cop's very large rifle.

"You must excuse my manservant," said Sothus to the clerk. "Itineraries aren't really his thing, I take care of all that." He turned to Nicco and frowned. "Nicco, my boy, I told you to stand in line behind me. Now look at all the trouble you're causing."

Nicco bowed his head in response. "Sorry, Mr Lubburon, sir."

"Come on, let me through. I can give you all the details."

The armed officer looked over to the clerk, who ran a hand through his thick black hair and sighed. He looked even more stressed out than Nicco felt, and that was saying something.

The clerk waved a perfunctory gesture and said something in Varnian to the cop. Nicco didn't catch it, but the result was good. The cop indicated for him to stand away from the desk while Sothus stepped up. The pod scanning Nicco's citi-card was finally showing green, and the clerk handed him the card. Nicco walked to where the cop indicated and waited.

Sothus smiled at Nicco, then walked to the desk.

"Manservant?" Nicco laughed.

"Hey, bluster's my forté, not blather." Sothus winked at him. "I get the feeling that's more your department, 'Mr Millurat.'"

Nicco peered at Sothus. The arms dealer's smile told him he knew Nicco was up to no good, and now that he saw him walk, Nicco realised what had struck him about Sothus' manner on the *Astra*. The confident stride, the short neat hair, the air of alertness... and the job, of course. Sothus was an ex-soldier, Nicco would have laid money on it.

"Well," said Nicco, "I owe you one. I can't honestly say I'll ever be able to repay it, but..."

Sothus took a business card from his pocket and pressed it into Nicco's palm. "Look me up when you get back to Azbatha. Assuming you ever go back, of course. I'm sure I could be useful to you some day." He clapped Nicco on the shoulder. "Here's to bluster!"

Nicco smiled after Sothus as he walked away. "And blather," he added softly.

The concourse was busy by Hurrundan standards, but to Nicco it was a breeze. He made it all the way down to the end, past the cargoed luggage retrieval pods and through customs without once having to dodge out of the way of an oncoming family, weave through a crowd of tourists or squeeze through a bunch of dead-from-the-neck-down gawkers. The port architecture seemed to be a queer mixture of utilitarian and baroque, basic materials and plainly shaped structures decorated with finely detailed patterns, intricate mosaics and ornate detail work on the walls and fittings. Once again Nicco was reminded just how alien Varn seemed to a city boy from Turith.

Not quite as alien, but bothersome nevertheless, were the two men following him.

He'd made them as he exited immigration with Sothus, falling in from either side of the concourse. They were both dark-skinned, native Varnians, wearing the sort of cheap suit ubiquitous to plainclothes cops. One was tall and burly, with a black moustache almost as prodigious as his gut. The other was short and wiry, with cheekbones that jutted like razor blades from his clean-shaven face.

The tall one carried a kit bag similar to Nicco's, casually shadowing him from twenty feet behind. The short one moved more randomly, scurrying back and forth across the concourse, pretending to be distracted by the gleaming windows of souvenir stores.

Nicco wondered if he'd been spotted leaving Azbatha after all. Perhaps Sergeant Patulam had contacts in Hurrunda. Wars were wars, but cops were cops; it wasn't that hard to imagine the two departments co-operating to catch him.

On the other hand, maybe he just looked a bit shifty. That wasn't hard to imagine, either.

He turned a corner and entered the airship port's main hall, a wide, low-roofed atrium with just one gallery floor above the ground level. Would they try to arrest him before he left the port? Or would they wait to see where he was going, perhaps hoping he'd lead them to the necklace? Nicco counted three black-uniformed police near the exit, idly fingering their entropy guns as they chatted.

He contemplated throwing in the towel and calling Bazhanka. He hadn't brought his phone with him. For one thing it would make his location traceable if Bazhanka was of a mind; but mainly because the skycomm network in Hurrunda was pretty basic, from what Nicco had gathered. If he wanted to call anyone, he'd have to find a street phone somewhere in the airship port.

He weighed the pros and cons. If he was arrested here in Hurrunda, he'd be deported back to the custody of some smug idiot like Patulam—worse, they might not deport him at all, if he couldn't produce the necklace. He didn't remember reading anything about capital punishment in Hurrunda, but he wouldn't put it past such a backward place. On the other hand, if he called Bazhanka, he could use the mob boss's clout to make the police back off; but he'd also have to face Bazhanka's wrath over his disappearing act, and that could be just as fatal. Neither option sounded very appealing.

So he ran.

Not outside. That would be too obvious, and mean somehow getting past the uniformed cops. And even if he made it past them, the undercover cops might have backup waiting on the street. The street was just too risky.

Instead, Nicco sprinted across the hall to a nearby elevator platform that patiently circled up and over, down and under, in an endless loop. They'd been common in Turith when Nicco was a boy, before grav tech was invented, but as he leapt onto the platform Nicco realised this one had no visible means of propulsion. It was powered by magic.

He jumped off as the platform neared the gallery level and hit the ground running, dodging through dawdling shoppers who barely registered his passing. Down on the ground level, the tall cop waited impatiently for the elevator platform to complete its cycle. His partner ran to the other side of the hall, where an old-fashioned moving staircase led up to the other side of the gallery.

Nicco suddenly realised he'd backed himself into a corner. There was no other way off the gallery, no branching corridors to break up the monotony of gift stores and cafés; in fact, no other exits on this level at all. He was trapped on foreign territory. He didn't know the layout, but the cops probably knew it inside out. He should have taken his chances on the street after all.

The tall cop knew it, too. He slowed to a walk, lifting his jacket briefly to show Nicco he was carrying a holstered blaster. Nicco checked behind him, but the shorter cop had already reached the gallery level, walking toward him purposefully.

He leant out over the gallery railing, checking the height. It was a six-yard drop to the ground floor, with nothing to break his fall. He'd almost certainly break an ankle, at the very least.

The shoppers had begun to realise something was going on. They backed away from Nicco slowly, allowing the two cops to pass.

"Salarum," said the tall cop, one hand outstretched in a calming gesture. "Come with us. You've got—"

He never finished the sentence, because at that moment the main hall exploded.

CHAPTER TWENTY

NICCO SAW A blinding flash of light, then heard a thunderclap. After that came complete silence.

He was thrown back by the force of the blast, lifted off his feet and hurled through the window of the storefront behind him. His fall was cushioned by the display of soft toys, but the shockwave itself stunned him and a storm of shattered glass rained down. Through the remains of the window he saw parts of the main hall roof crumble under their own weight, unable to support the structure now that a sixty-foot hole had been punched through it. He hoped there was no-one underneath the enormous falling chunks of masonry and steel. He didn't hear any screaming, but then he couldn't hear anything at all.

A second later he couldn't see anything, either.

Everything went black.

SOMEONE SHOUTED AT him. Whoever it was, he couldn't hear them properly. It all sounded like muffled gibberish. In a daze,

Nicco's mind was gripped by a terrible thought—he was brain damaged. He'd heard of people with head injuries who suddenly forgot how to talk, or understand language. Aphasia, it was called; a sort of aural dyslexia. By the watery saints, thought Nicco, I'll have to learn Turithian all over again!

Then he remembered where he was, and what had happened. *You don't understand them because they're not speaking Turithian, you bloody idiot.*

He opened one eye. Slowly, his vision focused on a man standing over him, shouting something in Varnian. Nicco lifted his head to get a better look around but regretted it immediately. Pain lanced up his spine, through his neck and into his skull. It felt like the worst hangover he'd ever had, times about a million.

Chaos surrounded him. Thick black smoke filled the air, and his lungs. Above him, through the smoke, was only sky. Dark, heavy clouds filled his vision. He blinked as cold rain splashed down on his face. At first he thought the roof had come crashing down around their heads, but then realised he couldn't see any walls, either. He was in the street outside.

The man standing over him noticed he was awake and shouted something Nicco couldn't understand to someone he couldn't see. The man wore a kind of bright yellow battle suit. Some kind of emergency rescue service, no doubt.

Nicco was lying on the ground, the hard street surface underneath his back. How long had he been out for? Long enough for some kind soul to carry him out of the airship port and onto the street. Was he injured? He must have been concussed by the shockwave from the blast—a Kurrethi bomb, surely—and been blown back into the store. Those stupid soft toys had probably saved his life. He turned his head to the side, with a little less pain this time, and saw more of the yellow-plated men carrying people out of the wrecked building.

He tried flexing his toes and fingers. They reacted, moving as he expected, though not without some pain. He tried lifting an arm. Pain again, but it worked.

The medic, assuming that was what he was, whipped out a small metal scanlite and pointed it at Nicco's eyes. A cool blue beam shone from the tip, blinding him. He tried to turn his head away, but the medic grabbed his chin and turned his head back to face the light. He moved the scanlite to the other eye, then grunted and said something to Nicco in Varnian that contained the word *fingers*. Nicco lifted his arm and flexed his fingers, and the medic nodded approvingly.

"Something something *bend* something something *legs*."

Nicco drew his knees up toward his chest. It hurt, but nothing felt broken.

"Something something *sit*?"

Nicco pushed himself upright into a sitting position. His abdomen ached, but looking down at himself, he couldn't see any major injuries. He had some minor cuts on his exposed skin from the impromptu glass shower, and he was covered in masonry dust, but besides that he seemed fine. Fine and very lucky.

"*You* something *okay*?" The medic turned away from Nicco and ran over to help two of his colleagues, who were wrestling with the unconscious form of an elderly lady.

Nicco assumed that meant he'd just been given the all clear. "Hurrka!" he shouted after the medic, and clambered to his feet. Bloody typical. He'd been in Hurrunda less than an hour and already he'd been chased by the police and involved in a terrorist bombing. Still, at least he was alive and apparently fully functioning. A quick change of clothes and he'd be right as the rain that was currently soaking him wet through.

Except, he suddenly realised, he didn't have his kit bag. Whoever had carried him out obviously hadn't brought it out with them. And why would they? Whoever it was, he was more concerned about saving his life than his lunch. He should be grateful for that. Nicco checked his jacket, and was surprised to find his wallet still in the inside pocket. Then he remembered he wasn't in Azbatha any more. Not everyone on these streets was a potential thief.

So he still had the cash he'd exchanged at the airship port. The exchange rate had been ridiculously low: a thousand lire, practically all the money he had left to his name, had got him eight million Hurrundan rakki. He hoped that meant the cost of living over here was low and not that a sandwich would cost him half a million.

Nicco looked back at the airship port building. The police and medics were turning everyone else away, pushing back the swiftly-gathered crowd of civilians come to see what the fuss was all about. Even the press were getting short shrift. There was no reason anyone would let him back in just to retrieve a bag. He'd lost his spare clothes, his fake citi-card and return airship ticket.

He had a feeling he wouldn't be needing them anyway.

Nicco pushed through the crowd of rubberneckers, trying to put as much distance between himself and the medics and police as possible. He hadn't seen either of the undercover guys who'd chased him, but if Nicco had escaped relatively unscathed then there was a good chance they had too. The crowd seemed to go on forever—people shouting above the wail of sirens, pushing and shoving to get a better view or to find some shelter against the rain... in some ways it was like being back in Azbatha. Nicco ducked and dived through the mass blocking the street, steering clear of the emergency vehicles inching their way through.

Halfway across the street the crowd still hadn't thinned out, and everyone seemed to be moving in one direction. Nicco went with it, figuring he could at least lose himself in the throng. There really were a *lot* of people shouting.

For the first time, he made an effort to listen to the voices. It was difficult to make anything out through the din. It sounded more like an angry mob than a crowd of concerned citizens. He heard someone shouting Werrdun's name, something about *government* and *traitors...*

By the watery saints, it didn't just *sound* like an angry mob, it *was* an angry mob! They weren't trying to get a better view, they were marching toward something, hundreds of them defying the weather, blocking the streets and carrying Nicco along on their wave. What was this all about?

Nicco remembered his conversation in the airship viewing pod with Sothus. *There's a big pro-Kurrethi rally scheduled for this evening. Rumour mill says Ven Dazarus himself is going to be there...*

Nicco tried to look over the heads of the crowd to get some kind of bearing, but the low-storied buildings of Hurrunda told him nothing. There wasn't even much air traffic to give him a clue. Were they headed into town or away from it? Where was this heaving mass carrying him to? Nicco suddenly felt stifled by the crush of people. He had no problem with crowds, but this one had a certain energy to it, a crackle in the air that made Nicco wonder. It felt like they could explode at any moment, like they were just waiting for an excuse to start something.

A riot was in the air. For the second time that day Nicco feared for his life.

And then a realisation struck him. Did it matter? He could have died back there at the airship port.

In fact... maybe he had.

How easy would it be to just vanish? There must be hundreds of people still trapped in the airship port. Many of them probably wouldn't make it out alive. They may not even be identifiable. Nicco could easily have been one of them. If the Azbathan police knew he was in Hurrunda, but never saw him again, how many conclusions could they draw?

It would mean never returning home, never seeing Tabby again. It would mean that Werrdun would die. But it would give Nicco his freedom, freedom from Bazhanka and that smug son of a squid Patulam...

An ear-splitting shout from behind him startled Nicco from his thoughts. The crowd had stopped moving, and him with it. They were in some kind of plaza, a small city square filled with hundreds of protestors packed in tight. Like fish in a vacpac, thought Nicco. And they were all facing the same way.

The crowd burst into raucous applause. Nicco stood on tiptoes and followed their gaze, directed toward one side of the plaza where an impromptu stage had been erected. A man wearing a long green robe, cinched at the waist with a length of rope, took to the stage and basked in the crowd's cries of support for a moment. He walked from one side of the stage to the other, waving to them all, and they loved it. In the centre of the stage was a single microphone. The robed man finally walked to it and began speaking.

Nicco's Varnian was rusty as ever, but he could follow the gist of the man's speech. He was some high-up representative of the Kurrethi, a colonel or something, and he was mocking Governor Werrdun's cowardice for not wanting to return to Hurrunda without his precious, devil-spawned necklace. He also made some insulting remarks about Turithians being congenital thieves and liars, that Werrdun was an idiot for ever trusting the "pale-skinned heretics," and that this was only to be expected of a man who took his orders from the demon Ekklorn.

The representative capped off his preamble by stating that only the Kurrethi could rescue Hurrunda from the demon-spawned chaos and depravity that the city had fallen into, by—of course—reinstituting their religious order and declaring Ven Dazarus as their Emperor. And if the Hurrundan police stood in their way, then the Kurrethi would fight to a glorious death, with Ven Dazarus himself at the vanguard of battle.

A roar erupted from the crowd at this last. Nicco looked around and realised some of the people here were wearing green robes like the man on stage. A few of them were waving placards, shouting Ven Dazarus' name and the glory of Kurreth.

The whole thing seemed absurd to Nicco. These people weren't revering a god, they were canonising some guy who, as far as Nicco could tell, just wanted to be a dictator himself. None of the placards, none of the banners hanging at the sides of the stage, made any reference that Nicco could see to their god. They all bore the same image, a stylised version of a man's face—presumably Ven Dazarus. What kind of hold did this guy have over his followers, wondered Nicco? What was it that drove people to actively want a dictator, to place their lives in the hands of one man and follow him without question?

Ven Dazarus himself didn't look like much. He looked like any of the hundreds of South Varnians you could find on any street—dark hair, dark skin, the same little goatee beard. The only thing that marked this rebel leader out was his eyes, piercing and blue. That was unusual, as most Varnians' eyes ranged from brown to amber, like Nicco's. Nicco figured the images were flattering toward this Ven Dazarus guy, they'd probably upped the brightness of his eyes to make him seem special. After all, if his eyes were really that colour, Ven Dazarus would look just... just like...

Watery saints!

"Xandus!"

CHAPTER TWENTY-ONE

HE COULDN'T BELIEVE it. And yet...

It made sense. If Xandus—no, Ven Dazarus—knew somehow that Werrdun's necklace was keeping him alive, and Werrdun was the last remaining obstacle to his own coup...

Nicco's mind raced with the implications of what he'd done. The pieces fell into place, and made him feel ill. He'd been used, not just so some small-time wizard could steal a magical bauble, but as part of a grander scheme—a plot that could bring about not only Werrdun's death but a full scale revolution, costing hundreds, thousands of people their lives. All because Nicco had needed a quick cash injection.

They would all be Varnian, of course; no-one from Azbatha was in jeopardy besides himself and Tabby. But the wars were over, now. These people, the baying crowd surrounding him, weren't his enemies anymore. Were they ever? He looked around at them. Ordinary people. Sure, they had some weird religious cult thing going on, but they were still normal people, just trying to get on with their lives, looking out for themselves. Just like him.

But that wasn't what sealed the deal for Nicco. It was something else entirely that made his mind up, drove him to a commitment to finish this game.

Revenge.

He'd been used like a common pawn without even knowing it. Nothing but a game piece in Ven Dazarus' play for power.

Nicco pushed through the crowd, shoving and squeezing his way toward the stage. Around him, the gathered crowd hollered and chanted, shouting the Kurrethi's praises and Ven Dazarus' name. As he neared the front of the plaza he saw Hurrundan police standing at the edge of the demonstration, a loose circle of men in primitive battle-suits modified for riots. Each man carried an entropy rifle. They looked distinctly uneasy, and Nicco wondered what it would take for them to start breaking heads. Probably not much.

A moment later, he was proved right. Hearing the sound of shattering glass, Nicco looked round, trying to find the source, but it was impossible. Then, in the corner of his vision, he saw a missile of some kind soar over the heads of the protestors and smash against the helmet of a riot cop. More followed. The cops stood their ground.

Then they opened fire.

The high-pitched shriek of entropy guns filled the air. People at the fringes of the crowd began dropping to the ground, some to avoid the riot cops' fire, some because they'd been hit. Their hair turned grey, their skin wrinkled, and men and women in their prime suddenly turned into frail, elderly octogenarians. They fell to the floor, rendered unconscious by the physical shock to their systems.

The effects of entropy guns were only temporary. Those hit would be back to normal within an hour or two. All the same, it made Nicco worry. The magical weapons weren't yet widespread in Turith, but now that peace reigned it was surely only a matter of time. The spread of cultural influence was inevitable.

Nicco dropped into a running crouch and weaved his way through the crowd. It had stopped raining, but the ground was still slick, slowing him. If he slipped here, he'd be caught in the crush and lose his quarry: the Kurrethi representative. But all the protestors cared about was avoiding the entropy gunfire, so they surged from the stage and away the police, leaving Nicco trying to move against the tide of bodies. The police had the whole plaza surrounded, but they ran all the same, and Nicco was almost knocked to the ground several times before he reached the front of the stage. The Kurrethi representatives had already left. Nicco whirled around, looking for their exit, and saw the man in the green robe jump into a large groundcar with blacked-out windows.

Nicco ran at the car, but as he reached the rear of the stage the vehicle's doors slammed shut and it sped off. The street in front was full of panicked people running for their lives but the groundcar driver just ploughed ahead, sounding the horn and revving the engine. People scattered out of its way, leaping into the gutter.

Nicco gave chase. The groundcar already had a good head start on him, but regardless of the driver's disregard for the safety of pedestrians, the crowd slowed it down. Nicco sprinted down the street, moving in the wake of the vehicle's street clearing efforts, and reached into his pocket for a tracking bug.

But his pocket was empty. The bugs had been inside his kit bag.

Nicco jogged to a stop, cursing the Kurrethi for all his troubles. The groundcar turned a corner onto a long, wide street where the crowd was thinner, and accelerated away into the distance.

Nicco leaned on a street post for support and panted. Ven Dazarus himself might have been in that car. If so, would he have recognised Nicco? Would he even remember the stupid thief whom he had manipulated so easily?

Nicco hoped so. When he finally caught up with him, he wanted Ven Dazarus to know his face.

He pondered his next move. He wasn't just taking on a charlatan pretending to be a wizard any more. This was the leader of a rebel cult, a veteran of the war who, according to what Nicco had read about the Kurrethi, commanded absolute loyalty from his men. Perhaps, on reflection, losing the groundcar was a blessing. After the violence they'd already perpetrated since Werrdun was confined to his bed, Nicco had no doubt Ven Dazarus' men would kill him outright if threatened.

He needed to find a better way, some way to infiltrate or sneak up on them unseen. To do that, he needed to know more about the Kurrethi than the fragmented overview he'd learnt when researching Werrdun.

THE CENTRAL HURRUNDAN library was as alien to Nicco as the streets outside. Dim and musty, with creaking shelves fashioned from dark wood and an atmosphere composed of equal parts air and dust, it felt like a relic from before the war. The shelves were stacked to bursting, permanently bent and bowed under the weight of old books and sheafs of printzines. Loose books lay on top of ordered books, pieces of paper lay forgotten on the thickly carpeted floor and not one of them looked like it was printed in the last century.

Even the Azbathan wizard's college felt more modern than this place.

A weight sank inside Nicco's stomach. He'd spent two hours just trying to find the library, and now he was here it all seemed for nothing. It could take days—weeks—to sift through all this stuff and find something valuable. Assuming any of it was valuable at all, and given the collection's age that seemed unlikely.

He walked past tables of people reading, all leafing through their ancient tomes in dutiful silence. Some of them were taking notes. Some of them looked like adepts. None of them was using a terminal, of any size. By the watery saints, he thought, it wasn't just cell phones that Hurrunda was slow in adopting. If this library was any indication, the city was as technophobic as Azbatha was arcanophobic. How in the fifty-nine hells was he supposed to find anything here? Even if he read Varnian fluently, which he didn't, it would take a day just to work out where everything was.

He walked down a corridor of high shelves hoping there might be a section of encyclopedias, maybe even one written in Turithian, when a heavy wooden door opened up ahead. A young man in grey robes walked out. An adept, maybe? Nicco didn't care. It wasn't the man he was looking at, it was the glow of an old-fashioned terminal vidscreen in the room behind him that caught Nicco's eye.

He caught the door before it closed and entered the room. A single terminal, almost as old as the books in the main library by the looks of it, sat humming on a dark wooden desk. Nicco sat down and scanned the vidscreen. He hadn't used one of these since he was a child, but it should have been easy enough to slip back into. The menu was all in Varnian, so he touched the corner of the vidscreen to look for a multilingual function.

Nothing happened. Maybe the options were laid out differently over here. He touched one of the onscreen options instead, trying to pull up a contextual menu pane. Still nothing. Nicco sat back and sighed in frustration. Surely it couldn't be broken. Hadn't that adept just been using it?

Then he saw the input board sitting on the desk.

Watery saints, when was this terminal built? Before the war?

Even the most basic of Turithian vidscreens were touch-based, and most terminals in his home country had abandoned flatscreens altogether years ago, replaced with motion sensing holovid displays. Werrdun might be doing a sterling job bringing Hurrunda into the modern age, but he was taking his sweet bloody time about it. Nicco reached out and touched one of the keys. It beeped at him, but the display remained the same.

He hit another key, and another, desperately trying to get a reaction—any reaction—from the display, when the door opened. He turned, hoping it might be an assistant or at least somebody who knew how to use the terminal, and asked for help in broken Varnian.

"Zandomon, bikka! Zenrrok firrom—?"

He stopped short. It wasn't an assistant, or a kindly adept, who had stepped through the door. It was the tall cop from the airship port.

"Salarum," he said in a thick Varnian accent. "You're coming with us."

CHAPTER TWENTY-TWO

THEY MARCHED HIM out of the library at gunpoint.

It was a normal blaster, not an entropy gun, but that wasn't what made Nicco suspicious. What gave him pause for thought was that the tall cop walked close behind him, with the gun pressed against his back, and his short partner walked in front. Not exactly police procedure. And neither of them said a word or flashed a badge during the walk.

Not police, then. Maybe they were government agents of some kind, Werrdun's own personal secret service. Mirrla Werrdun had got a good enough look at Nicco to give a decent description over a phone, and Nicco hadn't made any attempt to disguise his appearance when he arrived in Hurrunda. He'd thought he wouldn't need it. Strike one for overconfidence.

They exited the library, turned off the main street and into a narrow alleyway. They're going to kill me, thought Nicco. They're just going to shoot me in the street. The tall cop shoved him into the alley, while the other stood at its mouth and pulled out a cell phone. It was a bulky unit, an old model, but it was definitely a cell phone. It was also a cell phone in a city with barely any satellite coverage. He punched a number into the unit.

"I know where it is!" Nicco blurted.

The tall cop raised an eyebrow at him. "What?"

"I know where it is, or at least I know who has it. He wasn't a wizard—that was just a con, he was a fake—but I know who he really is now and if you kill me you'll never find out!"

The tall cop laughed, a deep, throaty laugh that just made Nicco worry all the more, and put the blaster away. "Calm down, Salarum. We're not going to kill you. We're here to take you back to Azbatha."

The short cop stuck two fingers in his mouth and whistled at his partner. The tall man grabbed Nicco by the arm and pulled him toward the mouth of the alley.

"Mr Bazhanka might kill you, of course. But we won't."

"Wait," said Nicco, "What do you mean, Bazhanka? You're government agents, you're not supposed to throw people to certain death! Turith doesn't have an extradition treaty with Varn! You can't do this!"

The tall man laughed again and called to his partner in Varnian. Nicco made out the words for *clown* and *idiot*. Then the big man turned back to Nicco. "Government agents, that's funny. No, Salarum. We work for Mr Werrdun."

The short man looked up as a sleek silver skycar descended toward the street.

Nicco's heart sank. "I knew it. That swine Patulam put you onto me, didn't he?"

The skycar landed at the kerb with the engine still running. The short man opened the back door, and his tall partner bundled Nicco inside. "Never heard of him," he said, sliding in beside Nicco. "Never heard of you until we got the call, either. But you don't seem so smart to me."

The short man closed the door, then walked round the skycar

and got in on the other side. As soon as all three of them were seated, the driver, unseen through a blacked-out glass divider, took the skycar back up into the air.

The short man turned to face Nicco. "Mr Bazhanka's very disappointed in you, Salarum."

"What? How do..." Nicco floundered. "Look, just who on earth are you? You're not police, you're not government agents, but you work for the governor? What are you, his private security force?"

The big man laughed again. "You could say that. But we don't work for 'the governor.' We work for Mr Werrdun. Just like you work for Mr Bazhanka."

The short man leaned forward and flicked a switch on the glass divider. A section of it flickered into life, revealing a vidscreen built into its surface. A beep sounded from unseen speakers, probably also built into the divider. The gear in this skycar was more like what Nicco was used to, much more advanced than what he'd seen elsewhere in Hurrunda. Evidently, 'Mr' Werrdun wasn't so altruistic as his hagiographers liked to think. He kept the best tech for himself. A second beep sounded, and a crystal-clear image appeared on the vidscreen.

Wallus Bazhanka.

"*Ah, dear boy,*" he said. "*I see you've met Brinno and Huwll. I do hope they've treated you well.*"

Nicco grunted. He didn't see a camera, but guessed there was probably a monocell hidden in the glass somewhere. "How did you find me?"

"*As I've told you before, Nicco, my reach is long. You were seen boarding the airship. While you were in the air, I called in a favour from my relative in Hurrunda.*"

"Your relative? These monkeys said they worked for..."

Bazhanka sighed and glanced from side to side at Brinno—the tall one—and Huwll who was the short one. "*Oh, dear. You weren't supposed to tell him.*"

Nicco gaped with sudden realisation. *Many of us run entire cities...*

"Werrdun's your relative! That's why you're so bloody concerned!"

Bazhanka shrugged. "*I suppose it was only a matter of time before you found out. Jarrand Werrdun is my grandfather, dear boy. Did you really think he turned Hurrunda around because people liked him? Dear, dear. So naïve.*"

"But why... why bother running for office? Why not just run the city from behind the scenes, like you?"

"*As I'm sure you've seen by now, Nicco, Hurrunda is a very different place to Azbatha. If Werrdun was not in power, the Kurrethi would be. And the last several hundred years have proven how bad that is for business.*

"*But all this is irrelevant. Tell me, what are you doing in Hurrunda? If you tried to escape me, you really should have run a little further.*"

Nicco considered his options. If he told Bazhanka the whole truth, the mob boss might yank him out of the city and put his 'boys' on the case instead. But if he lied, Bazhanka would just demand his return to Azbatha, and Ven Dazarus would get away with it. He couldn't allow that.

"I was looking for the necklace," he said to the screen. "And I think I've found it. I've found Xandus, at any rate."

"*The wizard? Are you sure? No-one I know there has ever heard of him.*"

"That's because it was an alias. The whole thing was a smokescreen."

"*Tell me more.*"

"No."

Bazhanka raised his eyebrows. "*I beg your pardon? Dear boy, perhaps you forget in whose skycar you are presently flying, and to whom you owe the pleasure of company.*"

The big man, Brinno, casually reached inside his jacket and

pulled out the same blaster he had pressed into Nicco's back in the library.

"I said no. I don't trust you, I don't trust your goons, and frankly I don't trust this entire bloody city. But you'll get your necklace back. Just leave it to me."

"*So you won't trust me, but I must trust you? Come, now...*"

"Look, you know I don't want Werrdun dead any more than you do. But I do want that conman. This is personal now."

"*If you've found him there, why don't you already have the necklace?*"

"Security issues. But I have a plan."

"*Then allow me to assist you. Brinno and Huwll are natives. They know their way around the city and can supply you with whatever you need.*"

"No. You know I work alone, and this pair would just be a liability. If you want that necklace, just let me get on with it."

Nicco could tell the two heavies weren't too happy about the comment, and Brinno still had his blaster in his hand, but they'd have to live with it. So long as Bazhanka told them to anyway.

The mob boss sighed. "*I confess, this isn't unexpected. Huwll?*"

Huwll reached inside his jacket. Nicco thought he might be going for a gun as well, but instead the short man pulled out a small red gem. "Here," he said and handed the gem to Nicco. "Take this."

Nicco did. The ruby crystal was no bigger than a coin, but masterfully cut, diffracting the dim evening light from outside the skycar even through the one-way glass. It glittered, the light seeming to move, swirling inside the sharply-cut facets—

"Aaaah!"

The gem suddenly burned hot, searing Nicco's palm. He tried to drop it, but it stuck to his hand like glue, jabbing needles of pain into his skin. He screamed again, staring at the gem as it burnt into his palm. Thin smoke curled upward, wafting an acrid smell across his nostrils that made him want to retch.

Then it stopped.

The crystal was firmly embedded in his palm. Nicco tried to prise it out, but his nerves shrieked and the gem didn't budge. He looked up to see Bazhanka, Brinno and Huwll all suppressing laughter.

"*It's a wonderful piece of Varnian technology,*" said the mob boss. "*Well, magic actually, but you get the idea. Think of it like a phone tracker. Except, as I'm sure you know, ordinary phones don't work very well in Hurrunda. But this does.*" He leaned closer to the screen. "*If you're lying to me, Nicco, if you try to run... I'll find you. If you lose yourself in the very wastes of Hirvan, I'll seek you out and bring you home. Magic doesn't need satellites. Understand, if Werrdun dies—and he won't last more than a few more days—I'll bring you back here and make you watch while I have that whore of yours executed. Then I'll throw you to the mercy of my grandfather's loyal subjects. Is that clear?*"

Nicco clutched his hand and nodded.

"*Don't fail me, Nicco.*" Bazhanka cut the connection and the vidscreen went dark, disappearing into the smooth surface of the glass.

Brinno put his blaster away and knocked three times on the divider. The skycar began to descend. "So," he said, "you're the one that stole Werrdun's necklace, are you?"

Nicco looked up at the big man with hatred in his eyes. "Yes. And I didn't realise what it was, so give me a break. I'm here to get it back from the son of a squid who hired me to take it in the first place."

"Right, I see."

The skycar landed in an empty backstreet and Brinno and Huwll got out. Nicco followed, flexing his hand and wondering if he could find a wizard somewhere in the city who could remove it.

"Right, then," said Nicco. "Now that you've mutilated me, just tell me how to get to—oof!"

Brinno punched him hard in the gut. Nicco doubled over and Huwll kicked his legs out from under him. He grasped at Brinno's sleeve to break his fall, but the big man took advantage and punched him again, this time in the face. Nicco saw blood spatter from his nose onto the street, and he followed it down.

He hit the ground with a dull thump. One of them kicked him again, he wasn't sure which, then the other joined in. Nicco curled up into a ball as they kicked and punched him again and again.

Eventually the blows stopped. Brinno grabbed Nicco's shoulder and rolled him onto his back. "'Mutilated'?" said the big man. "You don't know the meaning of the word. But if Mr Werrdun dies, you will. We could lose everything here, you idiot. Everything, do you understand? All because of a poxy pickpocket."

"I'm... considerably... more sophisticated than... a pickpocket," Nicco groaned. "I didn't... know... he'd die without the necklace."

Huwll leaned over him and grabbed him by the collar. "Well, now you do. And if Mr Werrdun comes back to Hurrunda in a box, you won't need to worry about Bazhanka. Because we'll take care of you before his airship even leaves Turith."

"Free of charge," said Brinno.

Huwll released Nicco's collar. He fell back, hit his head on the street and groaned. His ribs felt broken, there was blood in his mouth and he didn't dare straighten his back.

Huwll was still leaning over him. "Hang on," he said, "What's this?" He reached down toward Nicco's chest. Nicco brought his arms up instinctively, fearing another blow, but the short man wrestled them away and looked up at his partner. "Brinno, check this out."

Brinno crouched down. "Where on earth did you get that?

You're no Varnian! Steal that as well, did you?"

"What?" Confused, Nicco lifted his head. It hurt, but he could see what they were talking about—his father's pendant. It had slipped out from under his shirt while they were beating him up. Huwll peered at it. "No," said Nicco, "My... my father gave it to me..."

Brinno snorted. "A likely story. Who's your father?"

"I... don't know," said Nicco. "I never knew him. He was a sailor..."

Huwll stood up. "Sailor, my arse." He reached under his own shirt and pulled out a glass pendant.

"What...?" Nicco stared at Huwll's pendant. It was almost identical to his own, but the teardrop was a deep red instead of golden. "I... don't understand."

Huwll tuned to Brinno. "Show him yours."

The big man stood up. "I don't wear it. It's in a drawer at home."

Nicco sat up. His back and ribs protested, but this was too important. He had to know. "What is it? Xandus... he hired me to steal the necklace... he saw it too. He asked me... what it meant."

"And what did you say?"

"Nothing... My mother said it was just a... good luck charm."

Brinno laughed his deep, throaty rumble. "Then she's as stupid as you are. It's an army tag, you idiot. The Bishlurram army."

"Where's that?"

"I don't believe this. Here! Hurrunda is *in* Bishlurra."

Nicco sat still for a moment, trying to take it all in. His mother hadn't been lying when she originally said his father was a soldier. In fact she'd lied later. But Nicco had hired Birrum Razhko to check the military records and he'd found nothing. Had she lied about his father's name too? Could he still be out here somewhere, alive?

"You should get it read," said Brinno. "Find out what company he was in."

"Probably the bloody catering corps, if he's anything to go by," said Huwll, and both men laughed.

"But... where?" said Nicco. "How do you read them?"

Huwll rolled his eyes. "You go find a wizard down at the market, of course."

"But not before finding that necklace," said Brinno, wagging his finger at Nicco. The big man climbed back into the groundcar and signalled to Huwll. "We'll be waiting, Salarum. If Werrdun dies, you die. Even you should be able to get that through your thick skull."

CHAPTER TWENTY-THREE

HE'D LIED TO Bazhanka, of course. Nicco didn't have a plan at all. He didn't have the faintest idea how he was going to infiltrate the Kurrethi rebel camp and somehow get close to Ven Dazarus. One man, to achieve a task the entire Hurrundan force had repeatedly failed at? But he figured that if they couldn't find the rebels, Bazhanka's men wouldn't be able to help him either. At least on his own Nicco didn't have to worry about them ruining whatever plan he eventually formulated.

Besides, he didn't want Bazhanka spoiling his own personal revenge on Ven Dazarus. That was something Nicco wanted very much.

He also wanted to get to a market, to have the pendant read as soon as possible, regardless of what Brinno said. And in a place like Hurrunda, where the old world and its ways were clearly still a vital part of everyday life, the market might be a good place to hear gossip and find out as much as he could about the Kurrethi—and their new inspiring leader.

It was dusk when they left him in the street. He had no idea where he was, or how to get back to the centre of town where—he assumed—the market was located. It would probably be closed for the day by now, but he didn't even know how far he was from downtown. They'd been in the skycar for a while. It might take him all night just to walk back.

Nicco picked himself up off the street, wincing at the pain in his ribs and back. It was beginning to ease off a little, and now that he stood up he was pretty sure he'd been mistaken earlier about his ribs being broken. They just hurt like the fifty-nine hells. On the bright side, it was a sort of confirmation that at least he was alive.

Nicco smirked at his own cynicism, regretting it instantly when pain shot through his chest. He gasped, took a deep breath, and began walking.

"I DIDN'T EXPECT to see you here."

"Yeah, well. I didn't expect to find you still working here."

Lilla Salarum sat at her dressing table wearing a nightgown, slowly combing her long black hair. She looked at his reflection in the mirror. "You know better than that, Nicco. What else am I supposed to do, go work in a store? No-one would employ me even if I wanted to. Especially not now."

Nicco looked at the floor. He couldn't meet her eyes. "Is it serious?"

She didn't reply. He looked back at his mother and saw her sitting with her head bowed, her shoulders gently shaking.

Nicco would remember that moment for the rest of his life. It was the moment when all the resentment, all the contempt and anger that had boiled inside him for the past decade simply melted away, leaving a gaping hole in its wake. He closed the door and approached his mother, put his arms around her shoulders and leant his head against hers. He was surprised to find he was crying too. Neither of them said a word for five minutes.

Finally Lilla sniffed, wiped at her eyes with a tissue and smiled. "Still," she said. "It's not so bad. Madame Zentra allowed me to retire, but she says I can have this room for as long as I need it." She got up and busied herself around the room, straightening pictures that didn't need straightening, folding corners on bed sheets that were folded perfectly well already. "Have you spoken to her yet? I'm sure she'd love to see you again. Oh, look at you, all grown up and handsome."

"Mother, stop. Sit down for a minute, stop fussing. There's..."

"There's nothing else for me to do!" she shouted and began crying again.

Nicco had questions, so many questions, but couldn't bring himself to ask them. He could guess the answers anyway. Had she been for a second opinion? Of course she had. Madame Zentra herself probably paid for the best doctors in Azbatha to check his mother out, to protect her investment. Were all her affairs in order? Of course they were. Madame Zentra would have taken care of that too. Did she have anywhere to go? She was staying right here. She'd already said Zentra gave her the room for as long as she needed it, and Nicco had no doubt his mother would take her up on it. Since she was a teenager, Lilla Salarum had known little else besides this brothel, this room. It wasn't just like home to her, it was home. Could he do anything for her? She'd say no. They hadn't spoken in almost five years, after Nicco left to strike out on his own. What could he possibly do for her now?

But there was one question he couldn't guess the answer to. One question he had to ask.

"How..." His voice cracked, his throat suddenly very dry. He cleared it and tried again. "How long do you... I mean, did they...?"

His mother looked at him with sad eyes and smiled. "Maybe a year."

He took her to Tea for Turith that night, at the top of the Lighthouse Tower. She'd never dined there before. His mother was a pragmatic woman. She saw no point in wasting money on expensive nights out, unless a mark was paying for it, of course. All her money went on working equipment—clothes, jewellery or perfumes—or on Nicco. He may not have attended school like a normal child; his entire childhood was pretty far removed from what most people, even Azbathans, would consider normal. But he'd never wanted for holovids, storyvids, non-fiction magazines or books—anything he wanted to know or learn. His mother had given him a good education without his even realising it.

The watery saints only knew what she'd spent her money on since he left home. As they sat in the restaurant eating tanglefish, drinking purple Varnian wine and gazing out together over the silvery moonlit sea, Nicco absent-mindedly wondered if she'd been hoarding it, if he was about to receive a large inheritance. He cursed himself for thinking it as soon as the thought entered his mind, and swore that he'd make sure she spent it all on herself. He didn't need or want her money. All he wanted was to turn back the clock to that day he walked out when he was still barely a teenager, so full of anger and frustration, and change everything.

And that was impossible. But he could make sure he was there for her now, make sure the regrets and sadness were shared and maybe even resolved while there was still time.

As if sensing his thoughts, his mother turned from the window and smiled at him.

HE WOKE SUDDENLY, jolted from sleep by a loud metallic noise. He sat bolt upright, then regretted it as pain lanced across his chest and back. Squinting through his grimace, Nicco made out the large wheels of a groundtruck close by. The driver was unloading goods from the back of the vehicle, hefting them around on the heavy steel tailgate.

Nicco had walked for three hours before finally finding the market place. It should have only taken him two, but he had started out in the wrong direction. It wasn't until he came across a public information post—not an active terminal, just a printed sign—that he discovered he was heading toward the Hurrun Peaks, away from the city centre.

By the time he reached the market place, it was gone midnight. Nicco was surprised at how balmy the evening was, but he figured being almost a thousand miles closer to the equator than the Turithian winter he was used to had more than a little to do with that. The few locals he saw didn't seem to regard it as a particularly warm evening, especially as the night drew on.

The market place was closed, along with almost everything else in the city. Nicco had seen a few stores open for business during the walk, but they were almost exclusively restaurants, bars and groundcar hire firms. He'd bought something to eat, a fish and wheatgrass concoction that came in a cardboard box. The fish tasted of oil and brine, and the wheatgrass was limp and bland. Normally he would have thrown it straight in a recycan, but he hadn't eaten since the airship journey that morning. Besides, as far as he could see, recycans didn't exist in Hurrunda. People just threw refuse in canisters on the street and left it there to fester. When he first came upon one of these, he'd recoiled from the smell. It was clear that this city needed more than a new airship engine and terminals in the library. The whole basic infrastructure needed a serious overhaul.

The market place was a plaza, walled by rows of stores on all four sides. The stalls themselves were empty, just wood and steel frames with heavy cloth drapes for roofs, waiting for the traders to arrive and set up. Nicco didn't bother to count how many stalls there were, but it looked like a lot. Markets were extinct in Azbatha, and rapidly dying in the rest of Turith. They took up too much room for too little return. Besides, when you had holovids, computers, smartphones and a Shalumari payment card, why would you waste your time dealing in cash at some flea-ridden market? You could buy everything you needed, from food to wine to sex, without ever leaving your apartment. Of course, most apartments in Azbatha were so small that no-one *wanted* to stay in them, and spent all night pushing their way through the crowded streets instead; but it was a matter of principle.

In a way, he was looking forward to seeing a traditional market for the first time. But first he had to sleep. After a day of flying, being bombed and then beaten up—followed by hours of walking—he was desperately tired.

Nicco decided to join the rest of the sleeping city, and bedded down in the doorway of a store. He had no covering beside his jacket, but to his Turithian constitution it was more than warm enough to sleep. He dropped off as soon as he closed his eyes and slept through the night. Now it was a new day, greeting Nicco with the breaking of dawn and the slam of metal on metal. The traders had arrived to set out their stalls.

Nicco sat up, slowly this time. The ache from the gem in his hand had subsided to a dull throb, and his chest and back seemed all right so long as he didn't make any sudden movements. He checked his watch. Just gone six in the morning.

His stomach grumbled when he stood up, reminding Nicco that besides the horrid 'fish-in-a-box' concoction, he hadn't eaten anything for over twelve hours. He hadn't been able to make out the stores around the marketplace properly last night, as there was no street lighting in the square and the moonlight was subdued by thick cloud. Now that he could see, he spied a café on the other side of the square. He could while away an hour or two in there, getting fed while he waited for the traders to finish their preparations.

He walked through the plaza, wincing a little at his stiff legs as he maneuvered his way through the groundtrucks, carts, trolleys and crates. Traders shouted to one another over the din of groundtruck engines. Burly assistants carried boxes of spice, silks, fruit, newspapers and more, hefting them onto their shoulders like they weighed nothing.

"Look out!"

Nicco turned to see who was shouting, but in doing so missed why he was being shouted at and caught a sudden sharp jab on the side of his head. He looked round and saw a wooden box, lacquered with ornate brass fittings, hovering in the air just a few inches away. Ten more hovered behind it in a line.

"What in the fifty-nine hells...?"

An elderly man wearing grey robes ran over, shouting at Nicco in Varnian. He understood the words *idiot*, *look* and some variation of *go*. The meaning was pretty clear.

"Zandomon, bikka," said Nicco, rubbing his head. He didn't quite see how being clobbered in the head by a magical flying box was his fault, but he didn't want to get into an argument about it, so apologised all the same.

The wizard looked up at the flying box that had hit Nicco and whistled a short, high note. The box changed direction, flying around Nicco, and the others followed it. He waited until the strange caravan had moved on before resuming his journey to the café. He hoped there was more than one wizard at the market today.

Despite the early hour, the café was heaving with people, all working men by the look of them. Nicco guessed this was the market traders' regular haunt. He pushed open the door and squeezed himself onto the end of a bench occupied by a group of big men with rough hands. As he'd expected, the café's menu was simple, basic and hearty; just what he was looking for. The waitress, a twenty-something woman who would have been pretty if she didn't look as tired as Nicco felt, walked over as he sat down.

"What do you want?" she said in Varnian.

For everyone here to talk in nice simple words like that,

thought Nicco, it'd make my life a lot easier. "Tallus breakfast, please," he replied in Varnian. "And a coffee." If yesterday was any indication of how his time in Hurrunda would progress, he'd need it.

The waitress jotted down his order, then looked up, saw his face properly for the first time and peered at him. "Are you alright?"

Nicco put a hand to his mouth and found dried on his lips and chin. He probably had bruises all over his head, too. He wasn't looking forward to seeing a mirror.

He said, "I am well, thank you," and waved the waitress away with a smile, hoping she wouldn't feel the need to call the police. He turned back and saw that some of the labourers on his table were looking at him with similar expressions. He must have stuck out like a sore thumb, a newcomer in a regular haunt with a bloody nose and bruises. Very discreet.

A vidscreen, bolted to a bracket at the top of a wall, showed a news stream. The sound was off, but the lead story appeared to be yesterday's bombing at the airship port. An important-looking Hurrundan cop in full PR regalia was talking to a crowd of reporters while the text reported that the Kurrethi had denied responsibility. Twenty-three people were dead, dozens more injured. Nicco could only imagine what the death toll would have been if a similar explosion occurred at Azbatha International. Hundreds, at least.

The waitress returned with his breakfast, roast tallus with root vegetables and a thick meaty sauce. Nicco noticed it seemed much larger than the other meals he'd seen handed out, and wondered what was going on. The waitress patted him on the shoulder and smiled sympathetically. Then she really confused Nicco.

"No charge," she said in Varnian, and glanced at the men sat beside him.

Nicco followed her gaze and realised the labourers were all watching him carefully. One of them, a big man with a thick, dark beard, nodded at him. Nicco looked at his plate, then back at the labourers.

"Felishe, bikka," he said.

The bearded labourer nodded again and spoke in Varnian. Nicco made out the words *you*, *look for* and *work*, and it sounded like a question. Did these men think he was a labourer like them?

"Sakk," he said, smiling. No.

The bearded man leaned closer. He peered at Nicco and said, "Lok shazok Varnik?" *Are you Varnian?*

Nicco knew he wouldn't be able to fool these natives into thinking he was one of them. But if Brinno and Huwll were any indication of the prevailing attitude in Hurrunda, admitting he was from Azbatha could get him into serious trouble. "Sakk," he said. "Shazomon Turithik. Hun Turilum." He emphasised the last word, hoping they'd know the difference between Turilum and Azbatha, and began eating. The tallus was a little fatty, the sauce a little over-salted, but in his ravenous state Nicco didn't care.

The bearded man nudged one of his friends, a shorter, thick-set man with stubby fingers who'd just eaten his second helping of breakfast, and spoke rapidly to him in Varnian. The shorter man looked at Nicco and spoke with a very thick accent.

"Who hit with you?"

Nicco wasn't sure where this was going. Should he claim to be a tourist who had got beaten up because of his race? Had they noticed the red gem in his palm when he picked up his cutlery? Perhaps it had a deeper meaning besides just being a magical tracker. Telling them the truth was out of the question. But without some indication of the motive behind their questions, how could he be sure which lie to tell? He decided to stick with acts of the God, or rather Kurreth.

"Nobody," he said. "I was at the airship port yesterday, when the Kurrethi bomb exploded."

The labourer translated for his friends. Everyone at the table snorted and muttered.

"What's the matter?" asked Nicco.

"You should know," said the thick-set man. "This bomb is not of Kurrethi, no. Lies, they tell you."

"What do you mean? Who else could have done it?"

The man sneered. "Werrdun. His men, to hurt bad of the protest! Then blame Kurrethi, exactly."

"Werrdun bombed his own people? But that's..." Nicco stopped as the man's expression darkened. He was serious. Every man around the table nodded solemnly as the short labourer translated his words. Were they sympathisers? What about all this Hurrundan prosperity he'd heard so much about? Was it just more lies?

"Ven Dazarus is not killer. We know of the truth is, and hero is a man of God! Werrdun he is impotent and sick. His lies and tricks to make bad of Kurrethi. Kurrethi have the hearts of people!"

Nicco gaped. Was it true? Did the Kurrethi really have popular support? The protestors he'd seen yesterday in the plaza were certainly vocal and loyal, but how many had there really been? For all its problems, Hurrunda was a big city, almost as big as Azbatha. The population had to be around a million, if not more. It would take more than a few thousand demonstrators with placards and slogans to unseat a 'governor for life' who just happened to also be the local mob boss...

Wouldn't it?

The labourers stood up and began leaving. Nicco said nothing, returning to his breakfast as the men picked up their belongings and finished their drinks. The shorter labourer patted Nicco on the shoulder as he walked past.

"Always there is work for here, if you want it. No questions, not even for rules breaker, hmmm?" He touched Nicco's hand, the one holding the embedded red gem, and wrapped his thick fingers around it. "Market is good pay, no questions, exactly." He smiled at Nicco. "I am Julan."

"Nicco. And thanks, but I don't need work..."

Julan leant down, close to Nicco's ear. "You stay away of city lake today. Is the gala, many people. Nicco is maybe to be hurt again, exactly."

Then Julan walked out through the door and disappeared into the market, leaving Nicco staring at his violated hand and wondering how much more dangerous this trip could possibly get.

CHAPTER TWENTY-FOUR

MARKET SETUP HAD only finished fifteen minutes ago, but the plaza was rapidly filling up with shoppers. Clearly the Hurrundans loved a good bargain, and no threat of bombs or fanatics was going to stop them. Nicco strolled through the stalls, browsing with one eye on the wares and one on the lookout for a wizard.

The market was a riot of colour, sound and smells. Dark-skinned merchants in bright, gaudy clothes shouted their wares to the sky, their jewel-encrusted necklaces and bracelets rattling with every gesture. A fat grocer paced back and forth, encouraging passers-by to taste his fruits and dried vegetables. A butcher with arms as meaty as his stock stood at his counter and slammed a cleaver through shanks of flesh without missing a beat of his booming, incessant sales pitch. A short, wiry spice trader held small spoons with pinches of aromatic powder under the noses of customers, advising them on which spices to use with what meals. Nicco almost jumped out of his skin when he turned a corner and came face to face with the shaggy head of a Varnian tallus. The beast snorted and whinnied at him. He was about to shout for help when he saw it was part of a livestock farmer's stall, a miniature pen holding about a dozen different animals. The same man had glass cases of snakes, lizards and small, furry mammals that Nicco didn't recognise. In fact he didn't recognise even half of the animals, and the farmer pointedly ignored the chance to enlighten him. Evidently Nicco didn't look like a prospective customer, and he wasn't surprised. He hadn't washed or changed his clothes since yesterday morning, and the previous day's tribulations had left him stained with blood, dust, dirt and more. It was probably his scent that made the tallus uneasy.

In broken Varnian, Nicco asked the farmer where he might find a wizard. He didn't actually know the word for wizard, so he asked for a magus and hoped the farmer would understand. But the farmer just shrugged and turned away.

Nicco moved on, looking for the telltale signs of a wizard; floating ornaments, talking anti-theft purses, sudden flashes of light and colour. He didn't see any immediately, but he did see someone else he recognised. Sothus, the Azbathan arms dealer, was meandering through the marketplace with a young woman on his arm. She was dark-skinned and lithe, obviously a native. Probably a working girl, an escort Sothus had picked up in town.

He was surprised to find himself glad that Sothus had survived the explosion at the airport too, but didn't feel like making idle conversation. Nicco turned away, losing himself in the crowd. Or so he thought.

"Millurat! Hey, Nicco!"

Sothus shouted to him across the throng of shoppers and traders. Nicco turned to see the man walking toward him with a smile on his face, the woman in tow.

Nicco smiled back, feigning surprise. "Sothus! How good to see you! I thought perhaps you'd been caught in the blast."

Sothus frowned. "Already in a cab and away when it went

off. Heard about it, though. Awful mess. Were you still there?"

"Yeah." Nicco indicated his bruises and cuts. "But I'll live. So what are you doing here at the market? Thinking of setting up a stall for discount entropy guns?"

Sothus laughed. "Morning off, old boy. I'm trying to find something pretty for the wife before we go to the lagoon for lunch."

Nicco cursed himself for assuming the worst of Sothus so quickly. He'd spent so long lurking in the underworld, cynicism was just his normal state of mind. He smiled and offered his hand to the woman. "Nicco Millurat. Pleased to meet you. Your husband's a good man, he saved my bacon back at the airship port. But I'm sorry, I really must..."

The woman laughed. "I am not his wife, silly man," she said with a Varnian accent.

Sothus winked at Nicco. "No, no, this is Charruna. My escort."

Nicco deflated. Perhaps he should trust his instincts after all.

"And what about you, eh?" Sothus asked. "Enjoying your vacation?"

"Oh, yeah," laughed Nicco, thinking what a state he must look, "never better. But I really must be off. I have to find a wizard. Preferably one without flying boxes that clobber people over the—never mind, it's a long story."

Charruna smiled and shrugged. "Go to Hullorik," she said. "He is powerful wizard. Hullorik has many magics, exactly."

Sothus smiled. "There you go. Nothing like a bit of local knowledge, eh?"

"Where is he?" Nicco asked.

Charuna pointed to the other side of the market. "White hair," she said, pointing to her head. "He will burning, yes." She smacked her lips together, miming smoking a pipe.

"Looks like we'll say goodbye, old boy," said Sothus. "Take care, 'Mr Millurat.' See you around."

"Yeah. Goodbye, Sothus. Felishe, Charruna. Hurrka, bikka!" They faded into the crowd of shoppers.

Nicco turned and walked over to the other side of the plaza, following Charruna's direction and hoping it wouldn't lead him to the grey-robed man with the kamikaze flying boxes from earlier. It was about time he caught a stroke of luck in this place. If he'd been a religious man, he might have considered it an omen of good things to come.

He would have been wrong, of course.

Nicco reached the other side of the market, but didn't see anyone who looked like a wizard. Then he noticed a single stall, more like a tent, standing apart from the others on one edge of the plaza. The painted sign hanging from the awning read *BUSY DO NOT ENTER* in Varnian. A skull and crossbones was painted underneath the words. Lovely, thought Nicco. But he was pretty sure this was what he was looking for.

There was a trinket stall nearby, staffed by a man swathed from head to toe in bright orange robes. Only his face and hands, lean and hollow-cheeked, were visible. Nicco could clearly see the other tent's entrance flap from there, so he sauntered over and pretended to be interested. The stall owner smiled, revealing broken teeth, and enthusiastically encouraged Nicco to examine his wares more closely. Nicco browsed absent-mindedly, keeping one eye on the tent stall. The trinket stall was full of cheap rubbish and souvenirs—wooden versions of central Varn's famous white-stone statuettes that looked as if they were carved by a blind, one-armed Kyasi; oddly coloured crystals that, to Nicco's thieving eye, weren't even cut properly; charm bracelets and necklaces; head scarves embroidered with the Varnian flag; ceramic models of what Nicco assumed to be a notable mountain from the Hurrun Peaks; even replicas of Werrdun's necklace, which made Nicco laugh bitterly. He wondered idly if he could persuade the tent-dwelling wizard to enchant one so he could give Bazhanka that instead. It would save Nicco a lot of trouble, but he guessed that an enchantment to literally keep someone alive past their natural lifespan would be out of his budget. And even if Bazhanka was fooled, these copies wouldn't stand up to scrutiny by someone who knew the necklace well—like Werrdun himself.

The sound of canvas brushing on canvas caught Nicco's ear. He glanced at the tent stall. A young woman dashed out, sobbing, and quickly disappeared into the market crowd. A grey-haired man followed her outside and stood at the tent entrance. He wore bright yellow silk robes, all the brighter against his almost-black skin. The man watched the young woman go and rolled his eyes, then turned and removed the painted sign from the awning.

The trinket stall trader had noticed Nicco looking at the replica necklaces, and was trying to make him try one on. Nicco pushed the trader's hands away, apologised and walked toward the man outside the tent stall.

The owner of the trinket stall shouted after him. It was a rapid-fire shout, and Nicco had trouble translating, but from the trader's tone of voice he guessed that he wasn't the first customer to wait at the man's stall with no intention of buying. The grey-haired man glanced over and shouted back at the trader, dismissing him with a wave of his hand. Nicco understood the words *head* and some form of the verb *make smaller*. The trinket stall owner fell silent.

The grey-haired man reached into a fold of his robe and pulled out a long-stemmed pipe, watching Nicco as he lit it with a leafstick burner.

"Mekkla Hullorik?" said Nicco. "Zenrrok lok hulluda Turithik?"

The man smiled. "I am Hullorik. And yes, I speak Turithian... but it will cost you extra."

Nicco looked in the direction the sobbing young woman had gone. "What was her problem?"

"She could not handle the truth," said the wizard. "A card reader would have been better for her, I think. Then she would have heard only what she wanted to."

"Let me guess. Man trouble?"

Hullorik drew on his pipe. "Young people," he sighed. "Now what can I do for you, friend from Turith? Come inside where we may talk freely." He pulled aside the canvas flap and gestured for Nicco to enter the dim tent. Then he hung the *BUSY* sign back on the awning and followed him inside, puffing smoke as he went.

The smoke wafted over Nicco and made him cough. He didn't smoke himself, and preferred not to get it blown in his face, but as he crossed the threshold to walk inside the tent he saw he would be out of luck there. Incense and oil burners filled the wizard's makeshift store and he walked into a wall of scented smoke.

Then he realised it was heading straight for him. It coiled around him, mixing with Hullorik's pipe smoke as it circled Nicco's body, starting at his head and slowly drifting down. He felt a tingling, itching sensation around the red gem in his palm. He tried scratching, but it didn't help. Frustrated, Nicco clenched his fist around it and walked further inside the tent, trying to ignore the itch and hoping the smoke would disperse.

Looking around at Hullorik's paraphernalia Nicco was reminded of "Xandus'" place in Azbatha. And now that he knew the purpose of the fake wizard's hideout, he recognised the transitory nature of Hullorik's setup. Small sideboards and tables held ornaments and scrolls, bowls of brightly coloured powder sat alongside tomes of runes and sigils bound in thick tallus hide, a thick Praali rug lined the floor and deadened the sound within... It was all very familiar, and Nicco shivered. But unlike Ven Dazarus, Hullorik was clearly the real deal, and the reminder of how he was duped strengthened Nicco's resolve to see Ven Dazarus punished.

Hullorik tied the canvas flap shut and turned to Nicco. "You are a criminal?"

"What?" The question took Nicco by surprise.

The wizard sat down in a chair and indicated for Nicco to do the same. "It is all right. I do not care for myself. But I wonder why a Turith man comes to see a Varnian wizard. And then my home warns me he is with a following gem. And I think does he want me to remove this thing? Because it can be done, but the cost is very high. And my friend from Turith does not look a wealthy man."

Nicco sat down. "Your home warned you? That was what all that smoke was about?"

Hullorik gestured to the tent around them and smiled. "I am a wizard, friend from Turith."

Nicco placed his hand on the table between them, palm up. The gem was dull at the moment, the colour of dried blood. "So you've seen one of these before."

The wizard leaned forward and took Nicco's hand in his own. He had a firm touch. His fingers traced the gem's facets and it began to glow softly, warming and brightening to Hullorik's touch. He raised an eyebrow and cocked his head. "Interesting. Who put this gem upon you?"

"I don't know," Nicco lied. "I was in the bomb blast at the airship port yesterday, and when I woke up it was just there."

Hullorik snorted. "I am not one who asks questions lightly, man from Turith. You will tell me truth or you shall leave now."

"Look, this isn't why I came to you," said Nicco, noting the change from *friend* to *man*. "I'm not a criminal, or at least that's not why I've got this bloody thing in my hand. I wanted to ask you two things..."

"I shall tell you a truth, to make you understand, and in return you shall tell me the truth I desire. I can see now that this gem is not of the police. I know this because it is one of mine."

Nicco sighed. Why wasn't he surprised? "Then you probably don't need me to tell you where I got it. Who bought it, the gormless goons? Brinno and Huwll?"

"Exactly them, yes." Hullorik shrugged. "It is not the first time."

A sudden thought struck Nicco. "Wait a minute... If it's one of yours, does that make it easier to remove? Can you get it out now?"

Hullorik ignored the question. "Tell me these things you want to ask me."

"It can wait. Just remove this bloody gem!"

"Tell me."

Nicco sighed. "All right... The first thing I need to know is, this Ven Dazarus guy. Is he a wizard?"

Hullorik laughed, a deep rumble that shook the table between them. "Ven Dazarus? He is a soldier, not a magician. There is more magic in you, with that following gem in your hand, than in his entire body. Why do you ask this? Are you an agent of Werrdun, to know such men as Brinno and Huwll?"

"Never mind why. Are you sure he's not a magician?"

"Why would a man who controlled magic need a man like me to make thinmen for him?"

Nicco stared at Hullorik. Bindol had said something similar, but Nicco had already mentioned the thinmen by that point. He hadn't said anything about them to Hullorik. He suddenly felt very paranoid, and wondered if he was being watched. Had Bazhanka found him again? Perhaps he'd been recognised by one of the Kurrethi in the city. Even worse, maybe Ven Dazarus knew Nicco was on his trail...

"You made his thinmen." Nicco couldn't help but think of Clarrum. The poor bastard was only doing his job.

"Many times. I make the most accurate and reliable golems in Bishlurram. It is not the only service I perform for him. But I can see this surprises you. Why should it?"

"It's a long story. I'd been..." Nicco chose his words carefully. "I'd been led to believe he was a wizard."

"He is not. What is the second?" Nicco looked confused, so Hullorik leaned forward and spoke slowly. "You said there are two things you want to ask me."

"Oh!" The wizard's revelation had almost made Nicco forget why he came here in the first place. He reached into his shirt and pulled out his father's pendant. "I was told you could read this."

Now it was Hullorik's turn to be surprised. He took the pendant in his hands and turned it over, examining it. "Now why should a man from Turith be carrying such a thing? It is real?"

"So I'm told. It was my father's, but I never knew him."

Hullorik looked at Nicco in question. "And you are sure you want it read? If he was a stranger to you, it may not be all you want to hear. And you know already that Hullorik is not one to hide the truth."

Nicco took a deep breath and nodded. "I'm sure."

"Very well." Hullorik slowly closed his hands around the golden teardrop, shut his eyes and leaned back. Smoke from the smoldering incense and herbs around the tent seemed to seek him out, drifting over his hands and face. Nicco glimpsed soft rays of golden sunlight break through the gaps between the wizard's fingers, hazy and diffuse through the smoke. Nicco mentally kicked himself for never thinking to ask Bindol about the pendant. Though on reflection, he figured it was probably better to ask someone from Varn itself. Bindol might have misread it, or not know how to read it in the first place.

Hullorik opened his eyes and placed the pendant down on the table.

"Your father's name was Nicco. Nicco Miarrlak. He was a journalist."

Nicco stared at the wizard. The name fit, of course, but surely there was some mistake. "What? No, no, that's an army tag, the Bishlurram army..."

"Yes. He wrote for the army. Many countries sent reporters to live in other countries, to broadcast news streams. You are perhaps too young to remember."

"So he wasn't a soldier?"

"He was, but not as you think of it. It is doubtful he ever fought." He saw the confusion in Nicco's eyes. "I warned you it may not be what you are hoping for. You wish he was a brave combat soldier, yes?"

Nicco considered that for a moment and realised that the answer was no. He didn't wish that at all. If his father was a reporter of some kind, that meant his hands were clean of blood. That pleased Nicco. Perhaps his own distaste for violence was something he'd inherited from his father without ever realising it. He did regret, more than ever now, that he'd never met the man. He probably had some great stories to tell. Nicco felt a small pang of guilt at his own chosen profession. He felt unworthy next to a man who'd travelled into enemy territory just to send the truth home to his people.

But the feeling soon faded. Nicco had his own life to worry about right now. He could go on a guilt trip later, once his mission was complete. He picked up the pendant and replaced it around his neck. "Hurrka," he said to Hullorik. "How much do I owe you?"

"Ten thousand rakki, I think."

"What about removing this gem?"

"No."

Nicco blinked. "But you said it could be done."

"It can be. But I will not. Consider: I remove the following gem, and the man who gave it to you decides to watch where you are. He sees you are in the market place. Then later, he looks far for it again, and he sees you are in the market place once more. This is coincidence. But the third time he looks, you are still in the market place, and it is no more coincidence. He comes to me, to find you, but you are not here. What should I tell him? Hullorik speaks only the truth. And what of you? When he finds you he will punish you, and badly if you are so important as to require this thing. No, it is better that the gem stays with you."

"And have everyone think I'm a criminal."

"You would rather many assume you are a Kurrethi spy, sent from Turith to destroy our government? The man who gave you the following gem may have done you favours, especially now when the gala is at its height. A Hurrundan may feel very... patriotic at this time of the year."

"Now hang on a minute, you make thinmen for Ven Dazarus! You're a Kurrethi supporter!"

Hullorik raised an eyebrow. "No, man from Turith, I am wizard. Politics, bombs, governors and religion, these are nothing to me. I serve whoever purchases my services. It matters not to me who collects the taxes. And speaking of collection, you remain ten thousand rakki in my debt."

Nicco counted off the sea-blue notes and stood up. Hullorik had mentioned the gala, the gala at the city lake he'd been warned to stay away from... He stopped at the tent flap and turned back to the wizard. "Where's the lagoon? Is it anywhere near the city lake?"

Hullorik stopped counting his cash for a moment, looked up and shrugged. "They are the same. But few Hurrundans call it 'lagoon.' It is not the right word."

Nicco ran out of the tent. He needed to find a street phone.

CHAPTER TWENTY-FIVE

THERE WERE STREET phones in the marketplace, but the labourers he'd met in the café might still be somewhere around, and Nicco couldn't risk them overhearing his call. He ran out onto the streets and saw another street phone a few hundred yards away, on a busy corner. It would have to do, he may not have much time left. He kept running, searching in his pockets. By the time he reached the phone he'd found what he was looking for. Sothus' business card.

Nicco punched in the number and shoved rakki coins into the slot. There was a paypod slot too, but that would open the call up to tracing, something he couldn't risk.

Sothus' phone rang twice before he answered the call.

"Sothus, it's Nicco. Where are you?"

"...lo? Sorry, can't... this again?"

The line was awful, filled with static. Nicco slowed his voice and spoke as clearly as he could. "It's Nicco. Sothus, are you still going to the gala?"

"Gala? Yeah, at... lake. We're in... cab, on... now."

"Don't go! Turn around! Come back to the city, anything, but don't go to the lagoon!"

"...*what? Sorry... line's terrible, I... hear you. Cell phone coverage... bloody awful in... Anyway yes, we're... gala. Why, do... to come?*"

Passers-by on the corner were starting to give Nicco funny looks, he figured probably because he was speaking in Turithian. That and he looked like some kind of street bum.

"Turn around! Sothus, do not go to the gala! There's a bomb! It's going to be bombed! Do you understand?"

Nothing but static.

"Can you hear me?" Nicco shouted down the line. "A bomb!"

The line went dead.

Nicco hung up and rubbed his temples. There wasn't much more he could do, not without putting himself and his mission at risk. Not to mention everyone in Hurrunda, if Werrdun kicked the bucket and the Kurrethi took over.

"Excuse me, yes? I speak to you." The voice came from behind him. Nicco straightened up and realised that everyone on the corner was staring at him with expressions of hatred and fear, with not a lot in between. He turned to see a Hurrundan cop standing a couple of yards away, his weapon drawn and aimed directly at Nicco's head. Not an entropy gun or a blaster, either, but a good old-fashioned bullet slinger.

Nicco slowly raised his hands. "Shazomon Turithik," he said slowly. "Ikk shazor birrun?"

"What is wrong, man from Turith, is you are arrested, exactly. Come." Two more officers came into view, running down the street with their pistols drawn; the first cop must have summoned them. That sealed Nicco's fate. One cop, even with a gun, he could maybe escape from. But three, all with guns, in a city he still didn't know very well? Not likely.

The first man gestured for Nicco to get down on his knees. He complied, still holding his hands in the air. As he sank to the ground the cop noticed the red gem in his palm and gasped, shouted something in Varnian to the other two men, then stepped forward and shot Nicco in the chest.

CHAPTER TWENTY-SIX

HE'D BEEN WRONG. They weren't old-fashioned bullet-firing pistols after all. They fired some kind of electrical charge, a charge that slapped Nicco's already bruised ribcage hard and coursed through his nerve endings like cold fire. He couldn't breathe. He spasmed two, maybe three times in rapid succession.

Then he fell unconscious.

HE WOKE UP freezing cold. Soaking wet. Gasping for breath.

"Where's the bomb? The bomb! Tell us, you Turithian son of a squid!"

He was tied to a chair in a cold, empty room. Empty but for the two men standing over him. One of them stood a few feet away, holding an empty bucket. The other was just a couple of inches from his face, snarling through gritted teeth. Had to be police. Nicco felt water coursing down his head and face. He gasped for breath, sucking in cold air, and his teeth chattered.

"Lake..." he whispered. "City lake."

"Where?"

"Don't know... Guy at the market told me."

The snarling cop smacked Nicco in the face.

"Tallus crap!" Either this cop was Turithian himself, or he'd actually bothered to take lessons. His accent was perfect. "Who were you calling? Another Kurrethi? The one who planted the bomb, perhaps!"

Nicco shook his head and spat blood. They thought he was Kurrethi? What in the fifty-nine hells?

"How did you know I'm Turithian?"

The cop stood up and folded his arms. His sleeves were rolled up, exposing tattoos on his forearms of coiled, fanged serpents. "Your prints are on file, you idiot. Seems you have a reputation back in Azbatha."

Nicco groaned. Patulam. The Azbathan cop must have thought all his vacations had come at once when a Hurrundan officer told him they had Nicco in custody as some kind of suspected terrorist.

"So why would I be working for the Kurrethi? It doesn't make sense, can't you see...?"

"Same reason a Turithian would steal the governor's necklace, perhaps?"

Nicco couldn't argue with that. Or rather he could, but it wouldn't do him any favours. He had to assume he could talk his way out of this, somehow, and get back to finding Ven Dazarus... and the necklace.

"I had nothing to do with that," he croaked. "I'm a scapegoat. And I've got nothing to do with the Kurrethi either. I'm just here on vacation..."

The cop punched him again, and Nicco's head snapped back. It occurred to him, in the moments before his vision went black and he passed out again, that the Hurrundan force didn't seem as smart as he'd previously given it credit for. Perhaps they had earned their reputation not through superior intelligence and diligence, but by simply shooting first and asking questions later.

THIS TIME WHEN he came to he was warm and sitting on something soft. Perhaps they'd taken him to a hospital. That would be nice. He drifted on the edge of waking, allowing himself to feel comfortable for however long the feeling lasted.

Not long, as it turned out.

"He's awake," said Huwll and slapped Nicco around the face. "Come on, clown, wake up!"

Nicco opened his eyes. He was in the back of the silver skycar again, with Huwll and Brinno on either side of him. He had a terrible sense of déjà vu, and it only grew stronger when Brinno leaned forward and switched on the vidscreen set into the black glass divider.

"*Hello, Nicco.*" On the vidscreen, Bazhanka shook his head. "*You really are causing me a lot of trouble. What exactly did you think you were doing, shouting about bombs on a public line? Were you actually trying to get yourself arrested?*"

"I was trying to stop at least two innocent people from dying."

"*Well, you did a lot more than that. How you knew, I have simply no idea...*" Bazhanka held up a hand as Nicco began to interrupt. "*And I don't want to, I really don't. But you were right, there was a bomb at the lagoon. The police cleared the area and disabled it. You're a hero... or at least, you would be if the Hurrundans weren't convinced you planted it yourself.*"

"Which makes no sense. Why would I tell them about it if I planted the bloody thing?"

"*Perhaps you hadn't noticed my dear boy, but the entire city is somewhat on edge. The police cannot afford to take chances. It was a very foolish thing you did.*"

"Yeah, well at least I can sleep at night. Now get your goons to let me out so I can get the necklace back for you."

"You still haven't told me what your plan is."

"And I'm not going to, not yet. Especially with this pair listening."

"Brinno and Huwll are above suspicion, Nicco. Anything you can tell me, you can tell them."

"Not a chance. Let me out. I'll have the necklace back within twenty-four hours."

Bazhanka sighed. *"Very well. You're cutting it fine, Nicco. My grandfather is knocking on the watery saints' door, and they're going to let him in sooner rather than later."*

The skycar began to descend to street level. "How did you get me away from the police, anyway?" Nicco asked. "How did you even know I was there?"

Bazhanka smiled. *"Hurrunda is a small place, dear boy, smaller even than Azbatha. When word spreads that a Turithian has been arrested as a terrorist, there are only so many people it could be. And the following gem located you in the police station."*

Nicco looked at the red crystal in his palm, thankful for the first time of its presence.

The skycar landed and Brinno and Huwll escorted Nicco out. He half-expected another beating, but this time the men turned away without a word and stepped back into the car. If Nicco didn't get the necklace back, though, they'd surely return for him.

He watched the skycar soar into the sky and took stock of his situation. It still didn't look good. He knew Ven Dazarus definitely wasn't a wizard, for what that was worth. He also knew the rebel leader was somewhere in the mountains, but not even the Hurrundan police had been able to smoke him out. He could make an educated guess that the Kurrethi were simply waiting for Werrdun to die before they came down into Hurrunda and seized control of the city. Evidently there were plenty of locals who would support them in that endeavour.

Further, he now knew he'd been named after his father, who'd been a war journalist. Which was interesting, and went some way to quenching a thirst Nicco had endured for years... but didn't really help him at this precise moment.

He looked up over the city's low rooftops toward the Hurrun Peaks and cursed magi, mob bosses and dirty-minded businessmen from Jalakum alike. If only he hadn't touched that floating orb in the man's apartment, if only he hadn't listened to Tabby's bright idea to rob him in the first place... if only he hadn't dumped those skycars in the bay, before *that*, and gotten himself into Bazhanka's debt. One small action that crashed through his life and wrecked everything that had come after. If not for that, Nicco could have turned Ven Dazarus down and the rebel leader would have had to find someone else to steal the necklace. And it would be some other poor bastard standing here right now, wondering how on earth he was going to save his skin this time. Someone, *anyone*, other than Nicco...

And just like that, he knew what to do.

THERE WAS A cash-only phone in a corner of Fazikk's, a dark, noxious-smelling bar off a quiet street on the edge of downtown. The regulars didn't take their noses out of their glasses long enough to notice the smell. That suited Nicco fine.

Nicco walked to the phone, pushed coins into it and dialled Sothus' number again.

"*Lubburon.*"

"It's Nicco."

"*Nicco! Hey, did you hear about the bomb at the gala?*"

Nicco sighed. "Yeah, I heard. This line sounds a lot better."

"*I'm in the hotel. Better reception in the middle of the city. I've decided to stay indoors for the rest of my trip, it's not bloody safe out there!*"

"It won't be safe in your hotel soon, either."

"*What do you mean?*"

"Listen, you're in armaments, right? How quickly could you get hold of..." Nicco paused. If someone had told him two weeks ago what he was about to ask, he'd have laughed. But right now it didn't seem so funny. "A few hundred assault blasters."

"*Hold of what? Nicco, what exactly are you messed up in?*"

AFTERWARDS HE CALLED Bazhanka back.

"I need you to do something... Two things, actually. First, I need you to use your connections here in Hurrunda to get to the police."

"*Dear boy, have you been caught pickpocketing this time? How dreadfully boring.*"

Nicco grew weary of Bazhanka's constant jibes. He had one chance at this, and for once the mob boss had to take him seriously if it was going to work. "Unless you want to explain to your grandfather why thousands of his people died because you couldn't be arsed to listen, just shut up and write this down..."

A minute later Nicco hung up and left the bar. Time to get to work.

CHAPTER TWENTY-SEVEN

As THE PINK sun sank below the horizon and the moon rose in its place, the Hurrun peaks came alive. Here in the jungle-sided hills and mountains temperature variation between day and night was minimal, the dense vegetation and swampy ground trapping warmth and moisture in its thick, humid air. Surface clouds and mist permeated the tall trees, making navigation by any means other than satellite difficult at best.

Buzzing insects took to the air, grateful for even a one- or two-degree drop in the temperature. Scaly creatures emerged from their mud burrows, sniffing lazily at the scents of prey carried by the gentle breeze drifting through the jungle. Tree-dwellers slithered along the wide trunks and branches, their tongues flicking in search of the night's potential food. The last of the sunlight faded. Flowers closed their petals and retired for the day, conserving their energy for tomorrow. The Peaks belonged to the night now.

A man slowly picked his way over the roots and vines that lined the jungle floor, using a long stick to alternately bat aside giant rubbery leaves and give himself purchase on the slippery, muddy floor. Thorny branches snagged at his clothes, already damp and encrusted with dirt, and punctured the cloth with a thousand tiny pricks every step of the way. He was a man of average build and average appearance, with a short crop of thick black hair and skin too light to be a full-blooded Varnian. In the dark of the jungle, his only notable feature was that he was here at all, braving the Hurrun Peaks for his own ends.

He pulled a small object from his pocket and spoke to it in Varnian. A soft, blue-white glow emanated from the object, which he held in his hand and used to light his way. The glow would attract some insects, but repel the more dangerous nocturnal creatures. Hullorik the wizard had also promised it would not wake the rare carnivorous plants that could be found here in Bishlurra.

Not long after entering the jungle, he had reason to test that very claim. Stepping over a thick tree root, an orange insect flew toward him, its body bloated and heavy, its flight erratic and slow. It ignored the bright, magical light in his hand and simply hovered silently in front of his face, drifting to and fro with seemingly nowhere to be in a hurry.

The man stepped round it carefully, leaning his head and body away from the insect so as not to antagonise it. In fact, he was so focused on the insect that he almost trod on a large seed pod to the side of the trail, its skin so dark and hairy that it blended almost perfectly with the ground. He caught himself before his boot landed on the pod and stared at the millions of hairs on its surface. They were short and delicate here at the path's edge, but as his gaze moved along the pod's skin, following its curve into the undergrowth, the hairs became thicker and longer, more like spines.

He looked back at the insect. It was still there, hanging in the centre of the trail, silently dithering about in mid-air; but now he saw how it dangled by a gossamer-thin strand, almost invisible against the riot of colour and shade that made up the jungle landscape. As he raised the light orb to see, he saw the strand gradually become a thick green stem that arced over the path, high and curving, leading back to the 'seedpod' he'd almost stepped on.

Making sure his feet were safely and firmly in the mud and not touching any roots or vines, he moved the orb closer to the pod. Further back from the path its true size was evident, the thick, glossy skin continuing in wide folds to the plant's centre. There, the spines were thick as a man's wrist and as long as his arm, tapering to needle-sharp points at their tips.

Flesh-flowers, the Varnians called them. The orange 'insect' was bait. If it was disturbed, the folds in the flower's skin would open and stretch until it reached its victim with the millions of sticky hairs on its outer flank, then drag its prey back toward the thick spines. The sap it exuded would fatally poison anything smaller than a groak in minutes, then slowly dissolve its victim and over several days, right down to the bones. A single groak could feed a flesh-flower for two weeks.

But the flower was asleep, its maw closed and waiting for something to trigger the bait. The gentle glow of the light orb washed over the plant without disturbing it.

He carefully stepped around it and resumed his journey toward the summit.

An hour later, he felt no closer to the top of the Peaks than when he started. The sides had grown steeper and the ground became boggier with every step. He'd lost the trail half a mile back or more.

The noise of the jungle, a cacophony of buzzing that had long ago merged into an incessant monotonous din, grew louder with each step up the mountain. It was so loud he almost didn't hear the low, humming sound from up ahead. Almost.

The humming varied slightly in pitch, rising and falling at a slow tempo. He strained to hear it better, but the insects' drone blocked out most of the sound. Then he heard wet leaves rustling and slapping against one another, a sound that seemed to be coming closer. He pressed himself against a tree trunk and closed his hand around the light orb, enough to see a little as his eyes adjusted, but not enough to attract predators. He hoped.

Something was moving through the trees, heading toward him. The humming grew louder, and now he heard a rhythmic snuffling sound mixed with it, presumably from the same creature.

Just a few yards away the leaves parted, pushed aside by a wide horn. A low snort from the horn's owner ruffled the vegetation, and a head emerged from the undergrowth. Apart from the horn at the end of its snout, the high, narrow head— eminently suited to poking its nose through the foliage—was covered in a matting of thick, dark hair. Its large nostrils flared in time with its slow, rhythmical breath. Behind the nostrils the snout sloped rapidly upward to a brow of thick bone plates shielding small, yellow eyes. If it had ears, they weren't visible. Smaller horns and spikes protruded from the brow, protecting the eyes, and from a crest that ran up over the high forehead and disappeared down the back of the creature's thick neck.

The creature flared its nostrils, then gave another low snort and stepped forward. The back of the body was hairy, like the head, but the sides and belly were bald, revealing a leathery hide of brown scales as big as a man's palm. The creature's body was wide and heavy with muscle, and possessed six powerful legs as thick as a man's body. Its back arched high, the bony spines continuing down the length of its spine to a small, thin tail. The stomach was large and distended, hanging low and protected by its powerful legs. At the shoulder, it stood as tall as the traveller.

It was a groak.

It stopped humming and slowly swung its head from side to

side. He held his breath, hoping its poor eyesight would pass over him without remark. Insects buzzed around him, landing on his exposed skin. His skin was quite dry despite the heat, and he resisted slapping the insects away. Any sudden move would alert the groak to his presence.

The beast sniffed at the air and swung round to look directly at him, cocking its head to one side. As he watched, coiled and ready to run for it if necessary, the groak opened its jaw, exposing row upon row of teeth. Behind long fangs, suitable for tearing flesh, were dozens of smaller, sharper incisors for cutting and shredding meat and bone.

It yawned, finishing with a snap of its front teeth and a sharp snort into the man's eyes that made him blink. Then the groak turned and walked away, resuming humming as it continued its slow quest for food.

He waited for a minute, to let it move further away, then opened his hand and let the orb's light illuminate the scene. The groak's path across the trail was easily seen in the glow, a mess of crushed plants and ripped vines with deep footprints wider than the span of both his hands. He adjusted his grip on the walking stick and resumed his journey.

Hot breath struck his back. Slow breathing sounded loud in his ears. Cautiously, he turned his head to look back over his shoulder. The groak was less than three feet behind him.

He threw the orb to the ground and ran, frantically breaking through the undergrowth and hanging vines, looking for a tree to climb. But the jungle trees were too smooth-trunked here. The sudden loss of the orb left him blind in the jungle night, unable to see anything clearly. Vines, the only hanging plant under the canopy, slapped his face and body as he blundered onward.

The groak lumbered after him, crashing through the jungle with a deep, belligerent growl. It gained on him with every second. There was nothing else for it. He adjusted his grip on the walking stick, holding one end with both hands, and slammed the other end into the ground, vaulting himself upward. He grabbed at a vine, clamped his feet around it and started to climb. It was slippery, coated with moisture and sap, and for every foot he climbed he slid back six inches. It was already sagging from his weight, threatening to snap at any moment, but he ignored it and pressed on, because not climbing meant only death.

With a deafening roar the groak burst out of the undergrowth behind him. He made one last grasp as high up the vine as he could reach, clutched tight and pulled. The groak raised its head and snapped its jaw, missing his boots by a hair's breadth. He tried to pull himself up further, but his hands were too slick and couldn't gain any purchase. The groak waved its head from side to side, trying to catch his legs with its frontal horn...

Then stopped.

Another roar, louder and deeper, sounded from somewhere nearby. The groak dropped its head until it almost touched the ground, lowered its tail, turned its huge bulk around and trudged back the way it had come.

The vine snapped, unable to take his weight any longer. He plummeted to the ground and landed in the black, boggy mud, the broken vine still in his hand.

Two large, threatening horns emerged from the undergrowth. He tried to scramble back, but the mud sucked at his limbs and he only succeeded in collapsing onto his back as two groaks advanced out of the jungle together.

"Kollok shazoklok?"

He lifted his head and strained to see through the darkness. The groaks were directly in front of him, just a few yards away, but they'd stopped. Who was it that was asking for his name?

"Kollok shazoklok? Hulludok!"

He peered at the groaks and finally saw the source of the voice. Two men sat astride the backs of the beasts, riding them.

From that high up, they must have been able to see him over the tops of the undergrowth. He couldn't make out their dress, but it was a pretty safe bet who they were. And they were *very* keen to know who *he* was.

"Shazomon Turithik," he replied.

"Turithik! Ikk zenrrok lok?"

"Shazomon shlummok Ven Dazarus," he replied. It was grammatically awful, literally *I am the search of Ven Dazarus*, but the riders understood it well enough.

"Shazomon Nicco Salarum."

CHAPTER TWENTY-EIGHT

IT TURNED OUT that one of the riders knew a little Turithian, but not enough to say much besides *hello*, *goodbye* and so on. Through half-words and gestures, the rider made the point that Nicco was lucky they'd been patrolling the area, because a groak was only scared of one thing—other groaks.

The riders were Kurrethi rebels, wearing the same green robes Nicco had seen on the speaker at the rally in Hurrunda. When he'd mentioned Ven Dazarus, one of them dismounted while the other activated a light orb and levelled an entropy blaster at him. The one on foot frisked him for weapons, but found nothing. Then he tied Nicco's hands together with jungle vine and secured the other end to his groak's harness, a rudimentary arrangement of Tallus hide and steel rings.

Nicco was made to walk alongside the groak as the rebels returned to their camp. The riders seemed to control the beasts with a combination of tongue clicks and low whistles, but deciphering the commands while also trying to stay upright wasn't easy. Despite its bulk, the groak's six legs gave it a long, swift stride and an odd rhythm to its gait. For the first fifteen minutes Nicco kept losing time with the beast and falling to the jungle floor. After being dragged through the mud and foliage for the dozent time, though, he finally got it; by the time they arrived at the Kurrethi camp he was nicely in sync with the creature's rise-rise-fall-fall motion.

The 'camp' was more a loose patchwork of tarpaulins hung between tree trunks and over cave mouths in the mountainside, occupied by people who could have been normal Hurrundan citizens if not for the ubiquitous green robes they all wore tied at the waist. There was some light, from both magical orbs and flaming torches, but not enough to completely disperse the gloom—or to give away their position to anyone looking from above the dense jungle canopy. It set an ominous mood, which was only heightened by the ring of sentries at the outskirts. The sentries stopped the returning rebels and questioned them, before searching Nicco again to confirm he had no weapons.

Finally, a gruff middle-aged man with a white beard and no neck arrived at the sentry post and questioned Nicco in Turithian. It was the same man who had addressed the rally on Nicco's first day in the city.

"You!" said the man, recognising Nicco. "What you want here?"

"I need to see Ven Dazarus. My name is Nicco Salarum."

The man raised an eyebrow at his name. "So you are Salarum, coward! What you want, exactly?"

"I have a proposal for him."

"Tell me. I am second leader."

Nicco sighed. "No. I have to see Ven Dazarus himself. If you know my name, he must have mentioned me. Just tell him I'm here."

The rebel whipped out a blaster and shoved the business end in Nicco's face. "Perhaps I tell him you here because I show him your corpse, hmm?"

But Nicco didn't flinch. "You could, but I don't like to think what he'd do to you in response. Tell him Nicco Salarum has travelled here from Azbatha to see him. Tell him Nicco Salarum has found him, when all the cops in Hurrunda couldn't. Tell him if he ignores me, he will never take back the city."

The rebel grunted, looking Nicco up and down. Finally he relented, lowering the gun and taking a step back. "Come," he said and turned around, motioning for Nicco's captors to bring him along.

The riders had dismounted their groaks and given them to a Kurrethi who appeared to be in charge of the beasts, humming and whispering to them as he led them away to an area where more of the animals stood and rested. There was definitely something different about these, compared to the groak he'd encountered on the jungle trail, but when he asked, the 'second leader' refused to discuss it.

Everyone in the camp watched him with suspicious eyes as he was escorted through, and now he was inside the camp it became clear how much of an influence Ven Dazarus' military past had on them. One in every ten had the unmistakable look of an ex-soldier, an intense gaze that quickly assessed his potential threat.

They approached a large tent that in a clearing under a tree, its fabric the same camouflage green as the rebels' robes. Two sentries stood guard outside the closed entrance flap, entropy blasters in their hands and bullet-firing pistols holstered on their hips. The 'second leader' motioned for Nicco's captors to stop when they were ten feet away, and approached the sentries alone. He had a hurried conversation with them, inaudible to Nicco and the others, then pulled back the tent flap and walked inside. A moment later he reappeared and stood to one side next to a sentry.

The flap opened again. Ven Dazarus stepped out.

He looked quite different from how he did as 'Xandus' in

Azbatha, but not shockingly so. Facially he was the same, with the thick black hair and neat beard still present. But the pale make-up that hid his real skin colour was gone, revealing a true dark-skinned Varnian. His clothes were practical and militaristic, consisting of canvas trousers, boots and a plain collarless shirt. Curiously, he was one of the few people in the camp not wearing a green robe. The lights and flames of the camp reflected in Ven Dazarus' bright blue eyes as he stepped out of the tent and saw the pale-skinned, hollow-eyed, dirt-stained man held between the two rebel riders.

He laughed.

"By a groak's testicle, Nicco Salarum, you looking terrible! You have a long journey, exactly?"

"Hello, Xandus," said Nicco in Varnian. "I've been looking for you."

The rebel leader raised an eyebrow and replied likewise. "Now why on earth didn't you tell me you spoke Varnian? It would have saved me a lot of trouble learning that barbaric noise you peasants call a language. Oh, wait—that's right, you thought I was a Turithian wizard!" He laughed again.

"You don't seem very surprised to see me."

"Ah, Salarum. I am Ven Dazarus, leader of the Kurrethi and soon to be Emperor of the Hurrundan state. My eyes and ears are plentiful... including at police stations. When an Azabathan man called 'Nicco' is arrested, did you think I wouldn't know? That I wouldn't guess why you were here? You'd been released before I could get to you myself, but my men have been watching for you ever since. Surely you didn't think you could sneak up on me unawares!"

"Actually, I *wanted* you to find me. I was counting on your men bringing me back here."

"And yet, by coming here you've signed your own death sentence. You know I can't allow you to leave, not now. Not that you look like you'd last another day out here anyway.

You look awful—ill, in fact. Has our local cuisine not agreed with you?" He laughed again with a confidence bordering on arrogance. Or perhaps it had crossed that border long ago.

"We have unfinished business," said Nicco. "I've come to take the necklace back."

Ven Dazarus' jovial demeanour vanished as quickly as it had come. "That, my old partner in crime, is simply not possible. The old fool Werrdun will die soon—maybe tomorrow, maybe the day after, but soon enough. When he does, we shall ride down into the city and overthrow his council of cronies and crooks, with the masses of Hurrunda behind us. And as the whole city watches, I will crush that devil-spawned necklace on the Heart of Kurreth." He turned on his heel and began walking back to his tent. "We have no more business to discuss, Salarum. You and Werrdun will both die, and the Kurrethi revolution cannot be stopped."

"If you don't give me the necklace, your so-called rebellion will be crushed. You think they don't know what you're planning? You think they're not ready for your pathetic little band of curs and brawlers?"

Ven Dazarus stopped and turned back to face Nicco, his eyes blazing with anger. "This 'little band' are the true soldiers of Kurreth. And I have moulded them into an *army!* With the support of the people, we cannot be beaten!" He paused, peering at Nicco. "Who sent you? Who says they will crush us, hmm?"

"Why are you fighting, Ven Dazarus? Do you really believe in the Kurrethi cause... or are you just in it for the power?"

"Pah! Power is nothing, you fool. Werrdun's imminent death is proof of that. No, I fight because it's right. I fought for this country, this state. The people of Hurrunda were lucky—lucky!—because nobody thought they were important. Hurrunda was never invaded, never fought over. These very mountains saw to that, protecting the city as they've always done." He was ranting, equally blind to Nicco's indifference and the gathering crowd. One overweight man called out to him, but Ven Dazarus ignored him. "But when I returned from the war, I realised very few people understood that. For the first time, I saw how that mobster had made the city ignorant, blind to war and the true values of life. All anyone cared about was profit. Profit, while their husbands and sons were dying to protect their own country!

"Werrdun and his gang aren't fit to rule. They have no conscience besides the almighty rakki, no concern beyond their hoard of money and power. Power? No, Salarum, I don't want power. I want *justice!*"

"Lord Ven Dazarus!" It was the rebel in the crowd again, calling out. Ven Dazarus turned and shouted back.

"Who—oh, it's you, Gorrd." The crowd all turned to look at the man, an overweight Varnian with a thick black beard, shot through with grey. "Will you please be quiet? Whatever entrails you've thrown or cards you've read can wait, I assure you!"

"But, my lord—"

Nicco interrupted them both. "Just give me the necklace. I swear you'll regret it if you don't."

Ven Dazarus turned away from Gorrd and scowled at Nicco. "No, I don't think so. In fact, there's only one thing I regret." He walked back to one of the tent guards. "I don't know how, but clearly four thinmen weren't enough to kill you. I wish I'd left more."

He took the guard's pistol from its holster and turned back to Nicco.

"Goodbye, Salarum. May Kurreth have mercy on your soul." Then he shot Nicco between the eyes.

CHAPTER TWENTY-NINE

VEN DAZARUS WATCHED Nicco's body hit the ground with a dull thud, then turned on his heel and strode back to the tent. He held the pistol out for his guard to take, but the sentry wasn't paying him any attention. He was looking straight past Ven Dazarus, at something on the ground.

"Have to do... better... than that..."

Ven Dazarus turned to see Nicco struggling to his feet. Unable to believe his eyes, he raised the pistol again and shot Nicco three times, full in the chest. Nicco fell back to the ground.

Ven Dazarus walked to Nicco and stood over him, still aiming his pistol at the thief's head. How many people could take a bullet between the eyes and survive, even for a couple of seconds? Not many. Even now the thief was still breathing, hanging on to life with a preternatural will. Perhaps there was magic at work, although that seemed unlikely given how the Azbathans despised mages. Something had to be behind it, though, and there was no blood pouring from the pale-skinned thief's wounds...

"Ekklorn's hooves!" shouted Ven Dazarus. "This isn't Salarum... it's a thinman!"

Gorrd, the rebel who'd been trying to get Ven Dazarus' attention throughout the argument, ran over. "My lord, I felt something here in the camp..."

Ven Dazarus snorted at him. "You're a little late, wizard. I appear to have already found the source of your concern." He shouted to the crowd. "Search the camp! Every inch! There might be more of them!"

But Gorrd was still standing by the thinman, wringing his hands. "No, my lord, it was something else... I felt a following gem. There *is* an outsider here in the camp. Someone human."

NICCO SMILED. THE golem had been captured by guards, just as he'd hoped. When Hullorik had made the thinman for him, he'd instructed it to be as noisy and visible as possible through the jungle. It had almost got the golem killed by a wandering groak, but it had also paid off. He certainly hadn't expected the guards to be riding groaks, though. How on earth did they tame the beasts, let alone control them while riding?

He followed them up the mountain, keeping a safe distance. One of the riders was trying to speak Turithian, but clearly struggled. That was good—it meant there would be less chance of them trying to interrogate the thinman before they reached the rebel camp. It also meant the golem was doing as instructed and pretending not to speak much Varnian until he reached Ven Dazarus.

The camp was large and ringed by sentries, but to remain hidden from the Hurrundan security forces they had to keep it dark. That suited Nicco fine. He watched them question his thinman, then circled round to the other side of the camp. Everyone was far too busy looking at the pale stranger to see a dark, camouflaged figure in the thick of the jungle. He found a spot where the sentry's stations were almost thirty yards apart. It was his best shot.

Nicco threw a fallen tree branch into the undergrowth near one of the guards, but he didn't move. Either they were used to indigenous animals making noise out here at night or the buzzing drone of the insect population drowned out the branch's impact. He'd just have to sneak through.

He picked his way through the undergrowth, careful not to make too much noise. He watched the guards carefully, timing their patrols—five yards left, turn and look, back to position, pause and watch, five yards right, turn and look. The procedure was staggered, so that when one guard was walking the other remained standing at his post, and vice versa. It was effective, but it left a short period where the gap was thirty-five yards, with one of the guards facing the wrong way. All Nicco had to do was get past the other guard somehow.

Nicco reached into his shoulder bag and took out a woollen green robe. He'd had it made at a market stall run by a seamstress who was probably old enough to remember the city before Werrdun, although not too old to fleece a tourist. When Nicco told her he needed it done before nightfall, she cackled and charged him what he guessed was about three times the going rate. But need it he did, and his skin marked him out as a foreigner to be taken advantage of, so he paid up. If the plan didn't work, the money would be useless to him anyway.

He slipped on the robe and moved closer to the edge of the undergrowth. Not for the first time since he arrived in Hurrunda, Nicco bemoaned the loss of his kit bag and equipment. He hadn't brought much with him, just a few basic tools like a grav belt, omnimag grips and monofilament, but right now he could really have used some or all of it. Instead, he had to make do with what he'd been able to purchase at the market. Besides the green robe, there were other items he'd need to get inside this camp.

Like clockwork, one of the sentries began his five-yard walk. Nicco slipped on a pair of gloves, pulled the hood of the robe down and edged forward as far as the undergrowth could conceal him. He was less than ten feet from the stationary guard, but the night and jungle noise allowed him to remain unseen. All that remained between him and the guard was two long strides.

Nicco waited until the other guard walked four of his five yards, then stood and strode out of the undergrowth in one smooth motion, holding a thickly wadded cloth in one hand. The guard was startled, momentarily shocked by the sudden appearance of a man at such close quarters, and for that moment he hesitated.

It was all Nicco needed. He extended his free hand round the back of the sentry's head and pulled him forward, simultaneously pushing the wadded cloth over the man's nose and mouth. The strong, fast-acting anesthetic did its work: the sentry was asleep in less than a second. He fell like a stone, his body completely relaxed, and Nicco didn't bother to catch him. He was already stepping over the sentry and reaching inside the shoulder bag for one last item. He took it out, threw it next to the sentry and quickly dived behind the nearest plant.

The other sentry turned to walk back, right on time, and gauging from his puzzled shout, noticed his companion's absence right away. Nicco waited a few more seconds until he heard the man cry out again, this time in fear.

The livestock farmer in Hurrunda's marketplace had been only too willing to sell Nicco the small, vividly coloured snake. The sign on its case was at pains to emphasise that it wasn't venomous, but Nicco pretended he couldn't read it. Instead, he willingly played the part of clueless foreigner to keep the farmer from asking too many questions.

Nicco had to admit, if it hadn't been labelled he would have assumed the animal was venomous: garish yellow diamonds ran down its length, bordered in bright purple, and the whole topped off with a scarlet stripe from tip to tail. In fact, it was a harmless grass snake—the markings were camouflage for its natural habitat—but only someone versed in the animals would be able to tell, and by the sound of it the sentry was no expert. He yelped, turned and ran to his nearest colleague in the other direction, shouting for help.

Nicco smiled and emerged from his hiding place. The sentry would be out for at least an hour, and everyone would assume he was simply careless and allowed himself to be bitten by a jungle snake. By the time he woke up and told them what really happened Nicco would be long gone.

He pulled the robe's hood tighter and began walking through the camp, keeping to the shadows and carefully making his way toward the centre. If he'd judged Ven Dazarus correctly, the rebel leader would want to be as far from the perimeter and its dangers as possible. His assumption was confirmed a minute later when he saw the thinman being led toward a large tent in a clearing under a tree. The golem's escorts stopped while one of the rebels talked to the guards at the tent entrance, then went inside. He re-emerged and Ven Dazarus followed soon after.

That was Nicco's cue. Normally he would worry about being seen, but it was clear that all eyes in the camp were on Ven Dazarus and Nicco's doppelganger as they conversed. This was the thinman's final task, to keep Ven Dazarus talking for as long as possible. Every minute the rebel leader kept talking to it was a minute more the real Nicco had to find the necklace.

Hoping that Ven Dazarus didn't have concubines or worse, Nicco slashed a hole in the back of the tent and slipped through in one smooth motion.

There was no-one else inside. In fact, there was very little of anything inside. The tent was sparse, a marked contrast to the basement Ven Dazarus had used for his lair as Xandus. There was a rollaway bed, a wooden dressing cabinet of perfumes and toiletries, canvas chairs, a rack of clothes and a large table covered in old books and writing instruments. There was also a kind of natural rug, made of tightly knotted vines and leaves, that covered the entire ground area. It was surprisingly soft, and much to Nicco's delight completely deadened any sound his feet would have otherwise made.

But that didn't help him find the necklace. It had to be here somewhere. Ven Dazarus seemed too cautious, too paranoid to entrust the necklace to anyone else. Nicco was sure he'd insist on keeping it with him, to make sure it couldn't find its way back to Werrdun before the old man died.

He walked to the wooden dresser and pulled open the drawers one by one. Many Turithian women kept jewellery in their dressers, and if Ven Dazarus *did* have a woman, it might be the same here. But there was very little in the dresser at all, and certainly no necklace. Nicco pulled the bottom drawer out and checked for a hidden compartment in the body, but he felt nothing unusual. Next he checked the dressers's surface for the same thing, perhaps a recessed compartment under the wooden top, but drew another blank.

The next logical place would be under the bed. Nicco got down on his hands and knees and peered under the rollaway. There wasn't much room between the bed's base and the floor, but it would be enough space to fit a bag, or small box, with the necklace inside. All Nicco found, though, was a pair of boots that smelt awful. He braved the sweaty odour and shoved a hand inside each boot, just on the off chance, but they were empty.

Nicco's palm suddenly itched, the one with the ruby gem embedded in it, and he scratched it absent-mindedly. Then he remembered: the last time he'd felt that sensation was when he entered Hullorik's tent for the first time. There was no smoke, no incense burning, in this tent, but all the same, it doubled Nicco's resolve to be out of there as soon as possible.

He turned to the writing table, again checking for hidden compartments, but felt nothing. There were some ornaments on the desk, and they may even have been magical, but none was a necklace. He rapped against each of the desk's wooden legs—hollowed out, they would easily be wide enough to hide the necklace—but they were all solid.

The chairs were made of canvas sheets and tubular steel, both much too narrow to hide the necklace in. That just left the rack of clothes, but that seemed too insecure to Nicco's mind— certainly if he were in Ven Dazarus' shoes, Nicco wouldn't leave something as valuable as Werrdun's necklace in a coat pocket where anyone could reach in and find it.

But there was nowhere else. The tent was nothing if not spartan, a soldier's digs to be sure, and there just wasn't anywhere else that a necklace could be hidden. Nicco's heart sank. He was wrong, plain and simple. Ven Dazarus didn't keep the necklace with him, after all. Perhaps he entrusted it to one of his officers, or had it buried in the jungle somewhere. Or maybe he'd just dropped it in the Demirvan Sea on his way back to Hurrunda.

Bang!

A gunshot from outside the tent startled Nicco from his gloom. So the game was up. Whether or not he'd discovered the thinman deception, Ven Dazarus had decided it was time to end the trouble Nicco had caused him. He heard the golem's body hit the ground. Time for Nicco to...

The ground!

Nicco stared down at the thick, soft flooring. Vines and leaves, wrapped in a tight latticework that covered the mud and dirt of the jungle floor—or something more valuable. He crouched for a closer look, scanning the floor for a crack, a break, anything to indicate a section that had been removed or replaced. He didn't have much time; if Ven Dazarus had shot the man he thought was Nicco, he'd probably be on his way back to the tent right now. Although Nicco was dead anyway if he couldn't get the necklace back.

He heard another three shots. Either the rebel leader had figured out it was a thinman, or felt disproportionately sadistic toward Nicco. He swept his eyes back and forth across the floor, running his hands over the tightly woven surface...

There. Right there, a groove in the latticework that ran straight as a die, too straight to be a natural line. Nicco worked his fingers under the leaves on one side and pulled, holding his breath and trying to stay silent. It started to give, slowly bending back.

"It's a thinman!" Ven Dazarus shouted in disgust out in the camp. Nicco heard people gasp and shout, and a crowd begin to murmur and move. All or nothing. He heaved back on the bending leaf.

It came loose, and Nicco fell back on his arse. He might only have seconds before Ven Dazarus stormed inside the tent. He might even suspect the real Nicco was here, looking for the necklace.

And so he should, thought Nicco. Underneath the makeshift flooring panel was thick, black jungle mud, but resting atop the mud was a gaudy necklace of gold and jewels, glinting in the firelight. Nicco suppressed a laugh as he finally beheld his quarry.

Werrdun's necklace.

VEN DAZARUS TURNED to one of his tent guards. "You! Shoot it!" The guard stared at him dumbly, so he grabbed the entropy blaster from the guard's hand and fired at the thinman as it tried to stand again. The golem shrieked and crumbled to dust.

The rebel leader handed the blaster back to the amazed guard and flung back the entrance flap to his tent. The thinman had been dealt with, but a following gem in the camp? Just as an imposter of Salarum just happened to turn up?

Ven Dazarus didn't believe in coincidence.

He half-expected to see Salarum himself in the tent as he strode inside, but it was empty. He walked to his desk and pulled a smooth pebble from among the ornaments. It was enchanted, a tracker of sorts that could be attuned to a following gem by a good wizard. Gorrd wasn't a very good wizard, but he was good enough to manage this.

Then Ven Dazarus noticed the tear at the back of the tent.

On closer inspection he saw it wasn't a tear—it was a cut, made by a knife of some kind... He took two steps toward the centre of the room and fell to his knees, scrabbling at the removable panel in the floor covering. He found the edge and pulled.

It was still there. The necklace lay in the mud, just as it had since he returned from Azbatha. No-one knew its location, not even his most trusted Kurrethi officers. It was safe.

Very clever, Salarum, he thought. The thief had sent the thinman as a decoy, distracting Ven Dazarus while he snooped around for the necklace. But he hadn't found it, and now the deceit was exposed.

He replaced the panel and shouted for Gorrd. He'd enjoyed killing Salarum, even if it was just a fake. By Ekklorn's hairy hooves, he'd enjoy killing the real man even more.

NICCO HELD ONTO his hood, keeping it well over his face to hide his features, and walked through the camp at a brisk pace. The alarm had been sounded, much earlier than he'd hoped, and now his only option was to make his escape as quickly as possible. He had no doubt that if he was found, Ven Dazarus wouldn't hesitate to have him killed.

All around him, the Kurrethi were shouting to one another and mobilising, but it was chaotic. Most of them seemed to have no idea of what they were supposed to be looking for besides 'an intruder,' and Nicco was able to hurry unnoticed toward the edge of the camp. Soon the perimeter was in sight, but to Nicco's dismay the sentries were still standing at their posts, now turned to face into the camp. He'd hoped they might join in the search, but evidently their task was to stay put and keep people in as well as out. He hadn't planned on this; he'd hoped to leave while the thinman was still distracting Ven Dazarus. What on earth could Nicco tell the guards that wouldn't give him away?

"Har, lok!" someone shouted from behind him. "Farrdum lok dokoshok?"

Where are you going? Where indeed? Nicco ignored the man and kept walking, turning over scenarios and conversations with the sentries in his mind. If he could just get a few feet past the boundary into the jungle, he could get away. He may not know the area, but he'd seen enough of it on the way up here to know that finding a lone man at night would be almost impossible.

"Shazomon hulluda lok!"

A hand clamped down on Nicco's shoulder. He spun round, pulling on the strap of his shoulder bag and following through. Even with the robe and snake removed, it was still hard, heavy tallus hide. The corner of the bag struck his accuser on the side of the face. The Kurrethi grunted and reeled backward.

And now the game was up. Nicco glanced over at the sentries and saw two of them running toward him, shouting for him to stop. They'd left a gap in the perimeter, but to make it through Nicco would have to get past them.

He heard a deep roar to his side. The groak handler, who'd taken the beasts from his thinman's captors when they returned, was struggling to keep order in the groak pen. The animals were growing restless, probably unused to the commotion in the camp.

Nicco saw his chance. He sprinted toward the groaks, away

from the approaching sentries. One of the beasts reared up on its back four legs as he approached. The handler pulled at its reins and hummed urgently, trying to calm it down, but the beast was beyond calming.

The handler screamed, calling for someone called Gorrd.

It was the last word he spoke.

The groak slammed its front legs back down, one of them directly on the handler. Nicco froze in shock, unable to look away as the handler's chest burst open. The groak opened its mouth and roared, a deep bellow that Nicco felt vibrating in his chest. Maybe this wasn't such a good idea after all.

The sentries were closing in. They too paused at the sight of the handler's death. But these were military men, and they'd probably seen far worse on the battlefield. They recovered quickly.

More groaks were humming, now. Nicco could sense the unease growing among them. If they stampeded, the herd would trample them all, Kurrethi, Turithian and tents alike, and nothing would be able to stop them.

Nothing at all...

Nicco hauled himself up on the back of the groak that had killed its handler. If any beast was going to lead the charge, it was this one. It bucked and turned, trying to throw Nicco off, but he hung on to the harness, struggling to get his feet in the stirrups on either side of the beast's flanks. Holding on to the *Astra* ten thousand feet above Azbatha had been easier.

The animal roared and spun round, trying to dislodge its burden, and one of Nicco's flailing legs caught a sentry on the jaw. The other sentry backed away, circling, unsure how to approach Nicco without the groak striking him.

Nicco pulled himself upright, slotted his feet into the stirrups and pulled hard on the reins.

The groak bellowed, a deep, throaty sound that made the remaining sentry back away further. Nicco looked across the camp and saw dozens of Kurrethi running toward him, including Ven Dazarus. Out the corner of his eye, he noticed a guard raising his entropy blaster. One of his colleagues noticed and shouted to him to stop, but it was too late. The shot rang out loud and clear. Nicco sat frozen to the spot on the groak's back.

The blast shot past him, missing his shoulder by inches. A gurgling screech filled the air as one of the groaks behind Nicco reared up on its back legs. The shot had struck the beast in its thick, muscle-bound neck. The beast thrashed as the magical weapon's effect took hold. The thick brown hairs on its head and back turned grey. Its leathery scales shrivelled and dried, darkening to black. It collapsed, snapping at the air as it went down, and caught his mount on the backside—a bite that would ordinarily have ripped out a chunk of the beast's flank, but in its wizened state was nothing more than a nip.

It was enough. Nicco was thrown back as his groak suddenly bolted forward, charging out of the pen and into the jungle.

With a combined roar that made the ground shake, a dozen more followed. The groaks galloped out of the camp, their powerful legs pounding the undergrowth into mud. Kurrethi everywhere cried out and leapt aside as the herd began to stampede. Blasters and pistols rang out, but none of the shots struck Nicco or his mount.

At the head of the stampede, Nicco hung on to the groak's back for dear life.

CHAPTER THIRTY

HIS TEETH FELT like they were going to rattle free of his gums. The groak herd hurtled down the side of the mountain, heedless of everything in their path. Vines, vegetation, small furry animals—the creatures barely noticed them, much less slowed down for them. They thundered through the thick jungle, their multiple legs giving them an agility Nicco wouldn't have expected from such a large animal. At this speed he could be back at the city's edge before daybreak, much sooner than he'd expected and far quicker than the journey up the mountain.

Nicco was almost beginning to enjoy himself when the first shot screamed past his ear and blew chunks out of a nearby tree.

Nicco looked back and saw lights moving through the jungle, following the herd of groaks down the mountain. Following him. Shouts and more gunfire rang out as a rapid strobe of muzzle flashes lit up the jungle. The mountain was alive with gunfire and the roar of groaks. Nicco counted three Kurrethi, riding groaks—apparently some hadn't joined the stampede—and carrying solid ammunition rifles. Entropy blasts would be unable to pierce the foliage, and have little effect on the trees and jungle flora anyway. Evidently, Ven Dazarus was keen to kill him a second time.

Nicco ducked to avoid another barrage of shots. One of the groaks behind him shrieked, lost its footing and crashed to the ground, flattening a thorny bush as it fell. The rebel rider directly behind it pulled his mount up and leapt over the injured animal, still in pursuit.

Nicco had no idea how to control his own groak. It had been so spooked back at the camp, he wasn't even sure if it could be controlled. The groak handler had seemed to control the beasts by *humming*, of all things, but it hadn't prevented his death. Nevertheless, if Nicco wanted to make it back to Hurrunda alive he needed to learn how to ride this thing.

He leant forward and hummed a tuneless drone near where he imagined the beast's ear to be. If it heard him, it gave no sign. The air was filled with the sound of gunfire, galloping and splintering tree bark. Nicco hummed again, louder this time, and the groak cocked its head to one side and slowed, almost to a stop. It was a result, but not exactly what Nicco had in mind.

The rebel riders were gaining on him. If leaning forward with a low hum made it stop... He sat upright and pulled hard on the reins, humming at a higher pitch this time.

The groak snapped its head forward and launched into the jungle. Now he was getting somewhere. But that pause had cost him, and now the Kurrethi were hot on his rear. He heard one of them shout to the others above the gunfire, but all he could make out was Ven Dazarus' name. Whatever it was the rider had said, the gunfire stopped.

The first rider drew level with Nicco, shouting at him in Varnian to stop, and Nicco yanked the groak's reins to the other side, hoping his mount would understand what he wanted it to do.

It didn't. The beast kept running in a straight line, crashing through the undergrowth and sidestepping only to avoid trees.

The Kurrethi rider laughed and pulled his own animal over toward Nicco, with a pull on the reins and a low-to-high pitched humming sound. Nicco frantically tried to copy him, but the groak was having none of it. Desperate, Nicco leant forward and hummed low, hoping the groak was at least consistent. It slowed almost instantly, skidding to a halt and splashing black, boggy mud into the air.

The Kurrethi had expected Nicco to try and outrun him, not come to a stop. He shot past Nicco, the groak beneath him oblivious to his shouts of anger.

What happened next took even Nicco by surprise, but in hindsight he guessed it was why his groak hadn't wanted to turn when he asked it. The Kurrethi's mount continued forward, splintering vines and twigs as it blundered through the jungle. The Kurrethi leaned forward to give the stop signal, but it was too late.

Nicco saw a flash of something in the jungle night, something small and orange that struck the rebel rider as he shifted position in the saddle. Suddenly the vegetation itself came alive, billowing and flexing giant leaves around the Kurrethi and his mount. The flesh-flower's petals struck the beast's hide and rippled over it, and the rider barely had time to register what had happened before he, too, was struck, the blaster tumbling from his hand. Both man and beast were now stuck fast to the millions of hairs on the flesh-flower's petals, and immediately the plant began to contract again, pulling the unfortunate Kurrethi and groak with it.

Their screams and shrieks merged into one sound, a gurgling duet of death as the flesh-flower's largest spines ripped into them. The rebel was dead in a moment; his groak wasn't so lucky.

Nicco averted his eyes. There were still two other Kurrethi on his trail, drawing closer with every second.

The dead Kurrethi's weapon had landed in a thicket of leafy vines near the flesh-flower. Nicco moved his groak forward, hoping the plant would be preoccupied enough with its latest catch that it wouldn't care for another meal so soon. He ducked under the orange bug bait anyway, just to be sure, and allowed himself to slip sideways off the saddle. Holding on to the harness to make sure he didn't lose his mount, he reached out as the beast lumbered past the thicket and caught the blaster by its barrel. He hauled himself back up into the saddle and adjusted his grip on the weapon.

Nicco had always hated guns. A gun was the last resort of a man without wit: if you needed one, it meant your plan had failed. But right now he was guilty of that himself. If someone else had outlined what Nicco intended to do, he would have dismissed it as barely more than a sketch of a plan. At least half of it relied on sheer luck and chutzpah, a fool's game at the best of times.

Being chased down the side of a mountain on the back of a vicious, carnivorous beast, for example, was definitely not part of his scheme. But it was only the latest in a long line of miscalculations and errors he'd made.

He took the gun and raised it at the riders following him. One of the Kurrethi shouted when he saw the blaster, and Nicco almost laughed. He'd never taken a single shooting lesson in his entire life. The chances of him actually hitting anything besides trees were slim to none. Luckily, that was just what he intended to do.

Nicco squeezed the trigger and held it down, aiming ahead of the rider and sweeping it from side to side like a child playing at soldiers. It was a poor and inefficient way to hit your target, but Nicco's target was the entire ground. Even he couldn't miss that.

A volley of slugs ripped into the undergrowth and ground. Black mud and water flew into the air, splashing the Kurrethi and his mount. The beast faltered, startled by the sudden eruption of the jungle floor, and tried to take evasive action.

The groak's back legs tripped over its middle set. It reared up in an attempt to regain its footing and stay upright, but its own weight brought it crashing to the ground. The Kurrethi rider was catapulted from the animal's back; he flew over the undergrowth and struck a tree, then fell to the ground and was still.

The jungle was beginning to thin out, becoming less dense by the minute, and moonlight began to break through the canopy overhead.

Suddenly, the third Kurrethi rider burst through a bank of tall plants dead ahead. He must have spurred his groak on while Nicco was mucking about learning to control his own mount and circled round to cut Nicco off.

The rebel raised his blaster and prepared to fire.

Nicco ducked, bringing his body down close to the groak's neck, but remained silent. Even a moving target riding straight at the shooter would be a more difficult shot than if he came to a stop.

The Kurrethi fired. Nicco's whole body shook with a jolt from the impact, but he was unhurt. Then his groak roared and slowed, and Nicco cautiously looked up to see that a piece of the animal's brow, the outcropping of bone that protected its eyes, was missing. The beast roared again and shook violently, almost dislodging Nicco from the saddle.

Meanwhile, the Kurrethi rode past and turned like a jousting knight, preparing for another shot.

Nicco yanked the reins of his groak and hummed low-to-high; this time the beast turned. Now the groaks faced one another, their heads bowed low in what Nicco felt safe to assume was a hostile position. Before the rebel could fire a second shot, Nicco pulled back on his reins and hummed with the highest pitch he could make. Then he jumped off.

He landed in the thick, black mud of the jungle floor just as the Kurrethi took his shot. The bullet flew overhead and struck a tree trunk far behind Nicco. The rebel had no time to fire again. The groaks charged at full speed, emitting an urgent low hum as they prepared to lock horns and head plates.

The Kurrethi, caught in the middle of a bestial brawl, didn't stand a chance.

Nicco retrieved his shoulder bag from the mud and crawled through a patch of nearby undergrowth. He heard the groaks fighting from his hiding place, roaring and snapping at one another. The sound of splintering bone drowned out the rebel's cries.

He waited until the beasts fell silent. Then he waited a further five minutes, holding his breath every time a groak thundered past, not knowing if they were wild or bearing Kurrethi riders.

Finally he decided it was safe as it would ever be, and began making his way downhill through the jungle.

Dawn broke as he reached the edge of the city.

CHAPTER THIRTY-ONE

FAZIKK'S LOOKED EXACTLY the same as when Nicco had left the day before. It was almost ten, and he'd been in here for an hour. Three men were already installed at various points along the bar when he entered, their faces buried in their glasses, and he was certain he'd seen the same patrons in the same positions last night. Truth be told, he couldn't swear that they weren't wearing the same clothes.

A vidscreen in a corner of the room was showing some mindless soap opera. It appeared to focus on the daily lives of a bunch of ugly people who never actually went to work and spent all day in the local bar, which struck Nicco as both the same focus as every other soap Tabby had made him watch, and a particularly ironic choice for Fazikk's.

Fazikk himself, who looked as downtrodden and weary as his bar and its patrons, stepped out from behind the bar carrying a large platter of roast vegetables, fried tallus, broth and bread. Nicco ordered it the minute he stumbled into the bar, over an hour ago now, and if his stomach hadn't been growling at him the entire time he might have forgotten he ever ordered it. But as the food's aroma drifted to his nostrils—Nicco realised with a certain amount of embarrassment that he was salivating—the long wait was forgotten. He licked his lips and thanked the landlord, who grunted in acknowledgement and turned back to the bar.

It was ten o'clock exactly.

Later, Nicco would be amazed at the reaction to the news. Everyone in the bar, like the place itself, seemed so disconnected from the world at large that he expected them to shrug, maybe make a sarcastic comment, then return to their drinks. Far from it.

The vidscreen broadcast was suddenly interrupted. A harassed-looking news anchor appeared on the screen, seeming flustered and uncertain. The sound was off, so Nicco couldn't hear what the anchor was saying; but the headline across the bottom of the screen said it all for him.

GOVERNOR WERRDUN DIES IN TURITH

Nicco watched Fazikk. At first the landlord didn't notice. Then, perhaps noticing the urgent flickering from the vidscreen, he glanced at it from the corner of his eye and did a swift double-take. A barely audible croaking sound escaped from his lips, then he dashed back to the bar, leapt behind it—knocking over several glasses in the process—and hit a button to restore the sound to the vidscreen. The other patrons looked up at him in mild surprise. Nicco guessed Fazikk didn't normally engage in such blatant exercise. Then, as one, they followed Fazikk's gaze to the vidscreen.

"...was found dead this morning at his suite in Azbatha, where he had been staying since falling ill just a few days ago during a state visit to negotiate trade agreements with the Turithian city. A brief official statement announced that the governor passed away peacefully in his sleep during the night."

Nicco didn't understand all of the anchor's announcement

himself, but it was a by-the-book obituary. With the governor out of town—for the first time in years, according to Nicco's research—this was new, unfamiliar territory for the news streams. They'd probably practised and run through their 'Werrdun dead' scenario a hundred times, with cameras in place at his Hurrundan home and anchors standing by. It was standard procedure at any decent-sized stream station to do rehearsals of obituary broadcasts for prominent public figures. But none of those dry runs would have included overseas broadcasts, and it showed. The pictures they were showing now were standard stock shots of the Azbathan mayor's home, of Azbatha itself, and some re-run footage of Werrdun's appointments during his visit last week. Conspicuous in its absence was any footage or mention of his voyage on the *Azbathaero Astra*.

The next ten minutes were a condensed recap of everything Werrdun had done for the city of Hurrunda: the education programs, the social welfare initiatives, the technology and infrastructure improvements. Talking head after talking head appeared on screen, many of them looking like they'd just been woken up with the news themselves, and lamented the loss of their great leader. Some of them cried openly on screen, and in Fazikk's the reaction wasn't much different. The regulars were loudly grieving the loss, wondering how this could happen, if the son-of-a-squid Turithians were to blame, whether or not it was an assassination and what this would mean to the Kurrethi.

Nicco ate his breakfast and did his best to remain unnoticed. Even if his Varnian had been better, his accent—and his skin colour—immediately gave him away as non-local. It wouldn't take much of a leap for the regulars to place him as Turithian. The only saving grace was how filthy he was. He'd stopped off at a public restroom after entering the city and before making his way back to the bar, but it would take more than a quick strip wash to rid his skin of the filth and dirt he'd accumulated over the last two days.

And Nicco knew full well what Werrdun's death would mean to the Kurrethi. They would no doubt march into the city as soon as possible, led by a smugly triumphant Ven Dazarus. Nicco wasn't sure he wanted to be around to see that.

The main door opened and an overweight man stepped into the bar. He wore scruffy, threadbare trousers, a long overcoat that was a size too big and a shirt with food stains down the front. Under a floppy hat with ragged edges, his face was red and sweating from the morning heat, and he walked with a cane. But his pale complexion and expensive shoes gave him away. Fully shined and immaculate, they were worth at least a thousand lire—not rakki.

Wallus Bazhanka hobbled over to Nicco's table and sat down. "Good morning, dear boy."

"Morning. Is this your idea of incognito, then?"

"It suffices. Have you seen the news?"

"Yeah. It's funny, since arriving here I've seen a few different sides to all this. There's no question there's a power struggle going on over here, but it's difficult to tell who's got the most support. Given the choice, I'm honestly not sure whether most of the people here would back Werrdun or Ven Dazarus."

Bazhanka shifted in his seat, trying to get comfortable. "Well, that point is now somewhat moot. And I would like to know exactly why you demanded I come here in person. I gave you a long leash in this business, Nicco, and now I have nothing but regrets. I demand an explanation."

"Relax. Everything's going to... Ah, here he is."

Nicco looked over Bazhanka's shoulder as the main door opened again and another man entered. Bazhanka turned to see what Nicco was looking at.

"Who in the fifty-nine hells is that?" asked the mob boss.

Nicco smiled as the man walked over to their table and introduced them. "Wallus Bazhanka, meet Sothus Lubburon. He's in armaments."

CHAPTER THIRTY-TWO

VEN DAZARUS SMILED.

Behind him stood three hundred loyal Kurrethi, forty of them mounted on groaks. It wasn't as many as he would have liked, but during the stampede Gorrd's control over the animals was broken and the wizard had only regained a quarter of their original herd. But it would be enough. The groaks were more an intimidation tactic than a military asset—to strike fear and awe into the heart of any Hurrundan who stood against them—although the beasts' size and strength would be useful if they encountered heavy resistance from any police still loyal to Werrdun.

If anyone had seen Ven Dazarus in his tent that morning as he listened to the news stream announcing the governor's death, they would have seen a man uncharacteristically delirious with joy. He laughed out loud, punched the air and thanked Kurreth for at last delivering the blow that he needed to return power to the hands of Hurrunda's rightful rulers.

But no-one saw him. Part of Ven Dazarus' appeal to the

Kurrethi was his hardline stance on the Law of Kurreth, that was beyond doubt; there was also his enigma, his air of military knowledge and tactical planning that saw him secluded away from his followers for hours on end. It made him appear aloof, and that was no bad thing. In the days of sea power, before the Archmages came along with their airships and destroyed the natural barriers that kept races and countries apart, it had been standard protocol that the captain of a ship ate alone, or if he had companions they would be only his most senior officers. It drew a distinct line of separation between leaders and followers, a necessary aspect of military life. Any crewman who saw his captain with his guard down—eating, cracking jokes, even drunk—was more likely to question orders from the man. In a military situation, that could be disastrous. It was imperative that the crew did not think of their captain as a man, just like them, because he was nothing of the sort. He must be an unquestionable leader, whose authority and wisdom were so untarnished, so inspiring of loyalty, as to be almost inhuman. That was what it took to lead a crew into war.

The only people who understood that necessity outside the military were wizards. Civilians—like the original Kurrethi exiles—simply didn't get it.

For years, the Kurrethi lacked a leader who understood that essential facet of command. They had been too full of camaraderie, companionship and even—*Ekklorn's hooves, what were they thinking?*—democracy. And the rebels floundered.

Ven Dazarus had no time for such things. He was a military man, from a military family. Authority was not to be questioned, orders were to be followed without hesitation. When he first joined the rebels five years ago it was an attitude he espoused loudly, dividing the Kurrethi into two distinct camps. It had cost them at least a hundred members, men and women whose ego would not permit obedience. They abandoned their principles and returned to the city in disgrace. Ven Dazarus didn't mourn their loss, and over time the other rebels came round to his way of thinking.

The Kurrethi struggle was not as a fight by the downtrodden against an oppressor, but simply as a war between the good and the corrupt. Dazarus' unwavering devotion, his military precision and tactical mind had honed the Kurrethi into a guerrilla force to be reckoned with, more feared now than they had ever been since they were usurped by Werrdun and his heathen cronies. He had swelled their ranks with men he knew to be good soldiers, men from his own units during the war. They in turn recruited colleagues of their own whom they knew would remain loyal. Together, they had trained the civilian Kurrethi as best they could. The battle training had been difficult and slow without significant resources, but the rebels had no problems learning guerrilla tactics. Their bombing and sabotage campaign over the past few months had proven that.

And then came Ven Dazarus' masterstroke, the theft of Werrdun's necklace. It had been a risk, he knew, but in this new age of so-called 'peace on earth' it seemed that wizards and their like could get away with anything. When he learned that the governor's first foreign visit after Year Zero was to a society as ignorant of magic as Turith, the idea was born.

Salarum had almost ruined it, of course. Ven Dazarus didn't know how the thief had discovered the location of his hideout in Azbatha, but he'd left the thinmen there as a precaution against that. Kurreth only knew how Salarum had escaped their clutches and traced him back here. But Ven Dazarus didn't believe the thief had any solid proof. If he did he would have been working with Werrdun's own men, and the Hurrun Peaks would have been firebombed days ago to try and smoke out the Kurrethi once and for all. No, Salarum must have simply guessed his way to the truth. But that business with the thinman... Ven Dazarus should have seen that immediately. He was no wizard, but recognising a thinman imposter should have been child's play.

But it was the last thing he'd expected from a man like Salarum, and he'd almost paid the price. He thanked Kurreth the thief had somehow gained a following gem since Ven Dazarus had last seen him, and so alerted Gorrd to his presence in the camp.

None of that mattered now. Salarum may have escaped his clutches last night, but he'd failed to stop the Kurrethi. Failed to stop the revolution that was coming, as surely as day followed night. Werrdun was dead. By the time that moronic daughter of his brought the old man's corpse home tomorrow, Ven Dazarus would be installed as Emperor of Hurrunda. And his first act as Emperor would be to use all the resources now at his disposal, magical and otherwise, to track down Salarum and show him the error of his ways.

Ven Dazarus checked his watch. It was a little before two o'clock in the afternoon. He turned and shouted to the Kurrethi massed behind him.

"Let the revolution begin!"

THE REBEL ARMY marched forward into the city, moving first through the outskirts closest to the Hurrun Peaks. The streets here were almost empty. The sight of groaks walking down the road was impossible to miss, but only a few residents bothered to actually leave their houses and look on. Ven Dazarus guessed they were all watching the news streams, mourning their demon-loving governor and far too busy weeping to notice that the city was being taken right under their noses. The few that did come to their doors, or stopped in the street, just stood and stared. No-one protested or made a move to resist. A few dashed inside after realising who the rebels were, most likely to call the police, but Ven Dazarus gave no order to stop them. Let the police come; let them see how futile their resistance would be once the people themselves rallied behind the Kurrethi.

They moved on into more densely inhabited neighbourhoods.

At this point a quarter of the Kurrethi force on either side of the column split off, heading east and west to execute a pincer movement as they advanced toward the centre of Hurrunda. Though stronger as a united force, Ven Dazarus knew that a single column could be easily trapped if the police were quick enough to act. Splitting up in this way made the rebels more difficult to pin down, and meant they could besiege more key police stations along the way.

All three units' target was the same: the Heart of Kurreth, or 'City Hall' as Werrdun insisted on calling it, located at the very centre of the city. From its position, nine main streets stretched out through Hurrunda like the spokes of a wheel, stretching all the way to the Hurrun peaks north, east and west, and the shores of the Demirvan Sea to the south.

It was one such road they travelled on now, though Werrdun had also changed its name. In the days of Kurrethi rule it had been called the Eyes of Kurreth, the great North road that led from the Heart to the edge of the old trail over the Hurrun Peaks. Now it was called 'First Avenue.' The units that split off from the main column were also following two of these main roads, the Ears and Arms. There was no profit in subtlety or subterfuge, not today. For this revolution to succeed it was vital that the people bear witness; the Kurrethi must be visible and public, to show the city's inhabitants that they did not fear the late governor's forces.

It was here that they encountered the first signs of resistance. Civilian vehicles moved aside for them, their occupants staring in amazement at the army marching past, but at a junction ahead stood a squad of Hurrundan police, intending to block the rebels' path. Ven Dazarus ordered his men to keep going and ready their weapons. He would not shoot first, but would retaliate if the police refused to let them pass.

At least, that was the official policy. In fact Ven Dazarus had also sent his best men, all of them trusted ex-soldiers from his own army units, to scout ahead of the main unit. One of their tasks was to sabotage any serious police response. As the Kurrethi army approached the police line, Ven Dazarus caught a flash of movement out the corner of his eye, on a rooftop nearby. He turned back to his men.

"Stand by," he said. "Wait for the shots."

Two seconds later a burst of blaster fire rang out, echoing down the street. A burst of entropy magic slammed into the ground in front of Ven Dazarus' groak, leaving a blackened trough of crumbling dust.

"Return fire!" he shouted.

The rebels opened fire. Half of the cops were already lying withered and catatonic on the ground before they realised what was happening and opened fire themselves. The truth was, they hadn't shot first—one of the rebel scouts had, from a position behind the police line. It gave Ven Dazarus the deniability he needed.

Civilians scattered out of the road and into the nearest homes. Some dived for cover, or kept running into other streets.

When the dust settled, the police squad was defeated with just two fatalities among the rebels. Ven Dazarus was annoyed to note that the police were using bullet-firing rifles, not entropy weapons as he'd expected. Still, history was written by the winners; the story of this revolution, when told to the world, would ensure the Kurrethi were revered as heroes.

He ordered his men onward. The rebels stepped over the aged bodies of the fallen cops, or crushed them under heavy groak legs without a thought.

The battle for Hurrunda was underway.

A MILE FURTHER in, another unit of police tried to stop them. The rebels were approaching the business district now, leaving the residential areas behind. The street was empty of civilians.

By now word of the insurrection had spread, and the ordinary people of Hurrunda were hiding in their homes. Besides a few cheers and waved hands out of office windows, Ven Dazarus had hardly seen anyone on the street besides police officers; and not even many of those, which was a pleasant surprise. Perhaps support for the rebels was more widespread than even he had hoped.

This time the police had set up a roadblock using groundcars, accompanied by an airpod, a small four-person airship. Police used them primarily as reconnaissance and tracking vehicles, but they were light and maneuverable enough to also be effective as a firing platform for a trained gunman. The airpod swept over the rooftops and Ven Dazarus saw a gunner leaning out the side, rifle in hand, ready to lay down covering fire. He only hoped his scouts had seen it in time to get under cover.

He needn't have worried. As the airpod descended to back up the police, two men ran into the street from the entrance of a nearby apartment building. They wore scarves over their lower faces, obscuring their identity, and carried a large bag between them. Ven Dazarus watched as they took cover behind a parked groundcar, opened the bag and pulled out a miniature magmine launcher. An old-fashioned but effective anti-aircraft weapon, Ven Dazarus had seen it used many times during the war.

One of the cops spoke through a PA system. "*Halt!*" he shouted. "*This is an illegal demonstration, and you are all under arrest. Lower your weapons, dismount your animals and lay on the ground or we will open fire!*"

On any other day, Ven Dazarus would have laughed. Were they really that stupid? Did they think this was just a protest march? But not today. After all, this *was* a demonstration of sorts—one of Kurrethi strength and domination.

"Keep moving," he shouted back to the rebels. "Prepare to fire if attacked!" His troops raised their weapons, ready to 'defend' themselves.

But the men crouched behind the groundcar weren't part of his unit. They didn't know the rules. As the rebels and police both prepared to open fire, the masked men sighted up their launcher and fired. The shell rocketed into the air and burst open just a few feet in front of the airpod. The explosion itself was harmless, but it released the shell's contents; a dozen miniature floating magmines.

The airpod gunner recoiled from the blast and shouted to the pilot, who attempted to pull up and evacuate. But the magmines were too close. They homed in on the ship like moths to a flame, attaching themselves to the hull.

The airpod exploded in a deafening fireball. Below it, the police scattered for cover. They fired at the two men behind the groundcar and Ven Dazarus' men alike. One of the groaks crashed to the ground, crushing its rider as it fell. The beast had a leg injury—not enough to kill it, but it was out of action, as was the rebel lying trapped under it. The Kurrethi returned fire, filling the air with the shriek of entropy magic.

In less than a minute it was all over. The police lay fallen and slumped over their groundcars. The airpod wreckage burned in their midst, spreading fire to the other vehicles.

"Advance," shouted Ven Dazarus. "The fire's spreading! We must move now, before the groaks become restless!"

"Wait!" The shout came from the men with the magmine launcher. They'd survived the firefight, using the groundcar as cover. Now they approached Ven Dazarus, their hands in the air.

Friddin, the officer who had questioned Salarum's thinman, raised his blaster and ordered the men to halt. They did, and pulled down the scarves covering their features.

"Hail, Ven Dazarus!" one of them shouted.

The rebel leader laughed. The men were ex-Kurrethi, two of the members who had quit when he first rose to power in the rebel camp. "Well, well," he said. "I see you've picked a side after all. Are there many more like you?"

"Yes," said the man who'd hailed him. "Hundreds. The city will be yours within hours... sir."

Ven Dazarus smiled.

THE PRODIGAL REBEL was right.

By the time they reached the Heart of Kurreth, Ven Dazarus' unit had almost doubled in size, reinforced by insurgents from all over the city who had come to join the fight. After the airpod's destruction police resistance was minimal, and civilian resistance non-existent. In fact, it appeared most of the Hurrundan police had simply abandoned their posts. The units sent to besiege the stations reported later that many of them had only a skeleton crew of staff and surrendered immediately. Some of the police even welcomed the Kurrethi, vindicating once and for all his conviction that the Kurrethi had a legion of supporters who remained silent all these years to avoid persecution at the hands of Werrdun and his cronies.

When he reached the Heart, Ven Dazarus found that one of the flanking units had already secured it. They formed an honour guard from the plaza facing the building all the way up its stone steps. He dismounted his groak and walked into the building with his head held high.

It was four o'clock in the afternoon, and the revolution was already over. The Kurrethi had taken back their city.

CHAPTER THIRTY-THREE

AT SIX O'CLOCK Ven Dazarus stood on the steps of the Heart of Kurreth and faced the gathered crowd. His lieutenants had called every single news stream broadcaster in the city, and judging by the massive press presence at the front of the crowd, every single one had turned up. Not that he expected anything else. Behind the press stood thousands of people, ordinary citizens, waiting for him to usher in this new age.

He would not disappoint them.

"People of Hurrunda, great city of Kurreth," he began. "My name is Ven Dazarus, leader of the true Kurrethi and now your Emperor. Two hours ago we wrested control of the city from the grasp of those last, wretched few still loyal to Werrdun the Usurper. We did this with a minimum of violence that could only be achieved by a group who have the popular support of the masses. Even the police, who have hunted and oppressed us in Werrdun's name for so many years, came to their senses and laid down their weapons. Not a single man, woman or child died today, proving that the Law of Kurreth will usher in an age of peace, prosperity and spiritual well-being for you all." That last was a lie, of course, but those who had died were in his view soldiers, be they Werrdun's police or his own Kurrethi. No civilian had died. That was the important thing, and how he justified the lie to himself.

"This is a new beginning for the people of our great city," he continued, "and from dawn tomorrow we shall begin the immediate implementation of Kurrethi law and custom. We will not tarry, or delay, or renege. We will free this city of the corruption and perversion in which it is drowning. We will free you all from the inequality of capitalism and the fear of political correctness run rampant.

"We will free you to be true Kurrethi, and let your spirits be filled with joy."

He paused for effect and scanned the crowd for a reaction. The press hung on his every word. Dozens of vidrecorders watched and broadcast everything he did. Reporters without cameras held out audiopods or scribbled in notepads. He wondered how many of the cameras were streaming live. Probably all of them. What else was there to report on in Hurrunda today? Ven Dazarus and the Kurrethi weren't *on* the news stream, they *were* the news stream.

Behind the press, the civilian masses watched him with a similar rapture. He'd considered placing groak riders throughout the crowd, to ensure there was no trouble, but ultimately decided that could be interpreted as coercion. It was important not just to Ven Dazarus, but to the city and the world at large, that the people of Hurrunda were seen to support the Kurrethi without compulsion, as he had always known they would. Instead the groaks had been positioned near the building at the side of the plaza, inconspicuous but ready to quell any possible trouble. Gorrd stood with them, keeping the beasts tame despite the noise and crush of the crowd.

Some of the people burst into applause at Ven Dazarus'

words. The rest waited patiently for him to indicate he'd finished. He knew what that indication would be, what they expected of him. He'd waited for it himself, ever since joining the Kurrethi.

"There is one more thing I want to show you," he said. "Something that you will, I promise, remember for all your days to come."

He put a finger underneath his collar and pulled his shirt open. Underneath, resting against his skin, was Werrdun's necklace. He'd put it on the night before after nearly losing it to Salarum, and hadn't removed it since. It was the only way he could be absolutely certain of having it present for this historic moment.

"As you all know, this was the symbol of Werrdun's office. It was gifted to him by vile Ekklorn after a bargain was struck. In return for everlasting power, Werrdun allowed Ekklorn's influence to course through Hurrunda's veins like a foul poison."

Ven Dazarus removed the necklace, lifting it over his head and holding it up for all the crowd to see.

"It is the mark of a man who consorted with devils and darkness to maintain his power. I took it from him, to show you how false and passing that power was. Real leaders do not need trinkets to prove their fitness to rule! Real leaders do not need to bargain with Ekklorn! Real leaders need only one thing—the courage and strength to lead!"

He threw the necklace down on the steps. The crowd gasped. Ven Dazarus held out his hand to Friddin, who handed Ven Dazarus a heavy mallet.

He raised the mallet above his head, pausing just long enough to make sure that all the cameras were focused on him, that everyone present in the square would witness what he was about to do.

He swung the hammer down.

The necklace shattered. The gems split into shards. Thousands of fragments scattered down the Heart of Kurreth's steps like a waterfall of rainbows. The links twisted, burst and flew into the air before returning to ground with a hollow metallic ring.

The necklace was destroyed. Ven Dazarus turned to face the crowd.

He had expected them to applaud, or cheer, or at the very least be watching him. But they weren't. They were all looking up, every last one of them, at something above. He followed their gaze.

The sky was filled with airships.

Hundreds of men jumped out of the ships and descended on the plaza like a swarm of jungle insects. Flashes of light from the parachutists signalled a hail of bullets that smacked into the roof of city hall. Masonry and dust rained down on Ven Dazarus and the Kurrethi soldiers, and the crowd began to panic.

But he'd expected something like this. They were sitting ducks up there, and now that the rebels had taken control of the police stations, they had the firepower to deal with such an assault. "Return fire!" he shouted to his soldiers. "Call the stations and tell them to fire with everything they have. Kill them all!" All around the Heart of Kurreth, his soldiers raised their rifles and took aim. Ven Dazarus laughed. "Is this the best they can do?"

"Not quite," said a voice in the crowd. It sounded quite familiar.

Ven Dazarus turned. "Who said that?"

"I did. And so does my army."

Nicco Salarum stood on the stone steps, aiming a blaster at the Kurrethi leader. And behind him stood the entire press corps, brandishing assault rifles.

WEARING A LONG coat and hat, Nicco had watched Ven Dazarus from amid the throng of journalists and broadcasters. He was near the front, but the coat covered his filthy clothes and the hat hid his skin colour. The rebel leader hadn't even looked in his direction, much less noticed him.

Nicco had guessed Ven Dazarus would want to destroy the necklace in public. The rebel leader had made too much of its 'demonic' nature not to dispose of it. And Nicco already knew Ven Dazarus had a flair for the theatrical.

So when he saw a Kurrethi emerge from city hall carrying a large hammer halfway through Ven Dazarus' speech, Nicco knew this was the moment. He pressed a finger to the tiny radio in his ear and whispered, "Move in. Repeat, move in."

Above them, the entire Hurrundan fleet of forty-three airships soared in from over the sea and took their positions. Nicco heard murmurs from the crowd as they saw the ships block out the sun, but Ven Dazarus was oblivious to them. The 'emperor' was much too wrapped up in his moment of self-absorbed glory to pay attention to whatever was going on above him.

The airships came to a stop and hovered in the air just as Ven Dazarus brought the hammer down on the necklace. Once again Nicco pressed the earbud, and this time whispered, "Go, go, go!"

As the parachutists descended, firing on city hall to distract the Kurrethi, Nicco pulled a small blaster out from under his coat and raised it in the air. At that signal, the other 'journalists' pulled out their own assault rifles and blasters from their hiding places in coats, bags and even inside mockup vidrecorders. The press were in fact all Hurrundan police, every serving man and woman who'd managed to escape to a rendezvous with Sothus before the Kurrethi besieged the police stations. Nicco led them up the steps.

When Ven Dazarus turned and saw him pointing a gun in his face, Nicco smiled.

The rebel leader backed away slowly, his hands raised. Behind him the Kurrethi soldiers dropped their weapons at the urging of the Hurrundan officer. Ven Dazarus spat at Nicco and said something in Varnian. Nicco understood the basics, but he turned to Sothus anyway for a translation. The older man was standing beside him, expertly holding an assault rifle aimed squarely at Ven Dazarus.

"What did he say?" Nicco asked.

"He said you're a fool, that they've already won, and now that Werrdun's dead the people themselves will kill you. He says he won't have to lift a finger."

Nicco laughed. "Oh, really? Well, we'll see about that." He pressed the earbud one last time and said, "Bring him in."

From the far side of the plaza came the sound of two groundcars carefully making their way through the crowd. The engine noise was punctuated by bursts from their horns, and slowly but surely the confused crowd moved back to let them pass.

A minute later, the groundcars drew up to the bottom of the stone steps where the 'press' crowd had stood just a minute before. The rear door of the front car opened and Brinno emerged. The goon held the door open while Huwll emerged from the other side. On Brinno's side a cane appeared, followed by its owner: a large, pale-skinned man with puffy cheeks, thick pink lips and one wonky eye.

The crowd stared at Wallus Bazhanka, not recognising him. A murmur of confusion spread through the people.

Then the front passenger door of the second groundcar opened and a large, dark-skinned Varnian man climbed out. He moved to the rear and held the door open. Bazhanka walked over and offered his hand to someone inside the car. A bony, long-fingered hand took hold of Bazhanka's, and the mob boss straightened as his companion stepped out of the car.

Governor Jarrand L. Werrdun stood up and waved to the gasping crowd. Around his neck hung a gaudy necklace of gold and jewels.

His necklace of office.

* * *

"You're... you're dead..." croaked Ven Dazarus, staring at the governor as he walked up the steps. Bazhanka walked beside Werrdun, and following them were Brinno, Huwll and four of the governor's security team from his trip to Azbatha.

Nicco laughed. "First rule of warfare, Ven Dazarus—don't believe foreign propaganda."

Ven Dazarus turned to Gorrd. Like everyone else, the hapless wizard was staring at Governor Werrdun in shock. "Gorrd!" Ven Dazarus hissed. "Stop his heart! Take their guns away! Just... *do* something!"

But Sothus stepped between the wizard and Ven Dazarus, and moved his aim to Gorrd's forehead. "Hey, Nicco," he called. "Can wizards outrun large-calibre bullets?"

Nicco sucked air through his teeth and pretended to consider the question. "I don't think so, but I'm no expert. Perhaps you should conduct an experiment and find out."

"Not a bad idea," said Sothus, pressing the barrel of the assault rifle against Gorrd's skull, just above his eyes. "Well, wizard?"

Gorrd stared down the rifle barrel and began to sweat. "N-No..."

"Bah," said Sothus with a sneer. "You're no fun."

Nicco crouched to retrieve a handful of pieces of the shattered necklace. He held his hand out in front of Ven Dazarus, then let the fragments fall through his fingers like grains of sand. "Two hundred rakki from the city market. Pretty good likeness, though, eh?"

The rebel leader turned on Nicco with a murderous glare. "I will kill you, imbecile thief!"

Bazhanka took a step forward and scowled at Ven Dazarus. "Dear boy, the only execution around here will be yours..."

"No," said Werrdun, placing a hand on Bazhanka's shoulder.

"He's going to live." Werrdun turned to Ven Dazarus. "You'd like nothing more than to be a martyr, wouldn't you? But you won't get it. You're going to rot in a cell for the rest of your miserable life, you crazy fanatic."

The parachutists were landing, hitting the ground and rolling with a practised ease. Some came to rest on rooftops around the plaza, others in the plaza itself. The crowd who'd watched Ven Dazarus declare victory over Werrdun's men scattered as the governor's forces returned with a vengeance. Most of the Kurrethi were still in city hall, which was now completely surrounded. Those outside with Ven Dazarus had already dropped their guns and surrendered. The rebel leader may have trained them as soldiers, but they weren't suicidal. The remaining Kurrethi, occupying police stations across the city, would soon be dealt with and arrested.

Nicco allowed himself a smile. The idea had come to him at his lowest ebb, when he was running out of time and options. After Brinno and Huwll's last visit, he'd had the idea of using the thinman as a decoy while he stole the necklace; but he'd known that just stealing it would change nothing in the bigger picture. Werrdun would live, but Ven Dazarus would still be out there and the Kurrethi would still be active. And while that might have been fine for the governor and Bazhanka, Nicco wanted something more. He wanted revenge.

It was while feeling sorry for himself that Nicco remembered his despair at the Jalakumi businessman's fake gold bathroom ornaments, the despair that had left him with no option but to take the necklace job from 'Xandus.' Fake ornaments...

Nicco had already confirmed that Ven Dazarus was no wizard. And he couldn't be intimately familiar with the necklace, because Werrdun never removed it. So how would Ven Dazarus be able to tell a real from a fake sold in the marketplace?

Apart from Nicco's brush with death escaping from the rebel camp, it had worked like a charm. When he brought that hammer down, Ven Dazarus really believed he was destroying Werrdun's necklace. And that made Nicco enjoy what followed all the more.

Two of Werrdun's bodyguards took Ven Dazarus by the arms and held him fast while Governor Werrdun turned to address the crowd. He held up his hands for quiet. Despite the chaos in the plaza, with police seeming to appear from everywhere and the civilians wondering what on earth was going on, they quickly fell silent when they saw him.

"People of Hurrunda," he said. "My people of Hurrunda. What you have just witnessed was a shabby attempt to reverse this great city's progress to the dark days of an age whose time is passed, by an army of terrorists who would have removed the basic freedoms and rights which you have enjoyed for the past sixty years. Make no mistake, my 'illness' in Turith was no less than an attempt on my very life, carried out for the sake of one man's greed." Werrdun gestured at the rebel leader. "Ven Dazarus, mastermind of the Kurrethi, was willing to commit murder to style himself 'emperor' of your city. In that he failed, but he and his band of guerrillas are already responsible for the murder of many Hurrundan innocents. As we speak, the remainder of the terrorists are being placed under arrest. They will be tried within the week..."

A sudden shout from one of Werrdun's bodyguards interrupted his speech. "Suicide capsule! Stop him!"

Nicco turned and saw the bodyguard, one of the men holding Ven Dazarus, grip the rebel leader's jaw and try to force his mouth open. Everyone else had been so intent on Werrdun, they'd neglected to keep a careful eye on Ven Dazarus. Now the rebel leader was trying to outwit justice by killing himself.

Nicco leapt forward to help, and the other bodyguard holding Ven Dazarus joined in the struggle. Nicco wasn't going to let the rebel leader get away that easily, not if he could do something about it. He dropped his blaster, grabbed hold of Ven Dazarus' shirt arm, swung him round and slapped him hard on the back with his other hand. The bodyguard who'd noticed the suicide attempt still had the rebel leader's jaw gripped between his fingers, but Ven Dazarus was thrashing his limbs—whether to escape or because the poison was taking effect, Nicco couldn't tell—and the guard fell backwards.

Time seemed to slow down. The bodyguard fell into the crowd of people rushing to help. Nicco slapped Ven Dazarus on the back again. Ven Dazarus seemed to be falling with the bodyguard, his arms wrapped around the man's waist. Nicco lunged forward to catch Ven Dazarus. Then the rebel leader stood up straight and grabbed hold of Nicco's arm. He had the bodyguard's blaster in his hand.

He pressed the barrel against Nicco's forehead.

CHAPTER THIRTY-FOUR

"You wouldn't dare," said Nicco. "You wouldn't make it two steps before someone gunned you down." The pistol was a normal bullet-slinger, not an entropy gun. Evidently Werrdun had returned with no intention of taking prisoners.

"I think no," said Ven Dazarus in broken Turithian. "Werrdun say he will have me alive, exactly. Move!" He pushed the blaster barrel at Nicco's head, forcing him to step backwards.

The rebel leader was right. Governor Werrdun motioned for his men to stand back and let Ven Dazarus through. Nobody doubted that he had the guts to kill.

Nicco took slow steps back, down the stone steps toward the crowd. "What are you going to do, walk all the way back to the Hurrun Peaks with your gun pointed at me?"

"Maybe, exactly," said the rebel leader.

"Well, you'll be out of luck." Nicco looked over to Bazhanka. "When does the bombing start? Any time now?"

The mob boss nodded.

"You lie," hissed Ven Dazarus. "We are hidden well!"

Nicco held up his hand and showed the rebel leader the following gem embedded in his palm. "I'm guessing it was your pet wizard that got this tingling when I was in your tent," he said. "But you weren't the only ones following me."

Ven Dazarus' face darkened. "Then you are the fool."

He pushed Nicco back with the blaster again, and Nicco heard a deep-throated hum from close behind. The groaks.

"Get on," said the rebel leader. He turned Nicco round by the shoulder and pushed him toward the nearest of the beasts. "You can groak ride, I know this. Move!"

The animals were already agitated, snorting and milling around restlessly; Nicco figured it wouldn't help. He just hoped they didn't all stampede again. He'd only been in Hurrunda two days, and he'd had enough of groaks.

Ven Dazarus pressed the blaster further into the small of Nicco's back. "On," he hissed in his ear.

Nicco grabbed hold of the animal's harness, slipped his boot into a stirrup and hauled himself up into the saddle. He turned and offered his hand to Ven Dazarus, hoping to pull him off-balance and make him drop the gun.

Ven Dazarus wasn't fooled. "Put your hands on saddle and keep there," he growled. "Foot out." When Nicco had removed his foot from the stirrup, the rebel leader used his free hand to pull himself up behind Nicco. He kept the blaster aimed at Nicco the whole time, even as he swung his legs over the groak's back, and settled in on the back edge of the saddle. "Walk!" he barked in Nicco's ear.

Nicco took hold of the reins, snapped them hard and hummed. The groak stiffened, lurched to one side, then shot forward into the crowd. The people scattered, running and diving out of the beast's way. Nicco did his best to direct it, trying to avoid innocent bystanders, but the groak paid him no attention and just kept going forward.

Nicco glanced back over his shoulder. Werrdun's men were

running down the steps of City Hall. Were they going to try and follow him? Had they forgotten Ven Dazarus had a blaster pressed to his back? With a sinking in his stomach, he wondered if Werrdun had decided it would be worth Nicco's life to make sure the rebel leader didn't escape.

Ven Dazarus had seen it, too, and wondered the same thing. He turned in the saddle and raised his blaster.

Great, thought Nicco. It's going to turn into a shootout, and I'm the only one without a gun.

But the rebel leader didn't shoot at his pursuers. Instead he aimed for the already restless groak pack and shot three rounds.

Nicco didn't see exactly where they hit, but he heard the shrieking of wounded animals. Ven Dazarus was trying to start a stampede! With the groaks in a frenzy, getting through the crowd to follow Ven Dazarus—or save Nicco—would be impossible for Werrdun's men. Once again, he was on his own. You want a job done right... Nicco dropped the reins and turned in the saddle. Ven Dazarus was still aiming at the groak pack, preparing to fire another volley of rounds. It was now or never.

Nicco put one arm around Ven Dazarus' body and pulled him back, reaching for the gun with his other hand. Ven Dazarus shouted in protest and twisted his body away, pulling the gun free of Nicco's clutches.

Behind them the groak pack roared, broke ranks and stampeded into the crowd. By now many observers had already left, perhaps deciding that even an event so momentous just wasn't worth the risk. The crowd surged backward, scattering out of the rampaging beast's path.

Ven Dazarus threw a punch at Nicco's head. Nicco ducked and let go of Ven Dazarus' body, instead grabbing his arm as it swung. The two men half-faced one another, arms locked and straining. Nicco didn't stand a chance against the ex-soldier; he felt his arms begin to give way and the rebel leader smiled, confident of his victory. But when Ven Dazarus came within six inches from his face, Nicco snapped his head forward and headbutted the rebel leader on the nose.

Ven Dazarus cried out and jerked back, wrenching his arms from Nicco's grip and bringing his gun arm down. Nicco made a dive for the blaster but he overshot, slipping sideways in the saddle. Ven Dazarus fired and missed, hitting the groak in the neck.

The beast reared up on its back four legs. Nicco lost his balance completely and fell to the ground. He landed flat on his back, winded and immobile.

The groak reared again, twisting and bucking in pain. Ven Dazarus lunged forward, grasping for the harness, but missed. He slipped off the back of the saddle onto the groak's spines and yelled in pain.

Nicco gasped for air and looked up. The stampeding groaks were almost upon them. He struggled to his feet, trying to stagger away, but he was all out of strength.

Then, suddenly, the herd turned. As one, they swept round and headed for the groak he and Ven Dazarus had been riding. The rebel leader was slipping, one hand gripping the harness as his body slid down the beast's flanks. Nicco saw blood at the small of his back, spreading fast over Ven Dazarus' coat and trousers. The herd was heading straight for him.

Straight for the blood.

Nicco looked over at the wizard, Gorrd, on the steps of City Hall. Sothus still had the man at gunpoint, and the wizard was watching helplessly, horrified. He hadn't been able to fully control just *one* of the beasts when it went berserk back at the camp; there was no way he could calm an entire frenzied pack.

The groak herd crashed into their lone brother, bowling the beast over onto its side. Ven Dazarus went down with it, crushed under the weight of a hundred groak legs as the herd trampled over him, then stopped and circled round his limp and bleeding body. Nicco's blood ran cold at the roars, hums and shrieks from the pack as they fought over feeding rights.

The plaza was now empty but for the rebels, Werrdun and his men, and the feeding groaks. Nicco limped around the pack and made his way back to the steps. He heard one of the Hurrundan cops shout into a radio for animal handlers to come and subdue the groaks.

Nicco headed for Werrdun. The governor's face was black as thunder, robbed of his vengeance. Nicco wasn't sorry. Ven Dazarus had been scum, but everything he'd learned over the past two weeks told him Werrdun was no saint either. Nicco could imagine the torture he'd have put the Kurrethi leader through, and it turned his stomach.

"Looks like you won't be getting your pound of flesh," said Nicco to Werrdun. "Unless you fancy sifting through a ton of groak shit."

CHAPTER THIRTY-FIVE

THE MOON SHONE high and bright through the clear night sky. Ribbons of silver played on the water of the Nissal Straits like thousands of tiny fish darting in and out of the sea. A midsummer breeze blew across the mouth of the Nissal River, giving some relief from the balmy, humid night air.

Nicco stood on the observation platform of the small funeral skiff as it moved out from the mouth of the river into the Straits. Behind him, on the main deck, three men in all-white suits stood guard over a body draped in a white cloth. Each wore a cutlass, fixed to his waist and hanging down by his thigh.

Not that there was any need to guard the body these days, but it was a tradition dating back to the days before airships, when Turith was a nation of warring island states and warriors were buried with their valuable possessions and weapons beside them. The desecration of a corpse, or theft of the valuables, was a terrible affront. Not to the gods—Turithians had never had much time for religion—but to the warrior's reputation and respect, and the honour of the men who buried him. Failing *to defend the body of a fallen comrade was the ultimate black mark on a warrior's record.*

Nicco had been very clear that there would be no religious or spiritual element to this burial, but he had no problem with tradition. Lilla herself had asked him to bury her at midnight, which had been traditional for unmarried women for thousands of years. Legend had it that Babbola, the 'mother of Turith,' refused to marry any of the fathers to her children—of which there were twenty, fifty or hundreds, depending on which version of the legend you subscribed to. Babbola travelled from island to island, mothering a child on each one before moving on, in order to spread her family and genes among the nation. When her time finally came, at seventy years of age (or a hundred, or three hundred) her children all came to Turilum. Then, in silent agreement, they led a procession of her cloth-draped body to the shore at midnight. They set her adrift on the sea and returned to their separate islands without a word spoken.

The story was supposed to bring the disparate, isolationist Turithians together, to make them feel more like kin, because each of them allegedly had some of Babbola's bloodline in them. Nicco doubted Babbola ever actually existed, and regarded the whole thing as a bit silly. But the mythical woman had been adopted as an idol figure by sex workers and single mothers over the years, and Nicco was happy to indulge his mother's wishes on this of all occasions.

A small, slender hand slipped into his and closed around it. He turned to face Tabby. She wore a long white dress, and around her neck hung a small cameo pendant of Babbola. Nicco had never seen her wearing it before. But then he'd never attended a funeral with Tabby before.

Dozens of the women at Madame Zentra's, including the Madame herself, had asked to attend, but Nicco refused them all. He wanted a small, private affair and they reluctantly respected his wishes. Tabby had been insistent, though, and eventually Nicco relented. Now that they were here, he was glad of her company. Since his mother had become bedridden, he'd seen Tabby less and less, spending what time he could by his mother's side. Only Madame Zentra and the housekeepers disturbed him. Tabby left him alone, perhaps guessing that when the time came, he'd go to her. And he did, three nights ago, when Lilla Salarum breathed her last.

He returned Tabby's squeeze of his hand, and she leant her head against his shoulder. They were out of the Nissal Straits' river mouth and were now drifting on the open waters of the Demirvan Sea.

The Captain shut down the engine and the skiff slowed to a halt. The three white-clad guards turned inward to face the body, then looked up to Nicco on the platform. The one nearest asked him if he wanted to say anything.

"No," said Nicco. "I already said it all."

The funeral guards lifted his mother's body, still draped by the white cloth. One raised her by the shoulders, the other two took hold of her legs. Burial at sea was the most common type of funeral in Turith, the body embalmed to weigh it down.

The Captain pressed a button and a small section of the deck railing at the rear of the boat slid back, exposing a ramp angled down from the deck to the water. The guards carried the body to the opening and placed it on the ramp, legs first.

They let go and the body slid down into the water. Only the white cloth remained, floating on the surface of the sea. One of the guards took a long hooked pole from the side of the deck and leant over the side to retrieve it, but Nicco stopped him.

"No," he said. "Leave it."

Tabby looked up at him, confused. "Are you sure? Don't you want something to remember her by?"

"I've got half a room full of antiques and rubbish to remember her by. I don't need a piece of bloody cloth." The guard was still standing at the railing, pole in hand, looking expectantly

at Nicco. *"I said leave it. Let it join her in the sea. Just take us back."*

The captain did as Nicco asked, and soon they were heading back toward the bright city lights of Azbatha. Nicco held Tabby's head to his chest and gazed at the skyline.

Far behind them, a square white cloth drifted on the surface of the sea.

NICCO WOKE TO the sound of laughter. He blinked, momentarily forgetting where he was. Then he remembered: he was on a private airship bound for Azbatha. He'd cleaned up in one of the onboard shower units, then come through to the main lounge and fallen asleep on a couch.

Bazhanka, who'd chartered the airship, sat nearby flanked by a pair of bodyguards, as he talked to Sothus. The mob boss had ditched the faux-scruffy clothes he'd worn in Hurrunda, returning to his usual business attire. Sothus didn't seem at all fazed by Bazhanka, but Nicco guessed that a man in the arms trade—particularly one who could secure and distribute a thousand assault rifles in less than a day—had dealt with much worse. They were joking about something, and Nicco wondered how long it would be before Sothus began supplying Bazhanka's thugs with weapons.

The mob boss noticed Nicco had woken up and called over to him. "Nicco! Come and join us, dear boy. You're a hero."

Nicco walked over. He didn't feel like a hero. He'd just saved his own skin by returning a man as corrupt as Bazhanka—if not more so—to power in a foreign city that he had no right poking his nose into. A man who'd been perfectly willing to let him die, no less. His only consolation was that his debt to Bazhanka, and to Werrdun, had been declared void after they retook the city from the Kurrethi. Nicco could finally go back to being a normal thief again.

Sothus clapped him on the shoulder as he sat down. "That was a stroke of genius lad, well done. Pretty close thing at the end, I must say, but Werrdun's entrance was worth it. The look on Ven Dazarus' face! Ha!"

"Thanks," mumbled Nicco. It had been his idea to let the Kurrethi think they'd won and install themselves in power before showing any resistance. A pitched battle on the streets, even with the extra firepower supplied by Sothus, could have drawn out for days, even weeks. The entire civilian population of the city would be at risk.

Nicco was glad it hadn't come to that. He'd have enough trouble sleeping at night with even the small death toll the past days' events had caused.

Besides, this had to be a PR victory as much as a military one. It was important that Ven Dazarus be completely discredited. That was why they waited until he had destroyed the replica necklace before acting. He'd be forever remembered as a liar, exposed as a charlatan at his moment of supposed glory. And it had seemed to Nicco a fitting way to let Ven Dazarus know he'd been conned, just like he'd conned Nicco.

Still, the rebel leader's killing left a sour taste in Nicco's mouth. He took some solace in the knowledge that it was, at least, a quick death. His fate at the hands of Werrdun would have been much worse.

"It's true," said Bazhanka. "I had my doubts, as well you know. But the result was worth it, I think. The governor is reinstated, with greater support than ever before, and the Kurrethi are crushed. I expect they'll be completely forgotten within five years."

Nicco had his own doubts about that. There would always be sympathisers. Those labourers he'd met in the café, for example. Nicco wondered if they'd try to spin this against Werrdun too, perhaps claiming it was all a plot to get Ven Dazarus to come out of hiding so they could eliminate him.

They might have to go underground, and it would take a few years, but Nicco felt sure the Kurrethi would be back. Whether or not Werrdun would still be in power was another question. Surely the necklace couldn't keep him alive forever. Perhaps his daughter Mirrla would take his place. What kind of leader would she be?

"So are you going to remove this bloody gem, or what?" Nicco held out his palm.

Bazhanka snorted. "Ask Bindol. You seem to have discovered a fondness for magicians during your time in Hurrunda."

Nothing could have been further from the truth. If anything, Nicco's experiences had made him an even more serious arcanophobe than before. Werrdun's magical necklace was the root of all his troubles and Nicco swore to avoid any jobs to do with magic or enchanted items ever again.

There was, however, one enchanted item that still hung over his life. It was time to change that. He turned to Bazhanka. "I have a favour to ask."

The mob boss raised an eyebrow. "I have already waived your debt to me, dear boy. A favour could put you back where we started."

"Not this one. I think this is something you'll want to do." Nicco turned to Sothus. "Would you excuse us for a moment? It's a... family matter."

Sothus looked surprised. He was probably thinking that Nicco meant that he and Bazhanka were family, but if so Nicco wasn't about to correct him. A perceived connection to Bazhanka could do him good in the eyes of the arms dealer. Sothus stood up. "Fair enough. I'll go get a drink." He walked out of the lounge.

"Them too," said Nicco, indicating Bazhanka's bodyguards.

Bazhanka snorted, but waved the guards away then turned to Nicco. "A family matter?"

"Yeah. I think I've finally worked something out. I could

never understand why you've always been so interested in me. Asking me to work for you, paying those lawyers to come and get me off the burglary charge…"

"Dear boy, I take an interest in you because you are an exceptional thief. But your scope is limited. You are small-time, Nicco, but I could put you in the big leagues if only you would come and work for me."

"…the snide remarks about my mother."

"Ah." Bazhanka nodded. "Your mother and I were close once, that is all. Now that she is gone, I like to think I help to keep you out of trouble. I can see some of her in you. And I think she'd be proud of you."

"But what about my father?"

"I don't follow you."

Nicco took a deep breath. It was time for the truth. "You think you're my father, don't you?"

Bazhanka stared at him in amazement, and Nicco wondered if he'd crossed a line. The mob boss had never made a direct allusion to it, but Nicco had had a lot of time to think about his parents—particularly his mother's attitude to Bazhanka—during his time in Hurrunda. It seemed the most logical answer to all his questions. Why his mother never spoke of Bazhanka, and was so adamant that Nicco shouldn't work for him. Why Bazhanka claimed to have been 'close' with his mother. He couldn't imagine what in the fifty-nine hells his mother would have seen in the mob boss, but there was always the possibility that their 'closeness' had simply been part of his mother's work, and Bazhanka had got the wrong idea.

Then Bazhanka burst out laughing. His enormous body rocked and wobbled as he hooted and wiped tears from his eyes.

"Oh, dear, dear. She didn't… is that what Lilla told you?"

Nicco scowled, frustrated. "No, of course not. And what she did tell me was a pack of lies. I know you're not my father. In fact"—Nicco reached inside his shirt and pulled out the glass pendant—"this proves it."

Bazhanka regarded the golden teardrop. "Ah, the army tag. Brinno and Huwll mentioned it."

"I had it read by a wizard. I know who he was, and what he did."

"Really. And what was that, pray tell?"

Nicco relayed what Hullorik had told him about his father being a war journalist.

"I see," said Bazhanka when he'd finished. "Well, good for you. I hope you're happy. But I still don't know exactly what favour you want from me."

Nicco put the pendant back inside his shirt. "I want to know why my mother lied—twice—about him. Why was she so afraid of me finding out the truth? There's no shame in what he did. It's not like my mother was a rabid patriot."

"Dear boy, what in the fifty-nine hells makes you think I'd know?"

"Because you were 'close.' Don't bugger me about, Bazhanka, I know you know more than you let on."

Bazhanka leaned back, deep in thought. Nicco watched him carefully, trying to read the man's body language, but it was useless. Bazhanka had a perfect poker face.

"Perhaps it is time you learned the truth," said Bazhanka. "Lilla's long gone anyway, so the only person it can harm is you. And I think you've proven yourself... resilient enough, over the past week.

"You may not believe it, but as a younger man I was quite handsome. Yes, Lilla and I were lovers for a brief time. But I have never believed I was your father. In fact, it was your father who tore your mother and me apart.

"His name was Nicco Miarrlak, or so he told everyone. He was Varnian, everyone knew that, but living semi-permanently in Turith as a war journalist and thus tolerated by polite society, insomuch as there is such a thing in our fair city. But mark my words, Nicco, 'living as.' The truth is, he was nothing of the sort.

"One evening, Lilla accompanied me to a dinner party held by a neighbour of mine. This was shortly after Riverside had been built, and we fortunate few were getting to know one another as neighbours. Well, scoping one another out; one does not reach that level of affluence by accident, and allies are always useful. Your father was also there, as a guest of Drissen Faprassi, a manufacturer of weapons and armaments for the Turithian army. Your father was allegedly doing a story on Faprassi, knowing full well he would only be permitted to send back a propaganda puff piece.

"But that night, he only had eyes for Lilla. And much to my annoyance, the feeling was mutual. I can hardly say I was surprised when I discovered they had met again a few days later."

Bazhanka stood up. Leaning heavily on his cane, the mob boss walked to the lounge windows. Ten thousand feet below them, the Demirvan Sea gleamed and reflected pink sunlight.

Nicco joined him, gazing out across the water. Some of the larger Turithian islands—Turilum, Rilok, Kesam—could already be seen on the horizon. In less than two hours they'd be home.

"I was a younger man then," said Bazhanka. "And accordingly foolish with it. I thought I loved Lilla. Now I'm not so sure it was ever more than infatuation. But at the time, I was horribly jealous of this man Nicco. You must understand, Lilla's work meant nothing to a man such as me. But she was visiting with this man on her own time, and that incensed me.

"As you know, I am not without resources. So I put them to use. I wanted to discover everything there was to know about this 'Nicco Miarrlak.' Where he was from, where he had been, what skeletons were hidden in his closet. I wanted to destroy him in your mother's eyes, do you understand?"

Nicco nodded. Bazhanka was taking this in a direction he had never expected, and all he could do was listen.

"Ah, but the things I found... It took time, of course. At first, everything confirmed what he said about himself. He'd been allowed into the country as a journalist, so of course Turilum had done their own checks, and as far as they were concerned Nicco Miarrlak was clean.

"That was the problem, you see. He was *too* clean. He had no real past to speak of, no history with the Varnian police, no escapades or scrapes as a young man. It was too unlikely, so I kept digging.

"In a way, I wish I hadn't. Your mother was happy with him, and if I hadn't tried to tell her the truth... well, she might at least have deigned to see me once before her death. She never did, though."

Bazhanka turned and looked Nicco directly in the eye.

"Your father was a spy, Nicco. His name wasn't Miarrlak, it was Pallad. The pendant you have there, his papers and records, they were all forgeries made by the Bishlurram army. He was in Turith to pass secrets back to the Varnians, to sabotage the Turithian war effort and spy on the work of men like Faprassi. He was one of Varn's top men.

"But Lilla wouldn't believe it. I shouldn't have been surprised, of course, but as I said, I was young and foolish in those days. She insisted I had made it up, fabricated a reason for her to stop seeing 'Nicco' and return to my side. Eventually, I had the police follow them back to his house one night and arrest him on charges of espionage. It was the last time she saw him alive.

"Lilla never forgave me."

Nicco was suddenly very aware of the pendant's weight around his neck. He ran his fingers over it. "So what about this?"

"I expect she took it from his house. A keepsake perhaps, a memento of some kind. She named you after him, which

I think proves the strength of her feelings for the man. Lilla never believed the charges, you see; never stopped protesting his innocence. But it did no good. She received news he had been executed when you were about six months old, as I recall the date."

Bazhanka walked back to the table and passed it, heading out of the room. Nicco called out to him. "Wait! So what do I owe you?"

Bazhanka looked back from the doorway. "Nothing," he sighed. "I think you were right. That was one I owed you."

Then he turned and left, leaving Nicco alone.

CHAPTER THIRTY-SIX

TABBY WAS WAITING for him at the airship port.

Nicco had no idea how she'd known he'd be here, but Bazhanka probably had something to do with it. Whatever, he was just pleased to see a familiar face. He ran to Tabby, threw his arms around her and kissed her.

"By the watery saints, am I glad to see—"

She slapped him in the face.

"Ow! What was that for?"

"Why didn't you tell me? I had to find out from Madame!"

"Tabby, love, it wasn't safe. I was just trying to protect you."

She pulled herself away from him and pouted. "I don't need your protecting, thank you very much! I'd been trying to call you for *days*, and all this time you were over there! I didn't even find out until they said whatsisname was dead on the news stream. I thought you were gone forever!"

"Ah." Madame Zentra had kept her promise not to tell anyone; and when the news broke that Governor Werrdun was dead, why shouldn't the Madame have believed it? The only people in Turith who knew the truth were Bazhanka, the governor's security team and Mirrla Werrdun, who'd announced his death to the media. Zentra must have concluded that with Werrdun gone, Nicco would either be on the run for the rest of his life or already dead.

Clearly the Madame hadn't told Tabby about her own life being in danger, or she might be a bit more understanding. But at what cost? Even now that it was all over, Nicco couldn't bring himself to tell her. She was no innocent, but he didn't want her looking over her shoulder all the time.

He changed the subject. "How did your audition go, with that producer?"

"Don't change the subject Nicco. I'm still angry with you."

"I'm not, I... not exactly, anyway. How did it go?"

She looked down at the floor. "He was a scumbag."

Nicco chuckled. "I could have told you that. What happened?"

"He asked me to go down to his place in Riverside, and... well, I think he forgot I was there to audition as an *actress*. If you know what I mean."

Nicco smiled. She'd put herself in danger without even realising it, but Nicco couldn't help laughing.

"Hey, what's so funny?"

"Nothing," he said, still smiling. "I'm just sympathising with the poor sod. I'll bet you gave him a right earful..."

"Salarum!"

Nicco turned in the direction of the shout, immediately tense and ready to run. Recent events had made him jumpy.

With a face like thunder, Sergeant Patulam strode over toward them.

"Hello, sergeant," said Nicco. "How's that missing necklace case going?"

The sergeant wagged a finger in his face. "Don't come the smartarse with me, Salarum. I saw what happened over there. The Hurrundan police contacted me as soon as your fingerprints went in the system. And don't think I didn't see your ugly mug in the crowd during that news stream."

Nicco laughed. "Yeah, talk about an eventful vacation. Wrongfully arrested, then caught up in two revolutions. What are the odds?"

Patulam leaned in close and whispered in Nicco's ear. "You may think you're safe, but know this: Bazhanka can't buy *me* off." He stood up straight and scowled at Nicco. "One day, Salarum. One day people will start talking and you'll come a cropper. When you do, I'll be there with a nice pair of silver bracelets for you." He turned on his heel and left.

Tabby shrugged. "What is he, supercop or something?"

Nicco smiled. "Or something, yeah. Don't worry about it." He took Tabby's hand in his and started walking. "So are we all right?"

She raised an eyebrow at him. "That depends. How are you going to make it up to me?"

Nicco saw a flower seller out the corner of his eye, a middle-aged man in shabby clothes carrying bouquets in the crook of his arm. The man seemed to see Nicco at the same time, and walked over to intercept them.

"Flowers for the lady, sir?" said the man, smiling. "A selection from all over Turith and beyond, just ten lire a bouquet, excellent value. May I recommend the Hirvanian yelloweye here, a lovely complement to the lady's eyes if I may say so. Very rare but currently seasonal in these winters..."

"All right, all right," interrupted Nicco. "Watery saints, you don't need to give me the full spiel. Go on, I'll have the yelloweye."

The flower seller pulled out a bouquet of three of the vivid yellow flowers.

Nicco reached for his wallet, then stopped. "I don't suppose you take cards...?"

The flower seller laughed. "No, sir, I do not. Cash, if you please."

Nicco looked sheepish. "I've just stepped off the airship, all I've got is foreign money."

"No problem at all, sir. I take lire, Hurrundan rakki, even Praalian snowcaps if that's what you have. One learns to be adaptable, in my line of work."

Nicco produced a handful of rakki and dropped them in the flower seller's open hand. "Is that enough?"

The man stared at the coins in amazement. "This is ten times what I asked for, sir. Please, take..."

But Nicco held up his hand to silence the man. "Take it. Consider yourself tipped." He took the bouquet and handed it to Tabby. She accepted the flowers with a smile and sniffed them.

"Lovely," she said.

The flower seller produced a card and pressed it into her hand. "Please, miss, do call again. You have very good taste in men."

She giggled and took Nicco's arm, letting him walk her away. "Oh, look," she said, showing Nicco the card. "He's got a cell number. You'd think he could afford some better clothes in that case, wouldn't you? Hasn't put his name on it, mind. It doesn't even say he's a flower seller. How are you supposed to remember it's his card? Silly man."

She handed the card to Nicco to illustrate her point. The only text on the card was a phone number on the front side. But it was what was printed above the number—instead of a name or company—that stopped him in his tracks.

It was a symbol, a pattern of lines and curves. A symbol Nicco himself could draw from memory. The same symbol that was etched on the glass teardrop pendant he wore around his neck.

Was this some kind of sick joke? Were the Varnian military keeping tabs on him? He glanced back over his shoulder, but the flower seller was nowhere to be seen.

"Yeah," he said, shoving the card into his pocket. "Silly man. Come on, let's go get something to eat. I'm starving."

CHAPTER THIRTY-SEVEN

THAT NIGHT, AS Tabby lay sleeping in her bed at Madame Zentra's, Nicco paced around the room and stared at the card.

What did it mean? He tried to remember what the flower seller looked like, but Nicco had been so busy thinking about how to make it up with Tabby, and flustering about with the wrong currency, that he hadn't really paid attention. Middle-aged, average height, average build, with a scraggy greying beard... Just like every other street vendor and hobo in Azbatha. Nothing about the man stood out as distinguished or unusual. Expect the card Nicco now held in his hands.

One learns to be adaptable, in my line of work.

In Nicco's other hand was his phone. He stared at it, then back at the card.

Come on, just call it. It's probably nothing. Probably. Maybe. Perhaps. Perhaps not.

He dialled the number.

The other end of the line rang. Two rings. Three rings. It's nothing. He's asleep on a park bench somewhere, wondering why some idiot is trying to order a bunch of flowers at two in the morning. You bloody fool.

Just as Nicco was about to hang up, the ringing stopped. "Hello?" he said. "Look, if this is some kind of prank..."

The voice at the other end of the line was male, deep and calm.

"Hello, son. It seems you've made quite a name for yourself..."

ABOUT THE AUTHOR

Antony Johnston is a *New York Times* bestselling graphic novellist, author and games writer with more than fifty published titles, including *The Coldest City*, which became the hit movie *Atomic Blonde* starring Charlize Theron. His epic series *Wasteland* is one of only a handful of such longform achievements in comics, and his first video game, *Dead Space*, redefined a genre. He lives and works in England.

FIND US ONLINE!

www.rebellionpublishing.com

/rebellionpub /rebellionpublishing /rebellionpub

SIGN UP TO OUR NEWSLETTER!

rebellionpublishing.com/sign-up

YOUR REVIEWS MATTER!

Enjoy this book? Got something to say?

Leave a review on Amazon, GoodReads or with your
favourite bookseller and let the world know!

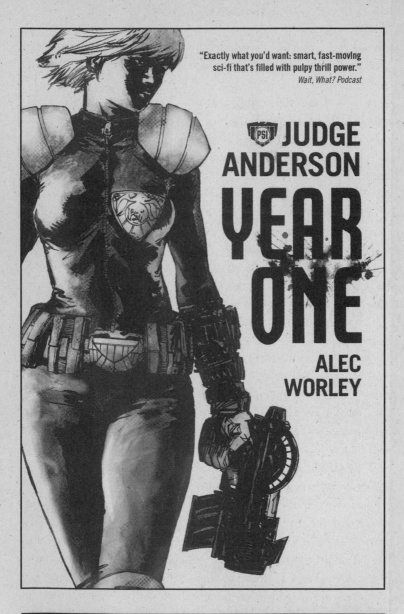

"Exactly what you'd want: smart, fast-moving
sci-fi that's filled with pulpy thrill power."

Wait, What? Podcast

PSI **JUDGE
ANDERSON
YEAR
ONE**

**ALEC
WORLEY**